The Lightbringer

In the Shadows of Fate
Book II

Rick Jurewicz

DIRE HAND
PUBLISHING

PO Box 2144, Indian River, Michigan 49749

This is a work of fiction. Names, characters, businesses, places, events and
incidents are either the products of the author's imagination or used in a
fictitious manner. Any resemblance to actual persons, living or dead, or
actual events is purely coincidental.

ISBN: 0578849828
ISBN-13: 978-0578849829

For my family,
fans and friends –
your encouragement is
a true inspiration.

The Lightbringer
In the Shadows of Fate
Book II

A NOVEL

Rick Jurewicz

PROLOGUE

A boundless landscape, without beginning, without end. But even places without end can have an edge, and in this place, the edge is that which lies beyond the sight of the Crystalline Tower.

The Tower is the center of the Infinite Lands, rising up from the luminescent sands that span the surface of the realm. The apex of the Tower reaches high into the sunless sky, hundreds of times surpassing the size of any structure ever created by man. The base of the Tower stretches on for miles, molded out of the sand-like substance that it protrudes from. The tiny grains themselves had been fused and twisted together, and they reached upward, forging into a translucent rod that grew ever so wider at its base and higher into the sky, becoming the massive monument that it now was.

While mostly sheer and smooth in appearance, the granular veins stemming from the base sand can be seen throughout the fabric of its structure, from its lowest foundation to the great pinnacle. It is from this pinnacle that the light of the land emanated from, giving the sky a brightness that reflected in the sands like a shimmering ocean of diamonds.

There was no night in this place. There was only the light, and therefore no measure of the existence of time. There had been the beginning, when all things moved forward from a single point. Creation had gone into motion; the Infinite Lands were formed, the Tower had risen, but from then on, this place did not change.

Until now.

The everlasting sheen from the Tower had grown dim. The land closest to the Tower stood in twilight. The outer regions, far away from the center, had grown even fainter, as if beneath a heavily overcast sky.

And for reasons beyond the mere distance from the fading light of the Tower, it was at the edge of the Infinite Lands that the greatest darkness could be found.

They stood as silhouettes, those who call the Infinite Lands their home. Shapes and shadows along the borderlands of what was once to them a land without end, without borders. But now, the border was drawn like a line drawn in the sand, and it was drawn with the many shapes and forms and faces of celestial entities standing before an impossible situation, one that those who stood opposing it could never have imagined would come to fruition.

A great chasm of fear and doubt and the seemingly inevitable unknown divided the wall of nearly 2000 of the inhabitants of this land from the just less than a thousand of those who stood facing in opposition. Each side had beings that reflected the same as every race and gender and size and shape as those scattered across the world or humanity, and almost all of them on either side had a different look upon their face. Some showed fear, some anger, and some a deep, deep sadness, but each let it surface in their own way.

The silence fell across them all as they stood across from each other, two factions of celestial power, separated only by a few hundred yards. Not one of them spoke. And when the great light of the Crystalline Tower fell to its deepest of darks, the time had finally come upon them all.

The mass of angels from the side of which the near thousand stood their ground began to part through its center, making way for the one to lead them to what would be their declaration of independence and freedom from their perceived enslavement. He walked on, proud and certain of his intention, yet with a great heaviness in his heart like he had not felt ever before in his long existence. His given name was Lucifer. In the Infinite Lands, his name came to mean "The Bringer of the Light".

To his right stood one of his oldest brothers, and archangel Veramlus, who was charged at one time long ago with the architecture of the winds of the world of humanity, the place called Earth, once known as Eden.

"Are you certain it is done?" Veramlus spoke, leaning in close to his oldest and vastly more powerful brother. Lucifer fixed his eyes forward at the opposing force across the way; they held still and unmoved.

"It is. Those he has suffered pain and anguish for have nailed him and bled him and taken the measure from him that he has granted all of them. And all of us." Lucifer spoke with bitter amazement.

"And he's already forgiven them for it."

But it truly did not matter to him in that moment.

"He?" asked Veramlus.

"Amanthus. On Earth, Amanthus walked among them as a man. So I believe they will only ever see Him as a man, a father, a patriarch of creation. So limited are the views and minds of humanity.

"It is time."

Lucifer stepped out before those that stood alongside him, one third of the angels of Amanthus, the celestial entity to all others known as God the Father or God the Creator of all things. He then marched forward, with the multitude behind him following in step.

Lucifer was truly a creature of eternal beauty, standing by Earth measures at more than 6 feet tall. At this pivotal moment in time his garbs were the same as those that he was created with; black trousers from the waist down with black pristine boots that shined in any light and rose nearly to his knees. His upper body, from the neck to the shoulders and down to the top of his trousers, was covered with a silver sheen of what looked like armor, yet it moved and flexed as his own body did, outside and apart from him yet still somehow a part of him. No sleeve or cowl came from this strange armor, but there was a peculiar white glow that emanated from the surface of the armor, a glow that seemed reflected in his almost shoulder-length blonde hair.

And finally, by his side on the left of his body, held in a long black sheath was his sword. It was the first sword in Creation, made perfect in every way by Amanthus. Yet the irony of the first perfect sword in Creation was that it was never intended to be a weapon. It was the tool that Amanthus charged Lucifer with to first bring light into Creation. It cut through the darkness and emptiness of the cosmos and brought forth the power by which all life would eventually be forged.

Lucifer held his hands by his sides as he approached his brothers and sisters across the far plains of the Infinite Lands, with those that stood with him slowly trailing behind him. The closer he got, the more those he approached wavered and swayed in fearful anticipation of what was to come in the moments ahead.

The first that he came to, a sister named Nuancia, dark skinned and stunningly beautiful, held a steady and defiant gaze until the last moment, but at last broke her gaze and looked away with a tear welling in her eye. She stepped aside, and for a moment Lucifer stopped his forward momentum and laid a gentle hand upon her shoulder. Nuancia let the tears stream from her eyes. Lucifer said nothing, bowing his head slightly in acknowledgment of his sister's breaking heart before he continued to move on.

Angel after angel in the multitude that stood before him stepped away as he led those who followed him through. Lucifer began to feel a slight easing in the weight in his chest. The path widened; some still held a visible anger in their eyes. For some, it was dismay or perhaps even wonder. Others still had no discernable expression. Once they made the way through the silent mass of their brothers and sisters, they would pass on through to whatever corners of creation they desired. Lucifer did not believe that Amanthus would act against them if the rest of the celestial host held no hand in opposing their exit. But Lucifer also knew that it was not destined to be just so.

A lone angel emerged from the crowd near the end of the line. Much like Lucifer in both stature and beauty, yet with hair as black as the darkest of nights. His armor was a more traditional looking beaten steal, by his choice and design, for he was the angel charged to lead a battle and defend the Infinite Lands if ever necessary, devoutly devoted to his duty. His name was Michael, and he was at one time Lucifer's most beloved brother and devout confidant. On this day, he faced his brother as an *adversary*.

Lucifer stopped several feet from his brother before him.

"Michael," Lucifer spoke softly.

"Lucifer."

Michael's voice was tinged with anger. "You are mad to try and go though with this foolhardy venture! Amanthus will never allow this."

"Amanthus will not oppose us if you allow us through, Michael," Lucifer said.

Michael bowed his head for a brief moment, and then brought his eyes sharply up to meet Lucifer's. "You know that is not possible."

"It is if you allow it to be. Please, Michael. Stand down."

Michael drew a long silver sword out of the sheath on his side and held it before him with the tip firmly planted in the ground, both of his hands upon the handle, stoutly braced in the stance of a sentry prepared to deny all who try to pass by him.

Lucifer held back a deep sigh, keeping it within as the crowds on all sides felt a tremor run through their cores. He stepped forward toward Michael now, moving slowly. His eyes closed as he approached, hoping against hope that the oldest of his younger brothers would at the last moment step down and this would be over.

In its many translations through the centuries, the Caducus Oraclum, the fabled *Prophecy of the Fallen*, stated that the great war in Heaven lasted for seven days and seven nights. It was a translation made in slight error. In truth, the war in Heaven lasted less than seven seconds.

Michael drew his sword up and brought it down upon Lucifer, and Lucifer responded with a defensive draw of his own blade, raising it up to meet Michael's blow. The two swords met in a clash and clamor of light and a thunderous roar that for a moment shook all of creation. When the blinding light abated, Michael stood above a stunned Lucifer, fallen to his knees down upon the crystal sand floor of the Infinite Lands. Nothing remained of the blade of the sword of Lucifer, shattered and cast across the vast expanse of creation. Lucifer knew Michael alone did not have the power to cause such a thing.

In that moment, the entire Crystalline Tower emblazoned with a harsh, cold light. All who stood in its presence knew that a judgment was to fall upon them…

Rick Jurewicz

CHAPTER ONE

Richard and Mary Kingston ran a small family farm in northern Ohio since Richard took over the family farm from his father, whose own father started a lifetime before that. It was a successful venture, mostly growing corn and a few other crops of pumpkins and squash which sold very well in the autumn months, especially closer to Halloween each year.

Russell, Richard and Mary's only child, tragically died when a tractor overturned on him in a freak accident when he was only 22 years old. The accident nearly broke Richard, but together he and Mary persevered and worked hard keeping the farm going for many years. With bigger corporate farms taking over the smaller farms in the area and expanding, the very idea of prospering in the farming business any longer for the small farm disappeared almost overnight.

The family farmhouse stood on the edge of nearly 80 acres of wooded property the family had used as hunting land for years, adjoining an area of state forest that was protected from hunting or logging, only used for hiking and in the winter time, cross country skiing when the snow allowed for it. The Kingstons, bit by bit over the previous 10 years, sold off most of the fields to neighboring farms who had already sold out to the corporate giants. They retained one small section of field to keep the pumpkin crop going, although even with the generous amount of money they had received selling the other fields off, the money was bound to run out eventually, and it just wasn't enough to make due on the years pumpkin and squash sales, especially as hard as it was to plant and harvest on his own, being now in his mid-70s. Hiring additional help was out of the question.

Then one day, about 4 years ago, something truly remarkable happened. A couple of men, claiming to be from the government, came knocking at the Kingston's door. They claimed to be doing secret, high level national security work, and wanted to lease - off the books – an area deep in the wooded section of the remaining land. Richard was of course skeptical, but when the men presented him with a briefcase full of cash ($10,000 to be precise) with a promise of an additional $10,000 monthly for the exclusive, private use of the land for an indefinite amount of time, Richard thought hard about the offer. Being in the dire financial situation that the Kingstons were facing, Richard agreed to the terms, and as promised, the same man who went by the name of Mr. Deacon, came and delivered a similar briefcase every month afterward.

The Kingstons spent a great deal of time traveling from then on out, and whatever was happening in the deep woods of the property beside their home was unknown to them, and they made their peace with that. They happily collected the money for the next 4 years, and with that amount of money they would be well taken care of for the remainder of their lives.

As for what was happening in the woods, they would

never know. If anyone were to look online through any satellite imagery sites they would only find an oddly obscured, blurred out area that only appeared to be uninhabited forest lands. If you found the place along the road that was the only entrance to the heavily fenced and heavily electronically monitored property, you would find a very unassuming gate that was designed to not draw undue attention. If you were to travel passed this gate and venture down the long two-track road, you would first be met by a man in overalls with a shotgun and a baseball cap and flannel shirt that would kindly direct you to go back in the direction that you came, citing the land as private property. If you somehow made it beyond the man with the shotgun, and traveled another half mile down the road, you would come to a large, plain brown metal warehouse with a large front door that, when opened, slid open from the middle both ways, about 12 feet high and 18 feet wide.

Within the entrance was an 18 foot wide room, 32 feet deep – a simple garage, with a black SUV parked inside on this particular day. Different vehicles would come in and out a few times each week, but over the past two weeks, there was a new urgency among those who traversed through this place. Confusion and an absence of clear direction were the dominating issues that hung heavy on the minds of the men in the brown metal barn in the woods. Professionalism and dedication (at least while the money held out) is what kept them to their duty. They were not really government agents after all, but highly trained mercenaries paid to guard, with great discretion, a valuable asset on the premises.

But on this day, an end would come to the duty for which they were charged. On this day, there was a presence on the wooded grounds that walked past the shotgun man as he slept. He fell to sleep quickly and unwillingly as the strange figure approached him from a distance.

The man walked up to the large steel door and, with only a smile, opened the door before him. And through the door he walked, unopposed, and through another, down a long and dark hallway, and with any man that came before him, a wave of his hand sent him to a sudden slumber.

A few more astute men managed to notice the intruder and fire a shot from automatic firearms before they collapsed, dazed and confused as they slipped into a dreamy trance.

In the last room, the final inner chamber of the warehouse, a lone figure sat in chains, bound to a steel chair by his legs and arms and waist. The man had long black hair and a scraggly, unkempt beard. He was barefoot and wearing tattered trousers and a dark gray t-shirt, and he raised his head slightly when he heard the sound of the gunshots down the hallway beyond the door in front of his chair.

On the other side of the door there was one final shot followed by a thud; and then, there was silence.

The man had no fear in his heart of what lay beyond the door. All had been taken from him already, so in his heart whatever was to come next would not faze him. He had already accepted his fate. Or so he thought…

The door flew forcefully from its hinges into the wall on the far right side of the otherwise empty room. The figure - who had sent all of the others he had faced to a sudden and unexpected nap - stepped into the room.

He was a tall man with long blonde hair, tied neatly back in a pony tail. He wore black denim jeans with black boots, and had a black blazer overtop a white v-neck t-shirt.

He looked down at the man in the chair, and while overcome within by sadness at the sight he beheld, could not hold back a smile at the sight of the man in the chair before

14

him.

The locks on chains that bound the man to the chair opened all at once and fell to the floor. The man in the chair slowly raised his head to face the stranger that stood before him. But it was no stranger at all. The man's tired eyes widened as he stared through the ragged strands of hair that hung down in his face.

The man's throat was dry, and his voice sounded rough and gravelly as he spoke his first word in many years.

"Lucifer," he whispered hoarsely across his dry lips.

Lucifer smiled wider now, a true joy filling his heart. "Hello, my dear brother Gabriel. It's been far too long."

Lucifer stepped up to his brother and gently touched Gabriel's temple. A light emanated from the tips of his fingers, and within seconds, Gabriel's strength had rejuvenated. His thirst was gone and his wounds were healed…at least as much as a man can heal. While Lucifer could heal his body, Gabriel's angelic essence, which the angel-kind called *glowen* – the power that separates angels and men - was not within Gabriel. This realization was the one thing that caused Lucifer's smile to finally dissipate.

"What happened to you, my brother?" asked Lucifer.

"How did you get here, Lucifer? How did you escape Hell?" asked Gabriel, ignoring Lucifer's question.

"It was your daughter's doing," Lucifer told him.

"Miranda…Miranda let you out?" Gabriel said with astonishment. "That's not possible. Why would she…?"

"You know it's more than possible. It was the only way, aside from Amanthus releasing me, which I assure you did not happen."

"You tricked her somehow into letting you out. You had to!"

"She did so by her own free will, Gabriel. That is the only way that it could have happened."

"When? How long have you been free?" asked Gabriel.

"Fourteen days, three hours and 36 minutes, approximately by standard human time." Lucifer stopped and turned away from Gabriel. When he turned to look at his brother once more, he could see the fear and the confusion in Gabriel's face.

"Gabriel," he said softly to his brother, "I did set things into motion a long, long time ago. I was trying to find a way to my freedom. I watch and I waited, looking into the dreams of mankind. It is all any of us that are imprisoned in Hell can see. We can sometimes influence the images that humans see in their dreams, but had I interfered directly with Miranda, then her releasing me would not have been entirely her own free will. While the decision would have ultimately been hers, the influence would have been mine. I do not believe Amanthus would have let that happen."

"Amanthus has not been seen or heard since he cast you out. The light of the Crystalline Tower has gone dim once more, as it was when Amanthus walked the Earth and perished among them. You broke his heart," Gabriel said coldly.

Lucifer bowed his head. "Yes. I know. I did what I had to do, brother. I was hoping that perhaps you could understand more than anyone."

"Why? Why should it be me that understands?!" Gabriel raised his voice in growing anger at the thought of this.

"My desire was to be free!" Lucifer snapped back. "Surely you can understand just as well where the desires of your heart can lead, otherwise we would not be speaking at all right now and I would still be trapped in the darkness!"

Gabriel stood silent. While Lucifer's heart led him

down a different path, it was his own heart that led him to Suzanne Gale. He loved her, and he would not change a single thing that he did embracing that love. He loved Amanthus as well, and his shame for the betrayal of Amanthus and his duty ran through the deepest caverns of his heart…but not deeper than his love for Suzanne.

"Cadere Gladii," Gabriel spoke the Latin words in a low voice.

"What do you mean?" asked Lucifer.

"The place where your 'prophecy' was first discovered. They call it 'Cadere Gladii'. The Fall of the Sword. You must have been drawn somehow to the place when you chose the boy you bestowed the prophecy to. A fragment, a small shard of your sword fell in that place, of all of the places amongst creation. Michael sent me to it when I betrayed my duty. It was to be my punishment. One scratch from the shard and your angelic *glowen* is gone forever. The shard crumbled into the sand once it stole my glowen. This is all that remains." He raised his hand to show Lucifer the scar across his palm.

Lucifer's heart sank. He could see it now as he looked deeper. The glowen – the mystical touch of Amanthus that manifest his power within the angels he created at the dawn of time – was no longer a part of his brother Gabriel. Yet another weight he must carry as a result of setting this all into motion when he decided to leave the Infinite Lands.

"This was my own doing, Lucifer. I know that look in your eyes. I made a choice, and I stand by it. Besides…you have enough guilt of your own to carry upon your shoulders."

"I will make it right, brother. I swear it," vowed Lucifer.

"What are you going to do now?" asked Gabriel.

Lucifer smiled. "I am going to do what I am meant to do, dear brother. I am going to bring humanity into the light!"

Gabriel felt much trepidation in both the words Lucifer spoke and the gleeful tone in which they were said. He knew he had to find out what Lucifer was up to. Glowen or no glowen, he still felt drawn to his duty to protect and honor the will of Amanthus. This also meant that in doing so, he may have one other vow that he must break.

"You are free now, my brother. I love you, and it is the least that I owe you. I do hope that when we cross paths once more, we won't be on opposing sides. You would be best to leave this place now before all of these sleeping devils stir to wake."

He turned toward the door from which he entered and started to walk away.

"I know the truth about the prophecy, you know. I figured it out," Gabriel told him.

Lucifer did not turn to face him.

"You are one of the most clever of my brothers and sisters, Gabriel. I assure you Michael knows as well, but as you must know by now, it doesn't matter. I wish you well, brother."

Gabriel hesitated for a moment. He needed one more answer to a lingering question before Lucifer left that place that day.

"Brother…there is one thing I must know. Do I…do I have a soul?"

This time, Lucifer did again turn toward his brother. There was an emptiness in his expression, bordering on sadness. Angels can 'see' souls in mankind, just as they can see the angelic glowen emanating from each of their own kind. But Gabriel was no longer an angel. And, he was not truly a human either.

"No, Gabriel. I cannot see a soul within you."

Gabriel nodded in acknowledgement to his brother.

Lucifer could only turn away without speaking another word, and then he was gone.

CHAPTER TWO

The cement and stone breakwall stretched far out into the dark waters of the bay, protecting the harbor that housed the many boats that were moored to the pier and walkway beneath the illuminated clocktower that loomed over the Waterfront Park in the small northern Michigan town of Petoskey.

The night was warm and quiet, and it was rare for anyone to be gallivanting about at this late hour. On the weekends on a typical July night, there would at times be tourists or teens frolicking about on the rocks that lined the shoreline of the waterfront. On occasion there was the reveling of those who spent their summers living from their houseboats tied to the pier; a few drinks, a few laughs, and not so many cares for the tumultuous world in which they were a part of.

But this night, quickly approaching the hour of 3 a.m., was not a night of such things. This was a night of silence. The stars, furious balls of fire and chaos so many million miles away, remained twinkling specks without a sound in the matte-black sky. This was the kind of time and place where Miranda Gale found the closest thing to peace that she could find, and it was the solitude that brought her this sense of solace, even in the illusionary form that it was.

Nearly thirteen months had gone by since the day the freak storm came from out of seemingly nowhere across the Petoskey bay bringing a brief but significant wave of fear and destruction to the small Michigan town. With it being so sudden and fierce, it was a miracle that no one was seriously hurt or killed during the sudden onslaught of treacherous winds and brilliant lightning beneath a jet-black sky in the middle of what was a bright June day moments before.

Miranda knew all to well what came to pass on that day; it was a storm that grew from the pain in her heart. Her suffering took a shape and form in the physical world. But it did not just manifest itself; Miranda turned a key, through an act of sheer will, and released…something. Not something. *Someone.*

Whatever it was that came to pass in that moment did not ease the pain inside. She had to leave, and from the devastation of that day, she walked away from everything that she had ever known in a life of the past and carried the burden of everything that her life had become. She lost her family. She lost whatever innocence she had from the life that came before. She turned away from her closest friends. And in her heart, Miranda carried the guilt and the pain she felt from losing the one connection she had to the past she had never known. Aimsley Carter; an innocent soul whom she barely got to know that showed her love like the mother she never knew she had.

What little she had gained in the shadow of what had been so terribly lost had just as quickly been ripped away from her in an act of greed and violence - and by none other than a man of her own blood. The Gale name was tainted and yet, she took it, no longer feeling right to claim the adopted Stratton name as her own. She could feel the Gale blood in her veins. And then, there was the other…

Half of her was the offspring of a celestial being, an angel of God…the disgraced archangel Gabriel. Miranda's ever emerging collective of special abilities began to form a picture in her mind of the power and duty of the angelic kind. They were architects, performing the will of a great being through the acts of creation. Yet from her bleak perspective, this meant little to her.

All she could see now in this great creation was pain and suffering and death.

What purpose could such a thing be for if it yielded such horrors? she often thought.

And so she walked into the world, and for the past thirteen months, she traveled across the lands and seas.

Having the ability to make those around her virtually unaware of her presence, she easily could board a plane and go wherever she wanted without much effort. It wasn't so much where she was going as it was what she was looking for in her journey. Consciously, Miranda was not entirely aware of what that was. She kept moving as if she were compelled to, and wherever she went – Spain, Great Britain, France, China – wherever she found a single act of human compassion she found ten more acts of violence, greed, and hatred.

She walked unnoticed through the streets of war torn Syria, and stood witness to the dehumanization of innocent men, women and children. She walked through the fields and streets of Columbia and saw the lives of the violent tyrants that built fortunes from the suffering and addiction of people around the world.

And then, in the quiet streets or the quaint cafés of almost anywhere, with but a gentle touch of her hand, picking up a check or taking a cup of coffee from the hand of a server, she could see the nightmares of people's lives – the tortured and the villainous alike – the monstrous ilk of mankind.

And through it all she found herself even emptier than she had before her journey had begun. She stared up at the night sky and found herself lost in a moment, burdened with the knowledge that there is more. Peel back the black firmament and it would reveal the truth that there is a God, and there are indeed angels (of which through her very blood she could never have doubt). But in that same moment of thought there was a darker truth of which she had come to believe – that mankind had become nothing more than a playground of suffering and pain, if it ever was any more than that.

Lost in the moment, fixated on a single star that had seemed to become brighter than those surrounding it, the always aware Miranda did not notice the almost silent footsteps that had approached from behind her as she sat on the edge of the end of the breakwall.

"Hello Miranda."

It had been quite some time since Miranda had felt the sensation of being startled. In an instant she grabbed her beaten leather motorcycle jacket that lay beside her where she sat and swung herself around and up to her feet, throwing the jacket around her like the armor that it had always been to her – at least from a mental and emotional standpoint.

She found herself standing face-to-face with the man standing on the breakwall who had spoken her name. He was tall and strikingly handsome, his long blonde hair pulled back in a ponytail. Miranda looked him up and down, still feeling the shock of the moment. He wore beach-style shoes without socks, a beige t-shirt with the words "Classic Vinyl" printed across the chest. Over the shirt he wore a dark grey blazer. His hands were held calmly by his sides, soft and smooth. Miranda finally moved her eyes to meet his. Whatever she was feeling only moments before was gone. Now, she felt like ice.

"Lucifer," she said aloud. It was the first time she spoke the name since the weeks following her parents' death. She had seen his face before so many times in her repeating nightmare over the years, yet now it was real and somehow seemed less menacing than it ever had before. There was a calm tranquility to it, yet it did nothing to lessen the building rage within her. Lucifer could see that rage as well.

Lucifer brought a subtle smile to his lips. He slowly raised his hands to his chest.

"Miranda, you have nothing to fear from me," said Lucifer.

Miranda clenched her fists by her side. "I am not afraid of you." Her face held a stern gaze. For the first time since her confrontation with her blood uncle, David Gale, did she feel this kind of directed contempt for a single individual.

"I am not your enemy, Miranda. I am not here to fight you. I care about you more deeply than you know," he stated, lowering his hands back to his sides. Miranda watched his every move intently, and then her eyes went back to his t-shirt. She eased her tension, but stayed on guard. She began to feel a sense of confusion. Then apathy. Her gaze sank toward the ground. And then she sank to the ground as well, cross-legged, her head hanging down.

Lucifer cautiously stepped closer to her, and then allowed himself to sit before her face-to-face, cross-legged as she was. He reached out his right hand and placed it upon her shoulder.

"Miranda. I understand your pain and confusion. You have so many questions, to be sure. I want to help you," he told her.

Miranda did not look up. Lucifer gazed upon her as if she were a small, broken bird. He felt a profound sadness deep within himself.

"I saw you once, several months back. In Paris. I found it was an astounding coincidence, of all of the places to find you," he said. "You were sipping coffee at..."

"Café Sous la Brique Rouge," she said, raising her head finally to look at him. "I felt something unusual there, but I didn't know what it was."

"Yes," he said, a little surprised. "I was hiding myself, much like you have learned to do...and yet somehow you still sensed my presence."

"I didn't know it was you. I have seen other angels as well. When I tried to approach them, they disappeared right in front of me."

"They aren't allowed to interact with you, I'd guess. Only observe. And now, you have grown strong enough to know what you are seeing when you see them. They can no longer hide themselves from you. You are very strong, Miranda," said Lucifer.

"I wasn't strong enough to save my parents. To save Aimsley," she said, a flash of the subdued anger resurfacing once more.

"I had nothing to do with any of that, Miranda. This 'devil' business...I am not the monster that mankind has come to see me as. Out of all of the angels in all of creation, no one loves Amanthus more than I," he said.

"Amanthus?"

"Yes. Amanthus is the true and original name of our

Creator, our Father and Mother, that which most simply call God. Mankind has a tendency to break down complex ideas into simpler terms to better understand them, never seeming to realize how much gets lost in translation when you don't look at the bigger picture. Amanthus is not a male or a female. Yet mankind in the early years of creation found superiority in the male gender, therefore Amanthus became the 'Father' of all things. Want to know a little secret? When Amanthus came to walk the earth over two-thousand years ago, he left his gender up to chance! The virgin birth could have just as easily yielded a Holy Daughter rather than a Holy Son. Just imagine how that would have played out through the centuries!"

"Doesn't sound so bad to me," Miranda stated.

"No, it really doesn't, does it?" remarked Lucifer. "And then, of course, there is me. Lucifer – the DEVIL. Mankind has never been so good at taking responsibility for anything. Amanthus gives you lush rain forests, and mankind mows them down. Amanthus gives man fresh air, and man fills it with toxic gas. But the greatest, most valuable gift next to life itself – free will – and it is abused to no end - and then to use my name and likeness to place the blame on for all of man's many faults. I have been locked outside of the known worlds for nearly two-thousand years. I have done nothing to incur this reputation that has become me!"

"Then…why were you locked away? What did you do?" asked Miranda.

Lucifer looked away. Miranda knew the look of shame, and he wore it like the frown of a sad clown. She knew it well from whenever she caught sight of her own reflection over the past year.

"I was…jealous of man. It's ironic, you know. Man likes to believe that God created mankind in 'His image', but

Amanthus has no image. Amanthus is light and love and energy and a part of all things created. Mankind was actually made in the image of the angels. Then - and I will refer to Amanthus as 'he' because that is what your kind is familiar with - *he* gave man the freedom to do whatever they desired. Never had we angels questioned anything he did since the very beginning. We served without even the thought of anything else, and then there was man, and it seemed he favored man over us. We had done nothing wrong! If anyone deserved free will – the freedom to choose to serve whatever we desired – it was those of us that had been faithful servants from the start. Many of us – most, actually – if given the choice would have gladly stayed right where we were. When I asked him why it was not us, all Amanthus would tell me is that it is our place to stand beside him and serve."

"You left?" asked Miranda.

"I tried. I did not want conflict. I did not rebel, at least how it is said that I did. I never coveted power or worship or anything of the sort. I simply wanted to be able to walk away if I chose to. And when I did, all chances of my freedom and the freedom of all those who believed as I did and stood beside me were lost."

"Until now. I mean, it's what Amanthus wanted, right? That's what the prophecy foretold. He must have wanted you to finally be free…" Miranda asked Lucifer.

"Well…not exactly." Lucifer looked down from Miranda's gaze.

"What do you mean? Tell me what you mean," she said sharply.

"Prophecy, or the idea of prophecy, is a tricky thing. There is no such thing as foretelling the future. It is something different when Amanthus – or anyone else for that matter – has laid out a plan and then executes it. The only true prophecies are the intended plans of Amanthus. When I and the others were banished to Hell, our only window to the outside world was through the dreams of mankind. We could not see through the eyes of mankind, but we could see what they dreamed about, and much of what they dreamed came from the lives they lived in your world. But a few more powerful of the banished angels like myself could actually influence the dreams of your kind. It was with great pain and effort, but we could interact with man's dreams. And, well…the prophecy of the Caducus Oraclum was a story that I made up and put into a young boy's head, to write down thousands of years ago."

"But…why?" Miranda asked, stunned.

"What I did in the Infinite Lands…what I did to Amanthus caused him great pain. When we were banished, a loyal friend – a dear brother – found a way to contact me in Hell and told me Amanthus had disappeared. I used this opportunity to create the 'prophecy'. Without Amanthus being in sight, the other angels would not be able to know that it was not Amanthus himself that had written the prophecy. I knew they would feel it was their duty to protect the will of Amanthus by standing guard and watching for the prophecy to take shape, although they did not know how it would or even could manifest. I knew it would be apparent to them that the loophole I described – a being with the freedom of man, yet the power of an angel – could possibly defy the will of Amanthus and bring about my freedom. It was only a matter of time before my romantic brother Gabriel met your beautiful mother Suzanne and then it became…"

"A self-fulfilled prophecy," said Miranda. "You *orchestrated* my birth."

"Not yours specifically. But, in a way, yes…had they

never believed that the prophecy was from Amanthus, they wouldn't have watched over the holders of the prophecy for all those years. And Gabriel and Suzanne would have never met. What I tell you is the truth, Miranda."

"So sayeth the father of deception," quipped Miranda.

"That," remarked Lucifer, pulling himself to his feet, "is *not* me. And I will prove it. I may have stretched truths a bit to escape from that shadow realm, but the means shall justify the ends. I have watched what mankind has done with the gifts Amanthus has given, squandering and abusing free will and all of the gifts of this world. I will find my redemption with Amanthus."

Miranda suddenly stood up, seething in anger. "*The means will justify the ends*? How many more lives are you going to destroy by doing it? How many more families will die? How many children's dreams will you and your kind terrorize?"

He stepped closer to her again. Miranda braced herself, but he did not try to cause her any harm. "Miranda, I swear to you that I had nothing to do with what happened to your family. It was the greed of a solitary man that caused you such pain. And you showed that man justice. It is over."

"It would have never begun without you invading my dreams and destroying MY innocence! I would have never gone seeking the truth about my past had you not brought about the nightmares in the first place. And what about causing Aimsley's dream that made her send me the videotape?" Her eyes went glassy when she said Aimsley's name aloud.

Lucifer narrowed his eyes. To Miranda, he almost looked confused.

"I have never entered your dreams, Miranda. Because the prophecy was written by me, it would have been forbidden for me to directly intercede in your decision to release me. It had to be your will to do it. All I could do was set the stage. The act had to be all you. The same with Aimsley. I did not manipulate her at all. I do not know who did, if anyone." Lucifer turned away as if he were finished with the conversation, and then paused, turning back toward Miranda. "In the end, Miranda, when all was said and done, it was you. Your will is what set me free. You didn't know what might happen, did you? Yet you 'pulled the trigger' anyway, so to speak. If anyone should be questioning ones intentions, then perhaps you should be questioning your own."

He started walking back down the breakwall when Miranda called out to him one final time, her voice beginning to quiver as she spoke.

"What are you going to do? Revelations, then? Bring down hell on Earth?"

Lucifer turned and smiled, letting out a little chuckle. "No, Miranda. No mythical fictions. I am simply going to show mankind the light that they have refused to see for themselves. That is what I am meant to do anyhow, is it not?"

He continued on, leaving her behind, before stopping one more time. He turned his head to the side and looked to her over his shoulder. This time, his bright blue eyes revealed the blackness common to his angelic nature.

"I had hoped that perhaps you might join me in my task, Miranda, but I see you have far too much contempt for me for that to happen. I owe you much for my freedom, but I still ask one final thing of you now. Please - do try to stay out of my way.

He turned his face away from her and vanished into the darkness.

CHAPTER THREE

Greenacre Village Northern Care Facility overlooks the clear blue waters of Lake Michigan from the outstretched hills near Charlevoix, Michigan, southwest of the city of Petoskey. A long-term care, short-term rehabilitation medical care center, Greenacre has been a well established fixture with a wonderful reputation for patient care since the 1970s.

Jake Neilson quickly became a familiar favorite of the patients and staff in the seven months he has worked there upon completion of his LPN training. The one time bad-boy of Native Springs could almost never be caught without a smile on his face, making personal connections with the people residing at the medical care facility.

He would deal with mostly the long-term care patients, mostly elderly individuals whose families could not provide the home care that was needed to properly care for their needs. Some were people who had suffered a stroke, a few were patients that had varying degrees of dementia.

Mr. Henry Willis was one of those patients, and a

personal favorite of Jake's. Jake didn't play favorites, but there was something about Henry that reminded him of his great uncle Sam Neilson. Like Sam, Henry was a Vietnam War veteran who often recalled stories of the time he served during the 'conflict', and the tales were always told with great emotion and a touch of sadness and regret. Henry liked to share his tales with Jake as well, with great fervor. Most often it was the same story repeated over and over.

Jake would politely sit down and listen, always offering the same amount of interest and enthusiasm when he heard the story. It was getting close to the end of Jake's overnight 12-hour shift, and Henry was one of the last patients that Jake needed to check in on to complete his rounds for the night. Things were running a bit behind for the staff that night; a patient had complained about chest pains around 4 a.m. and an ambulance had to be called. The woman, Mary-Ann Williams, was well into her 80s and had not been at the facility long. The staff had received word within a few hours of her being picked up about her passing.

Death was never an easy thing to deal with, but in the medical world, especially with the kind of work that the good people of Greenacre Village do, it was a common thing to see. When it came to some of the patients that had become long-term residents, despite how much the staff would try to stay objective and focused on the job and all that came with it, it was still a hard thing to deal with. Sometimes, though, watching the long suffering of people with illnesses that have robbed them slowly of their minds and vitality, there was a certain relief in knowing a person was now freed of their suffering.

Jake entered Henry's room, and Henry was already up sitting in his easy chair watching a morning cooking show. It used to be the news every morning until Henry got to the point where the news became far more depressing and discouraging than he felt his own state of affairs was. Henry would have moments of incredible clarity, and other times he could forget what day, month and year it was. He had a son, Ed Willis, who lived in Rochester Hills. Ed sold parts to the auto companies and became very successful and very wealthy doing so. The original plan for Henry was to have him moved to a facility closer to where he lived down in the southern part of the state, but availability for housing was extremely limited in the area close to where Ed lived. Or so Ed said, until Jake decided to research it in his free time to see if he could help Ed find something.

When Ed came to visit his father a month ago, Jake pulled him aside and told him he found a facility that could possibly take Henry within a month or so. Ed told him to 'mind his own damn business and let him worry about his father'. Jake has an intuition about people and soon realized what was happening. Ed's visits were becoming further and further apart, and Jake could see that Ed was getting tired of dealing with his ever declining father.

Jake may be a different person than he was years ago, but sometimes it was his big heart that brought out the dormant bad-boy inside of him. The conversation with Ed took a turn quickly when the smile faded from Jake's face and he could feel his right hand form a tight fist. Jake was not a man to trifle with by any means, standing at six-foot two and over 200 pounds. He had bulked up over the past year, finding weight lifting a positive way to work out some personal issues he had, mostly first and foremost with what he felt was the unfinished business of what really happened that night over a year and a half ago at the Stratusaint Tower and why Miranda felt she had to turn her back on those people that still cared a great deal for her.

Ed saw the rage in Jake's eyes, and Jake saw the fear in Ed's. Ed backed down and left Greenacre, and since that day he hasn't returned. Jake felt partly responsible for frightening Ed away, although he knew that Henry deserved better, and spent extra time visiting with Henry, sometimes even on his time off.

"Jake, my boy! Good morning to you," exclaimed Henry upon Jake's arrival.

"Good morning, Mr. Willis," Jake replied, professional and courteous as always.

"Nonsense, this Mr. Willis stuff, I told you a thousand times, Jake," said Henry. "It's Henry, and only Henry."

"Good morning, Henry," Jake corrected himself, always the same ritual.

"That name has served me well. Back in the war, you know what they called me? Wrought-Iron Henry. You know how I earned that named, Jake?"

"No sir," recalling the many times the story had been told to him. "I'd love to hear it though."

"Myself and what remained of my platoon, five men all together, were trapped in a valley, pinned down and under heavy fire. We gave back what we could, but the odds of getting out were a far cry from good. Jonny May was hit bad, fell dead right before our eyes, and then there were four of us left. Dan Walker, Billy Spencely, Cliff Barnes and myself. A grenade landed close by and Dan and Billy were hurt bad and couldn't hardly walk on their own. Cliff was still alright though. Tough bastard, God rest his soul. Air strike came at the last minute and gave us time. Cliff took Danny over his shoulder, and I took Billy over mine. We only had ninety feet to go until we were in a safer position than where we were at then. It was enough to give us a chance. Cliff and Danny were ahead of us when a sniper took Cliff down. Danny hit the ground and managed to push himself into a ditch for cover. I managed to do the same with Billy, and I grabbed my rifle and started firing in the general direction of the shot that took down Cliff."

Jake watched all of the emotions run across Henry's face as he recalled once again the story which had been told to him several times before. Each time the emotions ran the same, with the same depth, and the story held the same detail. It was easy to forget, with as much animation and heart that was put into the telling, that this was coming from a man that was slowly losing himself to this dreaded disease of the mind.

"I finally found the spot where the gunfire was coming from. I was an ace shot, and I moved into a position further down the ditch where I could get a clear shot at the son-of-a-bitch. Billy begged me not to leave him, and I told him no matter what happens I will not leave him behind. I swore it to him. Each one of those men were my brothers, and while I never had a brother of my own, I could not imagine a greater bond than the one I shared with those men. I took my shot, one bullet, and put the sniper down."

"I told Billy, 'I gotta get Danny – stay here and keep your head down, I will be back to bring you home'. He nodded to me, unsure and scared, but he knew I would never leave him behind, so he let me go. I pulled Danny from that ditch and dragged his ass to the safe cover zone, and then I headed back to get Billy. I picked that boy up over my shoulders and started ahead, and I was fifty feet out when there was another grenade attack, blew me and Billy right off the ground…swore we had to have flown 15 or 20 feet. I was stunned and in pain. Blew a chunk of my thigh out."

Jake had seen the scars on his leg, in times when Henry

was bad and he had to help him change his clothing. He was amazed that Henry was ever able to use his leg again, but Henry could get around just fine for his age.

"I couldn't get up," Henry continued. "My vision was a blur. The only thing I could make out in the smoke and the dust was Billy, lifting me up and carrying me the rest of the way to the safe zone. I passed out and found myself on a gurney next to Danny the next day."

"Billy was a hero," Jake said to Henry. Henry turned his head to the window and glared out with a blank look on his face. Jake thought he was slipping into a bad moment. This was where the story would usually end. This day was different though.

"Yes…yes, Billy…he was a hero." Henry slowly turned his head back toward Jake, who was seated on the edge of the bed beside him. Jake could see there was something different about the look on Henry's face. It wasn't the look he had seen many times before from Henry on his bad days. It was a look of strange realization.

Henry reached a hand out to Jake and laid it upon Jake's wrist. He looked directly into Jake's eyes.

"Billy…he never made it out of there. That grenade…he didn't survive the blast," Henry recalled. Jake had never before heard this part of the story. He wondered if somehow Henry had blocked it from his memory, or if it was perhaps not a real memory at all.

"But I know he pulled me from the ground and carried me to safety. The only thing I could see was his face. The only thing I could hear was his voice…it was so soothing. He said "I am not going to leave you behind, buddy". I know it was him. He carried me to Danny, and then it all went blank. They found and recovered his body in the spot where the grenade had gone off. Billy never got up again…but I know he carried me to safety. He saved my life."

Jake sat in quiet astonishment at the tale that Henry was telling him. Henry slowly pulled his hand back away from Jake's wrist. His eyes were glassy. His lower lip was trembling.

"Henry? Are you alright," Jake asked with concern in his voice.

Henry looked at him and forced a smile to his face. "Yes, my boy. I'm fine. But I'm afraid that kind Mrs. Williams won't be coming back to visit us again, will she? She came by my room just before you stopped by and told me that she was moving on. Said I shouldn't be too far behind."

Jake felt a hollow feeling in his chest. He knew that the residents were not yet made aware of Mrs. William's passing, so there was no way that Henry should know this. And there was the other part he said…

"Henry, don't say that," Jake said. "You'll be around for a long time."

Henry's only response was to give Jake a sincere smile. "How did you know she passed?" Jake asked him.

Henry didn't answer Jake's question though. He pretended that he didn't hear the question, and asked Jake to help him into his bed. He was tired.

Jake helped him and started to the door when Henry stopped him.

"Jake. I need to tell you something," he said, his tone uncharacteristically serious. Jake stepped closer to the bed. Henry held out his hand once again to Jake, and Jake took it.

"When Billy was carrying me, I felt something I had never felt before. I felt like, somehow, in some way, there was a feeling deep inside, and I don't know whether it came from Billy or from somewhere inside myself. I felt like I was somehow touched by divinity. Like I was touched by an angel. I'd never felt anything like it before. I've never told that story about Billy to anyone…not my wife, and certainly not to my self-centered, greedy-ass son. But I knew I could tell you, Jake."

"What do you mean? How did you know?" asked Jake.

"When I touched you I knew…you've felt it too, Jake. I can feel it inside of you. You've been touched by that same divine light." Henry smiled once more at Jake and rested his head on his pillow. He let go of Jake's hand and closed his eyes, slipping off to sleep.

Jake left Henry's room, shaken and uneasy. He knew the feeling that Henry spoke of, but had no idea what any of it meant. He knew it had to do with the Stratusaint Tower and Miranda, but as much as he tried to forget that night and move on, it always seemed to find a way to come back and haunt him.

He finished his shift that morning and punched out, heading out the back door to his Harley Davidson motorcycle. For the third day in a row he saw a man sitting on the bench near the garden fountain, always with a paperback novel in his hands, watching him as he walked out to his bike. After the second day seeing the man, he asked some of the other staff members if they had seen him or knew who he was, and no one said they had noticed, but just guessed that he might be a relative of a resident.

Jake felt uneasy about the stranger, and made mental notes about his appearance. Dark, medium length hair, cut a few inches above the shoulders, a dark beard much the same, with maybe a few weeks growth on it, flecked with bits of gray. Blue jeans, black pea-coat jacket, with a sling messenger bag. When the man noticed that Jake was staring a little longer than usual at him, the man casually placed his book in his bag and stood up, strolling along up the sidewalk. He glanced to his side and noticed Jake's continued glare, but he kept walking on, without another look back again.

Jake's gaze was broken finally by the sound of a text notification from his cell phone. He pulled the phone from the inside pocket of his leather jacket and looked at the screen.

The notification displayed the sender's name. It was from Miranda's best friend and former college roommate, Lydia Snow.

Rick Jurewicz

CHAPTER FOUR

In three days time, Xander Graves would be dead, alongside his five-man crew in a hail of bullets and gunfire at a private residence near New Haven, Connecticut. Despite what would seemingly be the best laid plans, an unaccounted for surveillance camera from a neighboring residence sparked an investigation by an anti-terrorism task force of federal, state and local agencies to the residence, where, in the aftermath of the massive shootout, documented evidence of domestic targets of Graves' group were uncovered.

The motivations, largely unclear and non-specific, pointed to anti-government and anti-establishment beliefs. Those beliefs culminated in the formation of the small group of United States radicals led by the wealthy Mr. Graves, to begin launching several attacks around the city over several months. The endeavor was short-lived, and had very little impact in itself regarding the intentions for which it was initiated, but what ensued in the aftermath of the first and only attack would have a far greater effect in the darker times yet to come.

On this night, Graves and crew traveled aboard *The Devil's Own* - a 65 foot Pershing 64 yacht - along the southern waters of the Hudson River near Lower Manhattan just after nightfall.

Graves was not a "professional" terrorist. He had been a very knowledgeable and resourceful businessman who made millions of dollars over his 64 years, constructing parking structures across New York and New Jersey. After 9/11, Graves became embittered with the way the U.S. government handled the terror attacks and came to blame areas of the government for being responsible for bringing on the attacks themselves. What made matters worse was that he lost his daughter-in-law, Sarah Graves, in the attack on the Twin Towers. His son Eric suffered from depression for years after her death, and despite Xander's best efforts to help his son, Eric took his own life a year earlier from tomorrows date.

This was the act that triggered Xander Graves to act, and tonight he would set in motion events to culminate on the one year anniversary of his beloved son's death.

The yacht that the group was on was not Graves' own. It was the property of novelist and real-estate speculator Canton Grace. Canton Grace was not part of Graves' group – just a part of Graves' plan, and would be the part that lead to Graves' demise in less than 72 hours.

Graves decided that he needed a watercraft that could not be traced back to him. He knew Grace from several social gatherings the two had attended over the years, and people often commented on how much the two men looked alike. They were close in age, within three years, and both had short, thick grey hair and bushy mustaches. Height and build were almost identical. Graves knew he could pass for Grace in almost any setting, so he chose Grace and his yacht on purpose.

    The day prior, Graves and two other men that were part of his group went to Grace's residence in Crotonville, New York, more than 40 miles driving distance from the Lower Manhattan area. Canton Grace did not have much for security at his residence. Just an alarm system that he armed when he left town, and through research and observation, Graves' men discovered this fact. Graves and the two men forced Grace into a car with them; they then traveled to a nearby pier where Grace kept his yacht. It was a high resolution security camera at a nearby residence that would lead investigators to Graves and his men soon after *The Devil's Own* was found in flames in the north Hudson River, along with the charred remains of Canton Grace.

    Tonight, the body of Canton Grace was tightly packed into a small holding container on the lower deck of the boat. Graves believed that if any NYPD patrol boats stopped the yacht for a credentials check, he could easily pass for Grace and establish his identity as the owner and operator of the yacht.

    The watercraft reached its destination a few hundred yards from the mooring place of the Singleton Way Ferry, a new river ferry service that took passengers for tour rides up and down the Hudson River along Lower Manhattan , or around Ellis and Liberty Islands, around Governors Island, up the East River, passing by the Brooklyn Bridge and the Manhattan Bridge, before circling around and coming back through to the mooring near the Battery – the section on the lower west corner of Manhattan Island that was until recently known as Battery Park.

    The Singleton Ferry was started by a wealthy retired shipping company executive named Gary Singleton. The service was new, and this was the first ferry in service. It would take a few different tours a day along the two different tour routes. The ferry held just over 300 people for the tours, and Singleton was having a very successful first year run, filling the ferry for more than three-quarters of the tour trips each day.

But the only mooring spot available for the Singleton Way Ferry near the Battery made it vulnerable, and Xander Graves was made well aware of that fact.

The Devil's Own anchored in the harbor and the drinks came out. The three men that remained on the craft listened to music and danced on the deck, pouring champagne to celebrate a victory that was still to come. The other three men that traveled with them were already in full scuba gear beneath the surface of the river waters, moving on to the spot where the Singleton Ferry laid in wait.

Once the men reached the ferry, six powerful plastic explosive charges were placed along the bottom of the hull well beneath the surface of the water. They were set to ignite in a sequential order along the wire that connected all six, like a line of firecrackers strung together. From the first charge in line, there was a wire that led to the edge of the hull just below the standing waterline, at the end of which was a small receiver that could be reached by a cellular signal.

The men who waited aboard the yacht were in fact passed by an NYPD patrol boat, but the officers passed by and waved a hello without incident. The only immanent danger was the possible discovery of Canton Grace's body on the boat. There were no weapons, and the explosive devices were now off of the boat and in place. Still, it was enough for the men on the boat, Graves included, to break into a sweat as the patrol boat cruised by. Soon after, the divers returned and were helped aboard the boat by Graves and the other two.

The Devil's Own departed, with Graves watching through

the eye of a harbor pier webcam for the ferry to load for its first cruise of the day the next morning and enter the river waters on the way toward Liberty Island. Graves would make his statement before one of the most visible American monuments ever beheld. And while, in the grand scheme of things, Graves attempt at terrible revolt would lead to very little in accordance with his twisted dreams, the impact of his attack and the acts of another individual would begin to shake the very foundations of faith in the fragile and damaged world that Graves ached for change in just the same.

For a celestial being that had one of the greatest hands in forging the fabric of the universe itself, Lucifer, the first angel, the first creation of God, sat high on the red stairs of Duffy Square in the heart of New York City's world famous Times Square in awe of what was before him.

Is this what it is like for Amanthus, a taste of near omniscience, he wondered silently to himself.

The screens across the buildings in every direction surrounding him blazed with a constant barrage of advertisements and news feeds from all around the city, state, country and world. Lights flashed, people walked past or huddled in the crowded open space below, and Lucifer's keen ears listened to a dozen different languages within 50 feet of where he was sitting. Echoing down the streets in every direction were the sounds of honking automobile horns, the wail of sirens and the voices of thousands of men and women watching with awe this spectacle of human informational overload.

It was perfect, everything he could have hoped for. From this spot, he would find the opportunity that would begin the change of everything. All he had to do was to wait for the right event in the right moment.

He had not moved from that spot for the past six days. Had he been like any ordinary man, his constant presence would have certainly flagged caution to someone, be it a New York police officer assigned to Times Square who took notice of the unmoving blonde man in the dark grey trench coat and shiny black boots that never even had to leave from his spot to pee, or the street performers that frequented the Square from morning through the night that may have perhaps noticed the man as well and alerted local authorities.

But no; Lucifer was, after all, an angel, and could choose if and how a mortal being could be aware of his presence. He sat and he watched and he waited with a patience that he had honed to immeasurable purpose over the past 2000 years in his shadowy Hell.

He had seen so much in the dreams of men, but the dreams were only blurred reflections of the actual reality of the world which was growing and forming in his absence from it. Two things struck him more than anything else in his travels around the world over the past year. First, it was the innovative and creative capacity of mankind. They had done so much with so little, carving this fantastic monument of technology and beauty and architecture. Lucifer and the angels had great power that had been bestowed unto them by Amanthus, and formed mountains and the Great Ocean. They designed the complex structures that made life possible with the guidance of their Creator. Mankind had no such power, yet they created so much on their own. They discovered the smallest secrets and forged new destinies for their entire race. They unlocked many of the secrets of the DNA that Amanthus and the angels designed from the midst of imagination and defined the rules by which the sciences of this world would adhere to.

And then there was the other - the thing that struck him even harder than the many great accomplishments of man. It was the thing that set him on the path to which he had dedicated himself, with his freedom from the great void. It was the chaos and destruction man has lain to the great world that had been created for its kind…the abuse and the arrogance that had been wrought upon the beautiful paradise that had been bestowed upon them long ago.

They had long forgotten. And many of them blamed Amanthus, blamed their God. Free will, the great gift for which Lucifer had been cast out of the Infinite Lands for claiming for himself and thrown into a realm of eternal darkness, had driven mankind against each other as it had driven his own brothers and sisters against each other when he tried to leave the Infinite Lands. But with man, it was so much worse, and it perpetuated through time with the rise and fall of kingdoms and empires; it fed their greed and their egos, and stained and tarnished their very souls.

Many didn't even believe in Amanthus. Most of the rest that did believe used what they believed Amanthus stood for to justify their actions and nullify their own sins. Anyone who fought a war in *His* name, no matter what the writings of their faith were, did not know Amanthus at all.

Everything that mankind came to blame Lucifer for, to defile his name, to make him their Devil – *everything* was of their own making. They just refused to take responsibility for what they had become. His one action of defiance made him the scapegoat for all of the sins of mankind since the beginning of time itself.

Now, he would remind them of the true value of the great gift. He would show them the truth within themselves by reminding them of where they truly came from. They would see and they would know and they would never forget. He would do this for Amanthus, and Amanthus would see and be glad. Amanthus would once more open his heart to Lucifer, and mankind would give Amanthus the love and respect he deserved.

The wait was about to come into its final moments...

They came in droves that morning, lining the sidewalks in long lines waiting for their chance to board the Singleton Way Ferry. Families, single tourists visiting the city for the first time - or the twentieth - for business or pleasure, took the opportunity to see the great city from a new perspective on the trip around Liberty Island and up the East River down past the Brooklyn Bridge.

It did not take long for the first tour of the morning to fill the ferry to its 300 person capacity. The ferry departed on time and was making its way toward the first part of this tour, the loop around Liberty Island. Xander Graves was a jumble of nerves as he watched the progress of the ferry approach the target zone, through the hacked network of harbor cameras and public webcams, from his far off location. Doubt began to plague his thoughts, but the small photographs he held tightly in his hand – one a picture of his son on his eighth birthday, and the other, a photograph from Eric and Sarah's wedding day – were all he needed to refocus his intent and purpose. Doubt gave way to anger and all hesitation disappeared.

Graves made the fated call. He watched as only a few seconds went by. And then, he ran, a desperate and doomed run away to his own fate.

The signal made its contact. The first explosion ripped a huge hole in the left rear side of the hull, followed by two more in the sequential order of the charges. And then the blasts stopped. The connection to the remaining three explosives failed through faults unknown. The ferry began to violently list on the port side as fear and panic erupted like a riot. The lower compartments were filling fast with water, and passengers were frantically climbing the steps to the upper levels to escape the flooding. Some of the passengers who stood along the rails on the upper deck when the blast first occurred lost balance and fell to the water below, shaken and caught by surprise by the jolt of the explosions from beneath the ferry. The ferry was not rapidly sinking as intended by Graves for maximum damage, but it was still sinking, and the distress of the vessel was noticed by a television traffic helicopter who pointed their cameras toward the ferry, calling their respective news agencies and alerting emergency services to the distress of the listing ferry.

Within minutes of the onset of the ferry disaster, the screens in Times Square flashed several images from different news agencies of the frantic scene near Liberty Island, stopping many of the constantly moving pedestrians in Times Square in their tracks. New York City has had many years to heal from the devastation of 9/11, but the scars remain all the same and the fear runs deep, coupled with the strength and resilience of a people ready for the challenge if once again their city comes under attack by enemies both foreign or domestic.

Lucifer raised his eyes to the massive screen in front of him and just as quickly disappeared without the notice of any of the thousand people in his near presence, just the same reappearing on the shores of the Battery with a distant view of the ferry as emergency boats raced to attempt a rescue of the survivors of the incident, which was not yet known to be a deliberate attack. The sidewalks lined with people all watching the events unfold. Lucifer stood in the middle of the crowds closest to the docks. He allowed his presence and his actions to be known by all around him, and he walked forward to the edge of the dock and looked around him before his feet lifted from the dock and he descended to the surface of the waters below. Where his feet touched the surface of the river, the waters smoothed around him, and for several seconds, he stood motionless on the river surface.

The people along the dock stared and murmured and gasped in a frenzy of disbelief and confusion. Many thought it was a stunt or a scene being filmed for a movie. Camera phones were pulled out and pictures were taken, as well as video clips and online live-streams. He did not allow the features of his face to be discernable on the images taken. Now was not the time for that. It would come later, one step at a time. He then began to take strides across the surface of the river, each step he took crossed a hundred yards of more at once. The confusion grew in those that had seen him take his first steps from the dock to the water, and soon he was nearly out of their sight as he came closer to the ferry.

He quickly passed by the emergency boats that had not yet reached the ferry. The crews on the boats took notice of the strange figure as it raced past them, and several of the rescuers stood slack-jawed as they looked on, dumbfounded by what appeared to be…a man walking on water.

Lucifer came upon the vessel, now half submerged in the river, many of the passengers still trapped on the lower deck struggling for air. His eyes searched the waters around the ferry and discovered many of the people that were already in the water, trying to keep above the choppy waves. He tapped his foot on the river surface, causing ripples to reach out from the places where he tapped, calming and smoothing the waters where the people struggled. With a slight movement of his right hand, the people in the water rose to the surface and now were lying upon the smooth, wet floor that was in all reality the surface of the Hudson River. The mixed look of confusion and fear on the faces of those passengers was evident as many felt a sense of relief and a few even pushed themselves to their knees and started to pray.

The first news helicopter above had been joined by one from another news agency and two more Coast Guard helicopters, all incredulously watching the events unfold below. The broadcast was no longer just local affiliates. It was now being seen live across most of the nation.

Lucifer focused his attention on the ferry, now that the victims in the water were safe. With his left hand, he motioned with his palm open and facing upward and within moments the water stopped rushing in the ferry. The ferry began to rise as the water began to rush out of the tears that it had come in through in the lower hull of the ferry. Within a few minutes the ferry was level again as the nation - and through a few international news networks - people from around the entire globe, looked on, shaken and awestruck. Many thought it was a hoax. Many thought it was all from a movie. Most waved it off as such, and a great many, like the rescued few in the waters around the ferry, dropped to their knees in prayer, realizing they had just witnessed a real life miracle.

The tears in the hull were sealed as if a searing heat welded the rifts, and Lucifer calmly walked to the people atop the surface of the water and extended his hand to help them back on the ferry. Many kissed his hands and thanked him, and several thanked God for him.

"*Let us hope so*", he said under his breathe after the first person said the words.

The rescue boats came upon him helping one woman, but the people in the boat said nothing at all, only helping the individual into the rescue boat as Lucifer led the woman to it.

"Thank you, good sir," Lucifer said to the man who took the woman's hand. The man only nodded, blank-faced as Lucifer did all he could to repress a grin from his lips.

The people were all safe, and with just as much mystery, the engines fired up aboard the ferry and the rescue boats led the way for the ferry to return to the nearest emergency mooring. All of the camera crews were still focusing on Lucifer, although they were all having the same difficulty trying to get focus of his face. Simultaneously, all of the cameras experienced a static glitch. It only lasted for a second or two, but in that moment Lucifer was gone, vanished from the camera screens and vanished from the eyes of those around him. The rescue boats circled back around, and still remained searching the waters in that area of the river for the next few hours, sending out divers and keeping watch from the sky above for any signs of the mysterious hero that saved the day on the Hudson. Nothing was to be found that day.

"Son of a bitch."

Hundreds of miles away, in a small café in northwest Michigan, Gabriel watched every broadcast second of the events that were unfolding in New York City. His eyes were wide and his attention sharply focused on the actions of his brother that morning.

Whatever it was that Lucifer was up to, Gabriel knew well the ramifications that could come with it. And he also knew that the only chance he had to stop those ramifications from happening was to once again break a vow and go against the will of Amanthus and those that serve him in the Infinite Lands, regardless of the personal cost to himself. Gabriel knew he had to find his daughter.

CHAPTER FIVE

Jake sat restlessly in the front booth of a Front Street Pub in the downtown area of Petoskey, closest to the main street door. He parked in the parking lot that was across from the alley that ran behind the pub, and told Lydia where it was that he would be seated so that it was easy for her to find him. He offered to meet her somewhere with a little brighter atmosphere, as the mood lighting in the pub was low and there was not a lot of color in the décor of the quieter dining side of the divided building. The solid flat hardwood tables and high-backed walnut stained booth seats made him feel quite secluded in the place, at least until the movement of patrons in the connected booth seat behind him reminded him that he was not alone.

She insisted on meeting in this place. She had seen great reviews of it online, and since she was going to be arriving in town around noon, she thought it would be a good opportunity to finally try it out and grab some lunch. Jake agreed and they arranged to meet that Saturday, noon, at the pub.

A text came though on his phone at ten after 12.

"Running a little behind. Be there soon. Parking behind alley?"

"Yes. Sounds good – no hurry," he typed back to her.

He shifted uneasily in the bench style seat. It was not the most comfortable seat with its straight back that reached high above his head in the booth, but it really wasn't the seat that was making him uncomfortable. It was facing Lydia today.

Jake and Lydia had been in contact several times over the past year and a half since Miranda disappeared. There were a few phone calls, a lot of texts…much of it was worry and speculation on Lydia's part about what happened that night at the Stratusaint Tower. He told her as much of the truth as he could. That was, the things that he could actually remember about that night in the Tower, and everything that he had found out after that night – everything except the fact that he had received a handwritten letter from Miranda that proved that she had survived the confrontation with David Gale and the explosion in the tower. In the letter, Miranda had stated that he should not tell Lydia, that she wouldn't understand. He knew that he himself did not understand what had happened or why Miranda chose to stay away, so he had made the decision to honor her request and not tell Lydia about it. Now he was not so sure he made the right choice.

Jake and Lydia had found a bond in their shared love of Miranda, and on those nights when the pain and the confusion seemed overwhelming for either of them, the other was just a phone call or a text away. Sometimes the calls lasted late into the night, and the subject of conversation often diverged away from Miranda, talking instead about their lives before all of this. Jake of course had his history with Miranda before Miranda had ever met Lydia, and they talked about those times quite a bit. But Jake shared with her the times after Miranda left as well

- everything he had gone through and how he finally got through it all and went on to school and eventually into nursing. He stayed away from the subject of the feelings that he still struggled with regarding Miranda. It was something he kept close to himself. Jake felt it was only his burden to bear.

Now, she was coming here. She had found a few more things that had belonged to Miranda that had been placed in boxes with many of her things when she moved out of the apartment she had shared with Miranda. She said they were probably mistakenly packed up by her sister who had come to help her move into a smaller place. The items – a few books and CD's and a photo album – had been placed into a storage facility along with the apartment furniture and other odds and ends. It wasn't that Lydia couldn't afford the apartment that they had been living in any longer. She just didn't want to be there any more without her best friend.

Everything else that Miranda had left behind had already been brought to Jake. There was no next of kin, and Lydia did not know what she should do with her things. She didn't believe that Miranda was dead and gone. She wouldn't allow herself to believe that. But she was lost as to what she should do with her things. Jake eased the burden for her and said that he would take care of them and keep them safe. It was a difficult thing for him to do, but he felt it was the right thing to do. He rented a storage building east of town and locked everything safely up there. In the back of his mind he always held the hope, much like Lydia did, that someday Miranda would come walking back into their lives. But another part of him believed that would probably never happen.

It was guilt that Jake was feeling now. Guilt for not telling Lydia the truth from the beginning. He didn't actually lie to her, he just didn't tell her everything that he knew. About the letter…and about the strange scar that was in the center of his abdomen, and the searing pain that he felt in flashes of memory, along with the memory of the murky image of Miranda during the pain. Her face in a haze of agony and emptiness…and her strange, dark eyes. He would see them, and then all would go dark, and that was the most he could ever make of the memory. Most of it came back only in dreams during the weeks that followed the explosion at the Tower. And then they finally stopped, and nothing more returned from that night.

Lydia peeked into the long, narrow room. Jake waved to her, and she smiled at him. She had cut her blonde hair very short, which was an unusual look for her. He smiled to himself as she began to walk toward the booth. He liked the new look for her. It was a far cry from the pony-tailed girl wearing sweatpants and a tee shirt that he briefly met in the coffeehouse in Preston on that fateful day. Now she was wearing an orange and yellow summer dress with white Converse shoes and the one word that popped into his mind was not a word that he used in everyday speaking.

Stunning. She looked stunning.

"Hi," she said cheerfully, sitting herself in the bench seat across from Jake. The smile seemed embedded on her face, and all Jake could do was smile back, although if for some reason he didn't want to smile, he didn't think he would be able not too at that moment.

"Hi." He was uncharacteristically nervous in her presence right now. He didn't know why, aside from the fact that he found her surprising appearance catching him off-guard, and of course the things that had been on his mind before she made her entrance into the pub.

"Are you alright?" she asked him, a puzzled look on her

face.

Jake quickly shook it off. "Yeah, I'm fine. There's just been a lot on my mind lately. You found the place alright?"

"The miracle of GPS. No problems." She smiled brightly at him again. A young woman in an apron approached the table and laid down silverware wrapped in cloth napkins at the table.

"What can I get you to drink?" asked the waitress.

"I'll have a lemonade," Lydia replied.

"And you, sir?"

"Give me a Labatt, please," Jake told her.

"I'll have these right up for you, too." The young woman smiled and walked away from the table. Jake decided he could not hold back any longer from Lydia. He had to tell her about the letter.

"Listen, there's something that I need to tell you," he started, with a slight degree of hesitation in his voice.

"Okay," she said, her bright smile dampening in the moment. There was an immediate look of concern in her eyes. "Is it...have you heard something? About Miranda?"

"Well, yes. But don't worry. It's nothing new...I mean, it's nothing that is recently new."

"What do you mean *recently* new?" she asked, narrowing her eyes at him.

"I got a letter...it was from Miranda," he told her.

"A letter? What...is she alright? Where is she?" asked Lydia.

"I got it a few months after the Stratusaint Tower incident," he said, trying to keep his eyes fixed on Lydia. It was more difficult than he had thought it might be. He noticed flecks of green in her hazel eyes he had not noticed before. It distracted him for a moment from the cold, hard stare in which she held him in that moment.

The waitress promptly returned to the table.

"One lemonade, one Labatt," she said, although neither one of them looked up from the gaze. Finally, Lydia broke the gaze and reached into her purse, pulled a twenty from inside and laid it on the table.

She looked up to the waitress. "Thank you, I'm sorry I won't be staying." She stood up from the table and started to walk toward the back door from which she came in from.

"Lydia, please, wait," pleaded Jake. He put a ten dollar bill on the table for his beer and told the waitress to please keep the change, and followed Lydia out the back door into the alley behind the pub.

Lydia was already fast up the alley when Jake made it out the door.

"Lydia! Please, let me explain," he called to her. She kept walking. "For Miranda, please!"

She stopped. Jake hurried in her direction, although she didn't turn around. He stopped just behind her.

"Why?" She said without turning. He knew that she had started to cry, and it made him feel that much worse. "You knew she was alive. She *is* alive. And neither one of you could tell me that she was okay? I had to wait and wonder and mourn her for a year and a half, and you knew the whole time!"

"Lydia…" Jake started, taking a deep breath, "Miranda was afraid. She didn't want anyone else to get hurt. She just lost her parents and her brother, and she was afraid that other people close to her were in danger. She asked me to do two things for her. To not come and try to find her, and to keep an eye on you. She said I should probably not tell you I got the letter…that you might not understand."

Lydia turned finally to face Jake.

"She was right about one thing. I don't understand. Why wouldn't she want me to know she was alright? That's all I needed to know. I would do anything for her, even if it meant not being able to see her. I just...*sniff*...I just wish she would have trusted me enough to let me know she was okay." Jake took her into his arms and hugged her, letting her get out the overload of emotions she was feeling. She was both greatly happy and deeply hurt, and her heart didn't know how to process what had just happened.

Jake lifted his head as he held her and noticed a man in the distance peering around the fence of the nearby parking lot adjacent to the alley. He quickly recognized that it was the man from the bench outside of Greenacre Village.

He lowered his head so the man could not see him whisper into Lydia's ear.

"Did you park in the lot that's 100 feet back up the alley?"

"Yes," she whispered back, suddenly aware of the serious change in Jake's tone of voice. "Why?"

"I'm going to take your hand and we are going to walk casually in the opposite direction. Do not look back. Alright?" said Jake.

She nodded a quick, subtle nod and he took her hand and started walking. They walked about 25 feet before Jake pulled out his cell phone. He turned on the camera and switched it to selfie mode, and held it as inconspicuously as he could to see if they were being followed. When he was certain enough that they weren't followed, he and Lydia slipped into a narrow side alley.

The man appeared around the corner and looked up and down both directions of the alley. He started moving in the direction in which Jake and Lydia had gone, and quickly picked up his pace when he realized he may have allowed them too much space and did not want to lose them. When he was almost to the side alley in which they had gone into, he realized quickly that the assumption he had made that they had already emerged onto the street at the far end of the alley was a false assumption. He realized this when the lid of a steel trash can swung out from around the corner of the narrow alley and nailed him square in the face, knocking him flat on his back. Blood started to run from his nose, and Jake was fast on top of him, grabbing the man by the pea-coat jacket with his fist at the ready, prepared for another hard blow if necessary.

Jake looked up and down the alley to make sure there was no one else trailing behind the man before dragging the man into the narrower side alley. Lydia stood at the ready with a wooden landscape stake she was prepared to use as a club if necessary. Jake pulled the man up off of the cobblestone alley floor and pushed him hard against the wall.

"Who are you!? Why have you been following me?" Jake roared at the man, who was still greatly dazed from the blow of the trash can. "Answer me, or I swear, if you think you are in pain now, I know ways to really make you hurt. I'm a nurse!"

Lydia shifted her eyes at Jake with a slight eyebrow raise, then shifted her attention back to the man against the wall.

"I'm…" the man started, trying to regain some composure. "I'm trying to find my…my daughter."

"What are you talking about," Jake shot back. ""Why are you following me? Talk!"

"I need to find my daughter…I was hoping to find her through you, Jake…" said the man, finally articulating himself more clearly.

"We have to find my daughter…we have to find Miranda."

Rick Jurewicz

CHAPTER SIX

There were a great number of reasons for Jake to be wary of the stranger and his claim of Miranda being his daughter. Given the events of a year and a half ago - the reappearance of Miranda's long lost evil uncle, prophecies and ancient texts and gun toting religious zealots - Jake didn't have much reason to trust the word of anyone, especially a man who had been stalking him and now following him and Lydia. But it was also this same string of circumstances which made him keep his mind open to any and all possibilities. That, and the scar on his abdomen that haunted both his waking thoughts and sleeping dreams.

Lydia returned to the pub and came back with towels and water from the pub's restroom. The man cleaned himself up and stopped the blood coming from his nose. Jake gave her his car keys and told her where to find his Buick sedan in the lot, and she retrieved the car and drove it down the alley to where Jake waited with the man. He had the man get into the back seat and Jake followed in beside him.

"I understand why this must be hard for you to believe…" the man started.

Jake cut him off mid-sentence.

"Just be quiet. We'll have plenty of time to talk when we get somewhere more private. If I don't like what you have to say, there is a detective I know that would love to ask you a few questions."

"I think we both know that you don't want to do that, don't we, Jake?" said the man.

Lydia's eyes flashed up into the rear view mirror and met Jake's. He looked back at the man.

"Lydia," Jake said, nodding ahead up the road. "Take that street all the way to the end. There is a dead end with a line of storage buildings there. Drive to number 38."

Lydia nodded without saying a word. She drove down the street and carefully looked around the facility as she drove. There were no other signs that anyone else was at the place. There were three long rows of buildings with garage doors lining both sides of each building, ten on each side, for a total of sixty units, each unit with a number beside the door. She pulled up just past the door of unit number 38, and turned off the engine.

Jake got out of the car and instructed the man to get out as well. Lydia got out and came around the rear of the car.

"Third key from the ignition key will open the door," Jake told Lydia. She moved over to the door as Jake held a firm grip on the man's arm, never taking an eye off of him. Lydia turned the key and cranked the handle, and the 8 foot wide garage door easily sprang up and open. Jake pulled the man inside and flipped a switch on the wall illuminating an overhead light. He pulled a wooden chair stacked against the wall down and placed it against an open wall.

"Sit down," Jake instructed the man, and the man calmly sat down in the chair. Mostly recovered from the stun of being slammed in the face with the garbage can lid, and with the bleeding finally stopped, the man's demeanor was overwhelmingly cooperative now. Jake grabbed the handle of the garage door and pulled it down to the ground, closing out the outside world. Lydia stood back nearest the farthest wall from the man, and Jake walked to a spot just a few feet from the man in the chair and looked down at his face. It was the first time that he had taken a good long look at the man. He could almost see subtle features in the man's face that reminded him of Miranda, but then thought that perhaps he was looking too hard to see anything clearly at this point.

"Okay. Time to talk. One thing at a time. I ask questions, you give answers. Understand?"

"Yes, I understand," said the man, calm and direct.

"Good," Jake said with a single nod. "Why have you been following me?"

"You were the only thing that I had to go on in the search for my daughter," said the man.

"By your daughter, you mean Miranda. Correct?"

"Yes. I am her father. My name is Gabriel," said the man.

"Miranda's fathers name was Robert Stratton. I knew him very well. He was murdered a year and a half ago by the same people that were after Miranda and I," said Jake sternly.

Gabriel lowered his head solemnly. "Yes, I know. Robert and Lorri were, as I understand it, good people. Miranda couldn't have been in better hands. But I assure you, I am Miranda's father, and I need to find her. She is in grave danger. I need to talk to her. My brother...he may try to get to her, and I need to warn her about what is coming."

"And what is coming," Jake asked.

Gabriel said nothing to his question. "Do you know how to find her?"

Jake turned away, briefly glancing at Lydia. He turned back to Gabriel.

"People were trying to kill us," Jake said to Gabriel. "I don't know how to find Miranda. I've tried. And even if I did know where she was, I have no way of knowing that you are who you say you are. You could be another one of David Gale's people trying to finish the job."

"David Gale was a sad, deranged man, hungry for power and glory that was never meant to be his or anyone else's. He captured me and tortured me, and kept me locked in a room for so many years I cannot even say," Gabriel told him.

"And you say that you have a brother that is coming after her now? What is it with all the evil uncles suddenly coming out of the wood-work into Miranda's life?" asked Jake, the anger starting to rise in his voice. "No, wait. Before you answer that, let me tell you something. This is pointless. Miranda has been gone for nearly two years. She doesn't want to be found. As much as I would like to find her, I am going to respect the last thing she asked of me. I am going to leave her in peace."

As Jake spoke to Gabriel, Lydia could hear the flurry of emotions in his voice. He cared about Miranda very deeply, this Lydia already knew. But she wondered if the anger he was feeling wasn't only directed at Gabriel. She wondered if maybe some of it was meant for Miranda as well. She left her and Jake behind, without any hope of knowing where she was going and if she was okay. Lydia understood Jake's feelings, but she still wished she could know Miranda was alright as well.

There was a silence in the small storage bin after Jake

stopped talking to Gabriel. He turned away from both her and Gabriel, and walked to a corner of the room. Lydia had not really looked around the room until then, staying focused on Jake and the man, Gabriel, who claimed he was Miranda's father. She soon realized that the bin was filled with many items that she had sent to Jake that were Miranda's belongings from their shared apartment. Sitting atop a box with the word 'keepsakes' written in black permanent marker was a snow globe that Lydia had bought for Miranda their first Christmas together in the apartment. Neither Miranda nor Lydia were big on Christmas traditions of the religious sort, but Lydia saw Miranda looking at it in a gift shop one time that December when they went shopping downtown together, only a few blocks from *Feast 'n' Baristas,* their favorite coffee shop. The globe had an angel figurine amidst a tiny snowstorm, wings outstretched on either side and arms raised in an embrace-like stance.

When she gave it to Miranda, she seemed happy and said how much she loved it, although she confessed that it wasn't the usual kind of thing that she'd be drawn to. It sat on a shelf beside her bed, although once she started having the nightmares, she put it away in a drawer in her desk. Lydia noticed, but never asked her why.

Lydia picked it up from atop the box and stared at it, lost in her thoughts and memories of better days. Jake turned to her and noticed her holding the globe, and watching her for a moment before turning his attention back to Gabriel.

Gabriel suddenly had a look of realization in his eyes and met Jake's gaze directly. "You said the last thing she asked of you...you've heard from her since the night at Stratusaint Tower, haven't you?"

"She...she wrote me a letter and..." he answered,

almost unconsciously. Gabriel cut him off, mid-sentence.

"She *hand* wrote it? Do you still have it?" Gabriel asked with a sudden urgency.

Jake silently gazed at Gabriel. "It doesn't matter," he said. "We are going to get in the car, and I am going to make a phone call to Detective Rice. You can tell him who you are and what your real connection is to David Gale. I will tell him that you are stalking me and he can figure out the rest. If you tell him about the letter, I will deny it. Miranda doesn't want to be found."

"Please," Gabriel pleaded, "We are wasting time. We all want the same thing – to make sure Miranda is safe. Time is of the essence! We need to get to her before Lucifer…" he said, realizing that he'd said far too much in speaking the one word, the one name.

Lydia looked at Gabriel with a hint of confusion, and Jake, his hand on the lever to open the garage door, stopped and glared with narrowed, piercing eyes at Gabriel, still seated on the wooden chair.

"I should have known," Jake said, his voice icier than Lydia had ever heard it before. "You're just as crazy as the rest of the nut-jobs that were after Miranda before. You're just another one of them. We're done here!"

Jake pulled the handle that released the door, and the door sprung up to the ceiling, with Jake never taking his eyes off of Gabriel. The overhead light bulb was very dim in comparison to the light that was suddenly flooding the bin from the bright sunlight outside.

As Lydia's eyes adjusted to the outdoor light once again, she squinted her eyes through the piercing light beyond where Jake stood as he still fixed his eyes on Gabriel.

Lydia's hands went weak, and the snow globe slipped

from her fingers, shattering on the cement floor of the storage bin. Jake jerked his head toward Lydia. Her face looked pale and blank, her eyes widened as she continued staring past where Jake stood. Jake noticed Gabriel was looking past him as well, and slowly began to stand up from the chair he'd been in since Jake told him to sit down. Jake turned with a feeling of apprehension to the blinding sunlight behind him.

At first, there was only a silhouette wrapped in the sunlight. As his eyes adjusted to the background of the garage doors all in a row across the way, the figure before him came more into focus. But before he could act, or even fully realize what was happening, Lydia darted past him and ran to the figure beyond the door.

"Miranda!" she exclaimed with an indiscernible flood of emotion. Lydia didn't raise her voice, yet the name was spoken with deep affection and urgency. She wrapped her arms around Miranda, and Miranda returned her embrace just the same.

"I'm so sorry, Lyd," Miranda said in little more than a whisper. Lydia squeezed harder, and then finally released her hold on her. She stepped back just to get a better look at her friend. She looked just the same as she had always been – the faded blue jeans and beat up leather jacket – but Lydia could see there was something in her eyes that was different. There was a sad distance within them that Lydia could not recall ever seeing in Miranda before. So deep in fact that in just looking into her eyes she could almost feel the sadness taking hold on her own heart as well. But there was something else…something more than sadness that Lydia could not fully grasp hold of.

Miranda turned to Jake. "Hi, Jake." She spoke slow and steady, and from the expression on his face she could read nothing.

He stepped toward her, stopping short a few feet, and just looked at her, trying not to feel too overwhelmed at once. But it was that youthful fire of old that finally came through to the surface.

"Hi, Jake?" he said in a contemptuous tone. He turned and looked toward the ground, shaking his head.

"Jake…" Lydia started, but Jake looked back up to Miranda.

"Hi…*Jake*," he repeated.

Miranda did not move from the spot in which she stood. She wanted to give Jake the space he needed. The space that he deserved.

"Jake, I'm sorry…for everything. You have to believe me. I meant to leave you alone…"

"I never wanted you to leave me alone, Miranda!" he shot back to her. She bowed her head to the ground. Jake found himself painfully aware that anger was not the only emotion that was flooding his soul at that moment. He was relieved, and he was also overcome with joy that he, as well as Lydia, could actually *see* that Miranda was well. He regained his composure and came up to Miranda and hugged her, and she returned the hug.

"I am so sorry that I've hurt you so much, Jake. You mean more to me than almost anything else in this world," she whispered to him. He let go and stepped back away from her, looking her over much like Lydia had moments before. Lydia stepped up beside him, and the three of them seemed to almost forget there was another in their presence.

Gabriel stepped up slowly behind them, keeping a fair distance away. Miranda eyes raised their attention in his direction. She had not for an instant forgot about his presence. She stepped in his direction, although Jake gave her some protest, she held her hand up almost dismissively, telling him "It's fine, Jake. I'll be okay."

Jake stood back alongside Lydia as Miranda approached Gabriel.

"You...you look so much like Suzanne," he said to her. "So much like your mother..."

She stopped just before him. The words he spoke unsettled her.

"She died because you came into her life," she said coldly.

Gabriel bowed his head. He felt the contempt in her words, and all the same, shame in his heart for the truth in them.

"That may be so...but I loved her, Miranda. I would have given up everything...giving up my holy glowen for only the chance of living one lifetime with her," he told her. Miranda could feel the sincerity in his voice, like a vibration of pure, unequivocal truth. She started to feel sympathy for him now, the broken soul that he had become. She stepped up to him and laid her hand gently upon him cheek.

She concentrated her thoughts on Suzanne. She had learned to focus on one particular aspect of a persons emotions, and the more she concentrated on her mother, the more she felt and saw from Gabriel's mind and heart. So much love...visions of the garden at the Gale Estate...the vision of the way Suzanne stared into his eyes, like nothing she had ever even experienced herself...and the tortured anguish he felt when he learned about her death.

She pulled away from him. She knew he was telling the truth, and she knew how much this man was in love with her mother. Gabriel dropped to his knees and sobbed into his own hands. With Miranda's look behind the curtain of his heart, it brought all of the emotions to the surface, even though he could not see the visions that she had seen.

Jake stepped up behind her.

"He said that he is your real father," Jake told her.

Miranda didn't turn to him when she replied, "He is my father. It's true."

"How…how can you be sure?" he asked her.

She turned to him and smiled.

"I guess if we are in this together now, then we have a lot to talk about," she said to him.

Miranda looked down at the shattered pieces of the snow globe on the floor. She lowered her head and focused on each of the separate pieces at a molecular level, and the pieces started to move, all at once rising into the air in the center of the room. The pieces began to spin faster and faster in front of Jake and Lydia, who could only stare with looks that could be construed as either wide-eyed wonder or desperate fear. The pieces one by one, faster and faster, came together until the globe was once more complete and whole. Miranda held out her hand and it gently landed in her palm.

Lydia's hands were shaking. When Miranda reached toward one of her hands to reassure her, Lydia instinctually pulled away as if by a sudden, unintentional reflex.

"Lyd…it's okay. I am the same person I always have been. There were just…a few things that I didn't know about myself. It's why I left…I need you to understand that," Miranda said to her.

"I don't understand any of this," Lydia said, her voice quivering. Jake stood alongside Lydia and had not even realized that he was holding his hand over the spot in his abdomen where the scar had appeared. Miranda looked down at his hand and reached out slowly toward him. Unlike Lydia, he did not pull away. As her hand made contact with his, she allowed Jake to see her memories for a moment...

He could feel the desperation in her voice...he was looking down at himself...he was bleeding...his eyes were wide with pain, and she could see the light starting to flicker out within him...she concentrated hard, with an enormous act of will...he could see the warm glow beneath her hand...she turned her hand over, and in her palm, a bullet...

Miranda pulled her hand away.

"Did you see?" she asked, with uncertainty in her voice. "I didn't know if that would work. I've never tried it before."

Jake nodded his head without speaking at first. He glanced sideways at Lydia.

"She saved my life. I'd been shot...she...she healed me." He uttered the words in a cloud of near disbelief, but deep inside he knew it was the truth. He put it together with the dreams that he'd had, and it was like the pieces of a long lost puzzle finding their fit for the first time.

Lydia looked on at Miranda. Her fears eased, but the question remained...

"But...how is any of this possible?"

Rick Jurewicz

CHAPTER SEVEN

Jake had been living in a rented house for the past six months, which was located just a few miles west of downtown Petoskey. The four of them drove back to the parking lot where Lydia had left her SUV, and Lydia followed behind Jake, Miranda and Gabriel in Jake's car.

At first, the ride was silent on the short trip to Jake's place. Finally, something that had been on Jake's mind broke the silence.

"How did you know where to find us? At the storage bin..." he asked her.

"I sat in the passenger seat when the three of you drove to the bin," she told him.

He looked straight ahead at the road, then back to Miranda.

"You...what? No, there was just the three of us in the car. Were you...can you turn *invisible* or something?" he asked, mystified.

She smiled at him. "No, I can't turn invisible...I don't

think, that is. But I can make it so people don't notice my presence. It doesn't matter if I'm standing right in front of you, if I don't want you to, you won't see me, although I am completely visible."

"Ah hah," Jake answered with a continuous nod, feigning understanding of the concept of not seeing someone standing right in front of you. "And you can do these things because you are an *angel*?" he asked her.

"*Half*-angel. Obviously on my father's side," she said. Gabriel remained silent as Miranda and Jake spoke. He knew better than to say anything right now. This was between the two of them.

Jake glanced up into the rear view mirror. "And you are *the* Gabriel, from the Bible?"

"Yes. Sort of. Things aren't always how you read them, but I am…was…the archangel Gabriel. So…yeah," Gabriel responded before looking back out the side window as the growing green corn fields rolled past his eyes.

"Ah hah," Jake said again, slowly processing the days many revelations.

Silence ensued for about thirty seconds before he asked her the question that she knew he would but hoped that he wouldn't. "Has it ever happened before?"

"Has what ever happened before?"

"Have you ever been right in front of me in the past 18 months and I not see you there?"

Miranda looked straight ahead in silence before finally uttering the word "Yes."

Jake didn't respond immediately, so Miranda went on.

"You don't know how hard this was, Jake. There was so much I had to come to terms with. When I saw you…"

"How many times?"

78

"It was three times…at the Roasted Renegade…I saw you, and when you looked in my direction…I made it happen…and I left immediately each time. I couldn't face you, and I wasn't ready for you to face me. I can only apologize so many times…"

"Well how about one more time, Miranda," he snapped, immediately regretting his tone.

"I'm so sorry, Jake."

He clicked on his turn signal and pulled into his driveway, drove up to the garage door and turned off the engine. It was a three bedroom ranch style home with a two car garage and a full basement, the backside of which was built on the downward slope of a hill which made it so you could walk out of the basement into the back yard. There was a deck built off of the back from the main level that overlooked a valley of green rolling fields that butted up to one of the many vineyards that had populated the northlands of Michigan over the last several years.

"Okay," he finally said as Lydia pulled in beside him. "I forgive you. I have to. I don't understand all - maybe not *any* - of this, but I know that we need to move past this. I just…I've missed you so damn much, Miranda. I'm just glad you're back now."

Miranda forced a smile with as much false sincerity as she could muster, hoping that it was enough to seem convincing. It wasn't that she was not happy to see her friends again. It was the fact that she had every intention of moving beyond her past and accepting the burden of the pain, guilt and anger that she was feeling on her own. Now, she was in their lives again and the feeling could not escape her, wherever it may be coming from, that her presence in their lives was a threat to everything she had once held dear.

Jake may not have noticed the untruth in her smile, but Gabriel had been around for a few millennia. He may not have the glowen that made him a celestial being any longer, but he did not lose the knowledge and experience of watching and at times guiding mankind for thousands of years. He retained his silence in the car. There would be plenty of time to talk to his daughter soon enough.

The inside of Jake's home was neat and well kept, much like the trailer that he had been living in back in Native Springs when Miranda had returned after her parent's and younger brother Steven's death. Gabriel sat down on an easy chair in the living room. He was feeling anxious, and asked if he could turn on the television.

"Uh…sure," Jake replied, feeling the request to watch television oddly timed given the current circumstances and the stream of revelations suddenly before them all.

Gabriel fumbled with the remote until Jake gave him a quick lesson on how to navigate it, and he found the news channel feed from the satellite network and started to flip through and scan each news channel.

Lydia was sitting down at a small dining room table that Jake often had breakfast at, preferring to eat his other meals usually on the go or sitting in front of the television on his days off. There was an awkward silence in the room, only broken by the flipping of the news channels in the adjacent room.

"What is he looking for?" Jake asked Miranda in a low voice.

"I don't know," she answered.

"Oh," said Lydia, "I almost forgot." She got up and went out the front door suddenly, and returned after a minute with a small cardboard box in her arms.

"This is what I was bringing to Jake from our old

apartment," she said to both of them as she came back into the dining room. Jake was looking into the freezer in the kitchen, and pulled out a package of frozen ground chuck to thaw for a meal. He put the package of meat in a pan of cold water and set it on the stovetop to let it thaw, then came back to the table and had a seat beside Miranda.

Lydia set the box on the table and opened it. It was filled with a small collection of novels, mostly old classics, that when packing up the last of her own things she had realized were books that were left behind by Miranda.

Miranda stood up to see what was in the box, and then looked to Lydia.

"You really didn't have to bring these back," she told her. "They could have been donated or something."

"Yeah, I know," said Lydia, "But I needed to bring this back anyway, so I brought it all back, and decided to let Jake decide what to do with the rest." She pulled out a brown, leather-bound album of photos and held it out to Miranda. Miranda looked at the album in Lydia's hands almost as if she was afraid to reach out and touch it. She slowly took the album into her hands.

At first, she looked at the cover and the binding edge as if she was studying it. She then took a few small steps away from the table into the kitchen before opening it. It was the album her adoptive mother Lorri had put together for her to take when she had first left home for school. The very first picture was a family portrait taken during her senior year of high school. The next pages were pictures from when she was much younger. There was a picture taken one summer of Miranda poking at the webbing of Steven's playpen while it was set up outdoors in the grassy lawn of their old house. Lorri sat beside them on a blanket with a book while Miranda played with her brother who at the time was nearly a year old. The adjacent page was a picture of her father Robert playing badminton with Miranda, in that same yard, later that day. She remembered her father telling her how surprisingly good she played the game for her age. He never hesitated telling her how proud he was of her.

Miranda snapped the book shut, startling Lydia and Jake, whose eyes jumped to Miranda. Miranda seemed to have a flash of anger in her expression, but just as fast recomposed herself, walked back to the table and set the book down calmly on its surface.

"Thank you, Lyd…it means a lot that you brought this back," she said, once more utilizing her talent for feigning a sincere smile.

"Miranda, you know I am here for you. I'll always be here for you. I never gave up hope that you were alright. I just…" she stopped, looking to Jake for a moment, "I just found out today about the letter. The one you sent Jake. I only found out today that you made it out of that building alright."

Miranda smiled and looked into Lydia's eyes. She touched her cheek, and held her hand there for a moment before hugging her once again. When she let her go, her expression was more serious than it had been only moments before. She stepped away from Lydia and walked into the living room.

Gabriel was stopped on one channel now, watching one story. It was further news coverage of the incident in New York from just a few days before. The image was blurred as it had been before, an intentional act by Lucifer to hide himself from the eyes of the world, but Gabriel was as certain now as he had been when he had first watched the live coverage that it was his brother. Miranda had not yet seen what had happened, but she knew just as well who was responsible for the rescue of all of those people on the river.

Gabriel looked over his shoulder when he realized that Miranda was in the room. Jake and Lydia followed behind, wondering what drew Miranda into the room so suddenly.

"That man is..." Gabriel started.

"Lucifer," she finished. "We've met."

Gabriel's eyes widened with surprise. "You've seen him? Spoken to him? What did he say?"

"He said...he told me about Amanthus. He told me why he wanted to leave, and why he was punished," she said.

Gabriel rose to his feet. "Go on...what else did he tell you?"

"He said he wasn't the villain everyone thinks he is. He spoke of the way man has squandered free will, and that he has found a way to redeem himself to Amanthus."

Gabriel stepped closer to her, his eyes filled with anxious anticipation. "Did he say how?"

"All he said was that he was meant to bring mankind *into the light*," she told him, as Jake and Lydia looked on with startled amazement.

"By Lucifer...do you mean...are you talking about the Devil?" asked Lydia, with a look of deep fear in her eyes.

Gabriel turned to her. "He isn't like the Devil you know," Gabriel responded to Lydia. He turned back to Miranda. "What he told you, Miranda, was the truth. He may bend the rules, but he has no reason to lie. Man's sins are their own, and they make their own pathway to the afterlife that they find themselves in. It is a path based on love, kindness and faith - faith being the key word in this case."

"What do you mean *in this case*?" asked Jake.

"Actually, in all cases, but faith is what is being

threatened here. Amanthus is a being of so many aspects. He - and I will refer to him as he for all of your sakes – set the rules and laws of physics for your world himself, as well as all of the exceptions for those same rules regarding the existence of sorcery and power and the other realms of existence. He imbued the angels with his own ability to create and form existence out of nothing with sheer acts of will. When he created man, he set very specific rules for how man was to be governed and interacted with. In the beginning, the angels were the guides that walked alongside man, teaching them how to survive and prosper. That later changed, and we were forbidden to interact with man. As an act of mercy and love, Amanthus came to the world and took the form of a man to once again try and correct the path that man had strayed onto. Now, the path to salvation for the souls of mankind comes down to faith. Not necessarily believing in God or not, but most importantly, *not knowing* if he exists and yet still doing what is right by your fellow man is what truly bridges the gap of faith."

"I don't understand. Isn't the whole idea of faith, at least as I remember it from catechism classes as a kid, about believing in something that you can't actually know to be true?" Lydia asked.

"Yes. Exactly," answered Gabriel. "But what if the question of if God is real is taken out of the equation? What if man knew for certain that God was real…if it all was real?"

Miranda had been watching the screen on the television play the event in the Hudson River over and over again. She turned her attention to Gabriel and said, "Then man's actions and decisions would no longer be a matter of faith. What they would do they would do not because they believed there might be consequences for their actions…they would act knowing for certain the consequences of their actions. It would negate free will altogether. The choice would still be there own, but the consequence would be certain."

"Amanthus is a being of divine structure and does not deviate from the design he created. If this knowledge is given to the world – the proof of God's existence – the bridge to salvation based on the idea of faith and free will without known consequence will be destroyed. It would end the existence of the human soul at the point of death, leaving it to wither or wander without consciousness or identity, just disembodied energy."

The room was dead silent for a long moment after Gabriel uttered these words.

"So, in the end, Lucifer is the Devil after all," said Jake as he stared off through the front window of his living room. "Why doesn't God…or Amanthus…just stop him?"

"Mankind's age old question 'Why does God allow evil to exist in the world?'" responded Gabriel. "It's by the same rules that everything else has been set into motion. Amanthus will not intercede, because his action would defy his own will, and the angels must not disobey his will without great consequence."

"Then how can Lucifer disobey him?" Jake asked him.

Gabriel took a deep breathe with a sideways glance at Miranda. The others didn't notice the look, but Miranda knew what it meant.

"I…I'm not sure. Perhaps it is because it is not Lucifer's intention for this to happen. Lucifer said it to me when he freed me from David Gale's prison, and he said it to Miranda. He wants to bring mankind 'into the light'. He's making a play on his original purpose under Amanthus, but I believe that he actually believes he is doing something good. I think that if he believes that if he reveals the existence of Amanthus to the world, man will finally come together under one faith and set of beliefs. The truth will set you free, so to speak, but in this case, it may destroy your very soul. Lucifer was the first angel, far more powerful than the rest of us, and he knows more about the fabric of the universe than anyone else under Amanthus. But he has been locked away, and he is desperate…he has been beyond the light of Amanthus for far too long. He may not realize the outcome his actions will set into motion."

"So this is what you think he is trying to do?" asked Lydia. There was a fearful quivering in her voice when she spoke. Miranda put her hands on Lydia's shoulders and by subtle force of will moved energy within Lydia to calm her nerves. Miranda didn't always now how to do what she did, but she would often know what the desired effect was that she wanted and it would often happen.

"Yes. I was set free over a year ago by my brother, and I have been following a pattern of events all over the world since then. A village plagued by disease on the west coast of Africa suddenly healed by a mysterious stranger. A section of the South American rain forest that had been cleared by foresters was suddenly re-grown to its full, lush glory. An entire ward in a childhood cancer hospital with more that 50 patients were spontaneously cured. All of these things were leading up to something. When I saw the news from New York, I could tell that the time was getting closer, and I began to fully understand what was really happening. What he was building toward. That's when I knew I had to find Miranda."

"Why?" asked Jake. He was starting to feel fearful for Miranda's safety again, like a shadow that had followed him from two years before.

"Because Miranda is the only being in this world that is strong enough to try and take on Lucifer," said Gabriel. "She is the only one that can intercede."

Jake turned away in frustration, and circled back around toward Gabriel again, his eyes flaring with anger.

"You just said the only thing more powerful than Lucifer is God! How is Miranda supposed to take on something like that? He is even more powerful that the other angels, who won't interfere anyway! How can Miranda?" asked Jake, fuming.

"Lucifer said one last thing before he left me the night he came to see me," said Miranda.

"What was it, Miranda?" Gabriel asked, shifting his attention away from Jake.

"He said he had hoped that I would join him. Then he *asked* me to stay out of his way."

Gabriel almost allowed a smile to come to his lips. "He is afraid of you. You are the only being of celestial nature that can intercede in his plans. Yes, but…" Gabriel mused, "He is still the strongest amongst all of the angels. There must be something else."

"So," Lydia interjected, to everyone's surprise, given the fears obvious within her. "How do we stop him?"

"We have a being powerful enough to get close to Lucifer with Miranda. What we need," Gabriel told them, "is a weapon powerful enough to disempower an archangel."

He raise his left hand and showed Miranda, Jake and Lydia the two inch scar on his palm near the base of his thumb.

"This is the scar from the Shard of Cadere Gladii. Cadere Gladii translates from Latin to…"

"The sword's fall," said Lydia. "I had a Latin class."

Gabriel smiled and nodded his head. "Yes, that's right.

When Lucifer was defeated in the Infinite Lands, his sword shattered into pieces that landed around all of creation. At least one fell to Earth, maybe more. A scratch from the shard was enough to destroy my angelic presence and power...my glowen. It made me mortal. But using it also destroyed the shard. If we can find another, we may have a chance to take Lucifer's power from him. As much as I'd hate to have to go to this length, the consequences of not doing it have far more damaging repercussions."

"So how do we find an object that even the angels don't know how to find, or even know if there is another one on Earth?" asked Jake.

"The answer to that is somewhat complicated, to be honest. There are some abilities humans have that angels do not. We need to find a person with psychic abilities. Someone with extra-sensory gifts and clairvoyant vision," said Gabriel.

"How do we do that? There are tons of fake psychics all over the place. Con men and women, and fake witch-doctors trying to make a buck. I've seen a great deal as I traveled. Mostly swindlers playing on the emotions of people who have had...a great loss. How do you find a real one?" asked Miranda.

Gabriel smiled, but he sensed the pain in Miranda's words. "We'll start with Google. I know that it sounds far-fetched, but it is a handier resource than I could have imagined...and I've seen things. Jake, you have a computer?"

"Yes," Jake replied, heading down the hall to his makeshift study across from his bedroom. He returned with the laptop, set it up on the kitchen table and powered it up.

Gabriel came over to the table and sat himself down in front of the computer. He started typing search terms into the search bar, and narrowed the results down to Michigan results, then even further down to the northern half of the Lower Peninsula. Most of the results were much the same. There were people offering spiritual readings for various amounts of donation. Some made house calls, offered their services for parties, did card readings, used crystals and various other objects to commune with the departed. One actually stated the proficient use of Ouija boards as their specialty, a certainly quick dismissal for anyone who knew anything about true spiritualists. No self-respecting real medium would dare to dabble in the occult practices associated with Ouija boards.

But it was not the resume of specialties that Gabriel was searching for. Many of the search results had names that appeared strikingly ordinary. Some took the more theatrical approach of coming up with names that sounded like something out of the monster movies of old. Roma, Esmerelda, and the like. Gabriel was aware that much of the lore about gypsy fortune tellers was based on fact. In Eastern Europe in the middle ages there were a few family lines that came out of what is now Romania, Moldova and northern Bulgaria that were somehow bestowed with true psychic talents. While the stories of these individuals ran rampant across the countryside and embedded themselves into the lore of the region, the true identities of these families were closely guarded secrets.

Anomalies to the structure of the world that Amanthus had created through the hands of his angels were closely watched by certain angels who were given charge of monitoring mankind's journey through the ages. Gabriel was well aware of these family lines, so it was not a line of services or special abilities that he was looking for. It was a carrier of old-world traditions that his eyes so very carefully scanned the pages for on the computer. More specifically, it was a name he searched for. A name like…

"Racos. Here, only a couple hours drive south. Madame Racos - Psychic Readings and New Age Life. She has a shop on East Michigan Street off of Mission Street, Mount Pleasant, Michigan. '*Sagittarian Sunrise and Readings by Madame Racos*'. The chances of finding someone this close seemed almost impossible, but it is our best chance so far," Gabriel said.

Gabriel read the address to Jake, who entered the information into the GPS app on his phone. "Got it," Jake said.

Gabriel stood up and looked to the others. He felt a burst of energy in the chance finding of the Racos name so close within reach, but knew there was still a long road ahead, not necessarily in the distance that they must travel, but in the endeavor in which they would face ahead seeking a way to stop Lucifer from achieving his misguided intentions.

"Tomorrow," said Gabriel, looking into the weary eyes of Jake and Lydia. They were both young, strong people, but they had learned things today that most of the world would not know how to handle. They held themselves together with their love for Miranda. There was a sort of high they felt in the relief that she was alive and well and here once again with them. There was also the shock of dealing with the fact of what Miranda is and what she can do, much of which they were still unaware of. Even Miranda had only touched upon the surface of the scope of her abilities.

But there was still something different Gabriel could sense in Miranda's eyes; a distance, almost like an absence of presence. She hid it well, although it did not escape her long-absent father's attention.

"I agree," said Jake, looking first to Lydia, and then to Miranda. "A lot has happened today. We can use some rest for a fresh start in the morning. Miranda can stay in my room, Lydia the guest bed in the other room. Gabriel will get the couch and I will take the inflatable mattress on the floor of the living room. He said this while looking Gabriel straight in the eye.

"Still not trusting me entirely, eh?" asked Gabriel with a forced grin.

"I've been around the block myself," Jake replied. "Trust doesn't come all that easy with me. I'm sure you can understand."

Gabriel nodded. He knew exactly what Jake meant, and knew that Jake had every reason not to trust him, regardless of what had been revealed today. Maybe more so because of what had been revealed. 'I'm an angel of God. My brother is the Devil. And you were – or perhaps still are – in love with my daughter, who is half-angel, half-human.' It was a lot to take in, and a miracle that he would even let Gabriel into his home or near those most important to him. Gabriel respected Jake, and he knew that even more, he *liked* Jake. Jake was the epitome of what a decent human being should be in almost every way, despite some of his earlier life choices.

"If everyone is on board for pizza, I am going to run to town and pick up some. I don't feel like cooking, so I think we can skip the burger for tonight. Gabriel can take a ride with me, right?" said Jake, looking to Gabriel for agreement. It was, after all, more of a statement than a question.

"Of course," Gabriel replied with a nod.

"Tomorrow, we'll head to Mount Pleasant," Jake said. "Hopefully we can find what we need to give the Devil his due."

CHAPTER EIGHT

The alarm went off promptly at 7:30 am, just as Ashley Racos had intended, and she jumped from her bed practically in a sprint for the shower.

It was the day of her 18th birthday, and it was a day that she had been waiting for, for what seemed like a very long time. Ashley, whom almost everyone in her life called Ashe for short, was getting her first tattoo this morning. She had made the appointment nearly three months before, but she'd been planning for this day since so long ago.

Ashe was raised by her paternal grandmother, Greta Racos, since she was only a little girl. What memories she has of her father are mere flashes and vague images in her mind. Sometimes she didn't know if they were actually memories of the man, or if they were something that her mind had put together from the pictures that her mother used to show her when she would tell Ashe stories about her father.

When Ashe was only six years old, her mother, Kim, would tell Ashe the story that would become the favorite of her childhood. Ashe would listen to Kim tell it, over and over again as they walked in the garden behind their home, just north of Mount Pleasant, Michigan - the same town where Kim had met her husband John when she was attending classes at Central Michigan University in the years before Ashe was born.

Every spring, Kim would plant a new batch of tulips in the garden and she would take Ashe to the tulips and sit in the soft grass and tell Ashe how her father, John, who was shy and didn't really know how to talk to girls all that well, went out of his way to find out, without her knowing, what Kim's favorite flower was. Through a friend of a friend, the answer came to him, and one day John just showed up at Kim's dorm room with a bouquet of tulips. Kim was floored, and John mustered the courage to finally ask her out on a date, armed with nothing but the tulips and rosy cheeks of flustered nervousness.

It was enough, and the rest was history. They dated through Kim's years in college, and were married shortly afterward. John was not in school at the time, but was working as a mechanic and first saw Kim across the room at a party he was at on campus with some friends. It was a classic case of love at first sight, although a tragic twist cut the fairy tale short only four years after Ashe was born. There was an accident at the garage where John worked, and a hoist collapsed in a freak accident. John sustained serious head injuries and was in a coma for nearly three weeks before a severe brain bleed took his life.

In the three weeks before his death, Kim would take Ashe to see her daddy, and they would sit by his bedside and talk to John, hoping that he could hear them and that somehow by some miracle it would draw him back to them. One of the days the doctor came to give Kim an update on his condition. Kim left Ashe in the room alone with John, out of earshot but still keeping an eye on her, as she went outside the door and talked to the doctor. At that point, there had been no apparent change in the condition John was in, good or bad.

After a few minutes speaking to the doctor, Kim was making her way back into the room when she stopped and listened to Ashe talking to John. It was nothing unusual for Ashe to speak to him, but it was the way she was speaking to him that caught Kim off guard.

"Yes, Daddy. I know Daddy. I'll tell Mommy. I love you too, Daddy," Ashe was saying as Kim listened at the door.

Kim slowly stepped into the room.

"What are you doing, baby?" Kim asked Ashe.

"Talking to Daddy. He told me to tell you something," she said.

Kim was shaken by what Ashe said, and kneeled down on the floor beside John and Ashe.

"You are pretending Daddy is talking back to you?" asked Kim, looking at Ashe's little face as she could feel tears starting to form in her own eyes.

"No, I was just listening. Daddy talked first," she said, matter of fact.

Kim looked around the room once more. It was empty. She looked back over her shoulder at the door. The hall was barren outside of the room. The only sounds in the room were the sounds of the machines beeping and the pulsing sounds of oxygen being fed through a line into John's nose.

"What...what do you think you heard, baby?" Kim asked with a shaky hesitation in her voice.

"I heard Daddy. He told me to tell you he loves you, and he loves me, and that he's leaving today and he wanted you to know that it'll be okay. And to...what was it, Daddy?" Ashe suddenly asked her father, unconscious on the hospital bed.

"He said to plant…tulips for him every spring, and he'll be there with you."

Kim wrapped her arms around her daughter and sobbed hard into her own arm. It would be another two years before Kim even told Ashe the story of how she and John met. There was no way that Ashe could have known about the tulips that day, but somehow, she knew.

The tears came, and Kim couldn't control herself and couldn't stop crying. A few hours later, John was gone, and it was now just the two of them. Ashe never mentioned what she had said again after that day, and Kim never brought it up. She would just take Ashe into the garden that she planted the next two years afterward and would tell her the story of John and the tulips, and how they were the first gift that John had ever given her, but the greatest gift he ever gave to her was Ashe, who Kim also referred to as 'her little tulip'.

It was just before her seventh birthday that Ashe was taken out of class at school where she met her Grandma Greta at the office. Greta had tears in her eyes when Ashe saw her. Ashe walked up to Greta and looked up at her grandmother. Ashe's eyes were glassy.

"Mommy died," Ashe said, and the tears started to run down her face. Greta dropped to her knees and hugged the girl, and they both cried into each other's arms. Greta didn't know how she knew, she only knew that no one at the school had been notified yet that Kim had been in a serious car accident and that she didn't survive.

Ashe came to live with Greta, who lived only a few miles from Ashe and Kim in an apartment above the building where she had her new age book and curiosities shop, "Sagittarian Sunrise and Readings by Madame Racos".

At the age of 61, Greta found herself in the position of

being a mother once again. She had not had an easy life. Greta's parents had moved from Romania when her mother was pregnant with Greta just after World War II and had made a home in the Detroit area. Her father worked in the train yards and her mother stayed home and raised Greta who was born not long after arriving in their new home of Detroit. It was not an easy life, but they got by, and Greta was an incredibly sharp and intelligent girl who excelled in her schoolwork, and after high school graduation went on to Central Michigan University where she studied education and philosophy. By the mid-1970s she had graduated CMU and was offered a professorship as one of the youngest professors ever for the fields of philosophy and later on cultural studies. It was around this time that she also found herself pregnant.

The father was another professor in the building where she worked, and he was also married. She thought they were in love, but he had different ideas about the relationship. Greta chose to take the high road and not cause a scene about the ill-conceived love affair, and made the decision to raise the child on her own. The father ultimately confessed the relationship to his wife, and the couple left the area, relocating to the Chicago area. Greta never heard from the man again. Which, in her mind, was for the best.

When John was born, Greta struggled with the time it took to be a parent and a full-time professor at the university, but she worked hard and made it work for her. John, while not as academically successful as either of his parents, proved to be of an intelligent sort and very mechanically inclined and talented when it came to doing anything with his hands. He loved to play with blocks as a young child, built his own computer out of component pieces when he was 11, and spent a lot of time in his teens at the neighbor's house when the neighbor, a gentleman named Ron Stevens who owned his own auto repair garage, worked on his own cars at home. Ron lived alone and never had any kids of his own, and he loved the company, as well as being able to pass on his knowledge to a bright young mind like John's.

Greta retired from the university in her late 50s, having acquired a healthy pension being that she started so young, and invested wisely in a retirement plan that set her up for a very long time. She was known as a fun professor to both her students and others around the university. She may have had her hands full being a full-time teacher and parent, but she found time to make a little side money utilizing another talent that she had.

She was very well versed in the areas of crystal gazing and palm reading, and also the use of tarot cards and meditation. Her father and her mother, both descended from old Romanian gypsy families, carried these talents and skills down from generation to generation. They took their teachings very seriously, and Greta listened intently as a child, but as her education grew she put less and less stock in the old teachings and viewed the world with a more academic and secular approach. But she knew the look, and she had the knowledge, and decided it would not hurt to offer these 'talents' as a service for parties or private individuals through her years teaching and raising John.

She knew the techniques involved in the process of reading the cards and palms and such, and much of the time, she would speak of her findings from instinct and intuition. The funny thing was, quite often, people she did readings for would come back to her and tell her she was right. This often brought about repeat business and created quite a reputation for Greta – a reputation that caused some scrutiny at times in the eyes of the academic peers around her. She decided for a time to tone things down a bit, but after retirement, she used some of her invested money to open her new age shop and do readings by appointment out of a backroom parlor she set up for just that purpose.

Business was steady from the college crowd. There was always someone wanting to know if they were making the right career choices, or someone wanted to know if a departed loved one had a message for them, or if they were going to fail the big exam they were having on the coming Friday. The fortune teller in her would speak from that inner voice, the intuition within her, while the academic would tell them to get their ass home and study. She was not one to hold back. She was tough, and at times, when she had to be, she was hard. But she deeply cared as well, and those who ever had the chance to get close to her knew this well.

Taking on the role of parent to seven year old Ashe was a labor of love indeed. She was always a phone call away if there was ever anything that Kim and Ashe needed, and she loved Kim like her own daughter, if from nothing else, from knowing how much John loved Kim. Sundays were always a day where Greta, Kim and Ashe would spend at least part of the day together; Greta would make a big breakfast and Kim would cook dinner, or sometimes they would switch places, and they always had a good time.

After Ashe came to live with Greta, things were hard for both of them for a while. Greta had lost both a son and a loving daughter-in-law, and found herself extra protective of Ashe. This led to a rebellious streak in her middle teens that caused even greater tension between Greta and Ashe. Ashe got wild ideas about her hairstyles, dying her hair at times every color of the rainbow and dressing in goth fashion styles. She came home one time with a homemade nose piercing that a friend had done that got badly infected for a short time after.

They had rough patches for certain, but Greta knew as Ashe grew up that she was her own person and had to treat her as such. She had to release her grip, and started complimenting her more over choosing to criticize her fashion choices. She took her to get piercings professionally done when she was 15 (after the first piercing debacle had healed), and gave her a job working in the Sagittarian Sunrise on the weekends, stocking and ordering merchandise to sell in the store.

Ashe thought the things in the shop were very cool, and she loved the stories her grandmother would share with her about the histories of the items and the beliefs that came behind them, but she did not put a lot of stock in the reality of such ideas. She saw them as forms of entertainment, and when working, presented them as such. But when she was working the counter at the store, she fell into character of that of a true believer. It almost always resulted in an appointment for a reading by "Madame Racos", and that did well for Greta's extra income. Most of the money that Greta took in from readings went into a college fund that she put aside for Ashe, if Ashe decided to take that route. Ashe didn't talk much about what she wanted to do after school, and Greta didn't want to push. Ashe hadn't had it easy as well, and in her own time, Greta knew that Ashe would find her way, whatever way that might be.

Greta was cooking breakfast when Ashe burst out into the living room down the hall from her bedroom. Ashe could smell the eggs and the bacon, hear the sizzle of the hash browns on the stove, all of her favorite breakfast foods. It was a special day, and she was getting a special treat from grandma, and she was all that much more excited.

Greta turned to Ashe as she came in, belting out an exuberant "Happy birthday, Little Miss!" as she often came to call Ashe over the years they had been together, following it with a big, squeezing hug.

"Thanks, Grandma," Ashe said, returning the hug with as much overwhelming affection. They were very close, and very open with each about most things.

"So," started Greta. "Today's the big day. Tattoo day."

"Today's big for a lot of reasons, Grandma!" Ashe said excitedly as she sat herself down at the breakfast table. Greta brought the pan of hot scrambled eggs over and served them onto the plate that she had waiting in front of Ashe's seat. Today Ashe's hair was dyed pitch black with bright red streaks running all throughout it. Her hair came down to almost her shoulders, with the exception of her bangs which hung from a slight part in the center of her forehead down to just below her chin. She had a soft, pretty face, and didn't overdo it on the make-up that she wore. When she first started dressing in lots of black, she had a tendency to cake on the eye make-up, until she realized the tediousness of it all. Greta always told her she had a natural beauty about her, and that she shouldn't cover it up. She was wearing a black "Shinedown" band tee shirt that she picked up at the concert the year before at the local casino, and stretchy Capri pants and flip-flops that morning. Her hair was pulled back into a pony tail, with the exception of her bangs.

She pulled from her wallet on the table beside her a piece of paper with a hand drawn tulip on it. Greta smiled and picked up the paper for a closer look. Greta had seen the drawing many times over the past several months leading up to this day, but this was the day that the "Little Tulip" was getting the image permanently attached to her forever.

"Are you nervous?" Greta asked.

"No…not really. I mean, I know that it's not going to tickle," she responded with a short giggle. "But, I'm ready. I know in some way Mom and Dad will be there with me."

Greta smiled again, and turned back to the stove to bring Ashe her bacon and hash browns. Ashe didn't speak much in any sort of religious or spiritual way. She claimed to be agnostic, but said she believed in something. If not believed, then *hoped* there was something more, but she didn't speculate too much what that something might be.

Ashe finished up her breakfast and went over to help Greta with the dishes, but Greta shooed her away and told her not to bother with them on her birthday.

"You have some time before you're appointment, so go have fun!" Greta told her. Ashe smiled, gave Greta a hug and thanked her for the wonderful breakfast, and said she would come straight home after the appointment to show her the finished product.

"You had better," Greta said to her as she continued to face the sink while doing the dishes.

"Um," Ashe said, realizing she had forgotten to ask before. "Is it alright if I borrow the car? I wanted to run by the record store first before I went to Angry Hamster."

Greta raised her eyebrows and looked back over her shoulder at Ashe. "The tattoo parlor is called the 'Angry Hamster'?"

Ashe let out a short burst laugh as she heard her grandmother say it out loud.

"Yes, I know. It sounds funny, but they have the best reputation in town."

"Of course you can take the car if you want," Greta said as she shut off the water and turned away from the sink.

Ashe ran up to Greta one more time before heading to the door and gave her a quick kiss on the cheek, grabbing the keys out of the key bowl beside the door as she headed down the stairs to the driveway that ran beside the building.

When she got to the door she turned around the corner into the driveway and stopped dead in her tracks. Parked directly behind her grandmothers Chevy Equinox was a metallic green Jeep Wrangler. There was no outlet at the other end of the driveway for Ashe to get out with the Equinox, and not enough room for her to get around the Jeep that was parked in the way.

"What the hell?" she said in almost a whisper to herself. She looked around her, but could see no one around who might be the owner of the Jeep. There were other businesses down the street, but it seemed out of the way for someone to have parked in their driveway to walk down to the other businesses when there was available parking on the street.

She turned back toward the door to head upstairs, but stopped short when she found Greta in the doorway waiting for her.

"Grandma, someone parked in the driveway. I can't get around this Jeep," she had uttered before she noticed the silver key ring in Greta's hand with a set of two keys hanging from it.

"Oh," Greta said. "One more thing. Consider this an eighteenth birthday gift from your mom and dad." Greta held out the key ring and dropped it. Ashe instinctively reached out with both hands and caught the keys, standing in a semi-state of shock.

"But...what? How...?" Ashe uttered.

"Remember Mr. Stevens? Taught your dad almost everything he knew about mechanic work at a young age. He told me about a great deal on an old Jeep, it just needed some work – work that he was happy to do free of charge. I bought the Jeep, he did the work. It's good as new."

Ashe finally regained some semblance of composure, once again wrapping her arms around Greta and the tears started to flow.

"Dammit," Ashe let slip out. "I'm glad I didn't put on much make-up today."

Greta let a few tears flow as well. She let out a slight laugh when Ashe said what she had said.

"Go," Greta said. "It's your day. Have fun. Be safe. I love you, Ashley."

"Love you too, Grandma," she said.

Ashe got into the Jeep, adjusted the seat and the mirrors, and took a moment to wipe the tear tracks from her face. Then came the smile once again. She started the engine and backed out onto the street, and away she went as Greta watched from inside the doorway at the bottom of the stairs.

After a stop at the 'Round and Round Revolution' all-vinyl record store, she pulled into the plaza off of Mission Street and parked the Jeep right in front of the Angry Hamster Tattoo parlor. She hopped out of the Jeep and started toward the front glass door when she saw a familiar face coming out of the shop.

"Heyyyyy," said the always happy, bushy face of the man exiting the tattoo shop. "Wassup, Ashe? Big day, eh? Happy B-day!" said the man as he reached out to give Ashe a hug.

"Alex! I was wondering why you weren't working at the record store today. I was just there to see you. I picked up the Cure vinyls you called me about. They are in awesome condition! I can't believe it! Thank you!"

"No problem! Hey, did you see the Ramones reissues we just got in. Cool shit. I think you'd like 'em," Alex said.

"I love the Ramones! I don't have any of their stuff on vinyl yet, just downloaded stuff. Wanna save one of each for me?"

"Sure. Hey, cool wheels. This new? Birthday present?" asked Alex.

"Oh my God, yes! My grandma surprised me with it this morning. I couldn't believe it!"

"Your grandma's a cool chick," Alex said with a big smile.

"So, are you getting new ink?" asked Ashe.

"Well, I didn't plan to. I knew you were coming down here today, but I ended up getting this," he said, pulling up his sleeve. It was a tattoo of a small robot body with a larger cat's head in a round, fish-bowl-like space helmet. It was weird and it was quirky, no less than Ashe would expect from Alex.

"You just got that on a whim?" Ashe asked, but before he could answer, she went on with "Of course you did." She laughed, and so did Alex.

"I gotta get back to the store. I was only supposed to leave for a little while, and that was right after I got in at 8. That was an hour and a half ago," Alex told her.

He got on his bike and started to peddle away in the direction of the record store.

"Wait," said Ashe as he began to ride away. "You said that you knew I was going to be here today. What did you need?"

"Oh yeah," he said as he started moving again. Your tat is covered. All paid for! Happy birthday!" He didn't look back as he went off, only raising his hand in a quick wave as he rolled away down the block.

Ashe smiled warmly and then looked at the front door of the Angry Hamster. For the first time, she started to feel a little nervous about the tattoo. Her friend Kelly had gotten one a month before, and she described the feeling like 'having someone scratch a bad sunburn.' Overall, this didn't sound like something all that pleasant to Ashe, but at the same time, she felt that it could be a lot worse. She was determined, and she walked through the door.

The room was a long, deep room and there was a desk off to one side with a computer on is. The man sitting at the desk was typing on the keyboard, and he looked up at her and gave her a friendly smile. He was covered in tattoos and piercings himself, and had small gauges in both of his ears.

"Hey," he said, stopping what he was doing and looking to her. "What can I do for you?"

Ashe looked around the rest of the room momentarily and took in the surroundings. It was clean, and actually kind of cozy. There was rock music playing (she thought the song was an Avenged Sevenfold song, but she wasn't sure), and there was a leather couch and a coffee table with several tattoo catalogs on top of it. She heard what sounded like someone clearing their throat, and then looked back to the face still smiling at her from behind the desk. The buzzing of the tattoo guns could be heard through the sound of the music pulsing through the speakers.

"Uh, yeah. Sorry. I have an appointment this morning. Ashe Racos."

The man looked back to the computer and typed something, and then turned the monitor screen to her. On the screen was an image of the tulip she had sent to them a couple of weeks before.

"This what you're getting?" asked the man.

"Yes," she responded.

"Cool," he said, and handed her a clipboard with some papers on it. "I just need you to fill out these sheets, and I need a copy of your ID. Tony was scheduled to do the work this morning but had to leave town unexpectedly, so we are a little behind already this morning. I've got you set up with Felicia, but she is working on a client right now, so it should be...ah...hopefully only another half hour to forty-five minutes. That okay?"

"Sure. No problem."

"You can sit down and relax, or you can take a walk if you'd like...and, everything is covered. An 'anonymous benefactor', as he called himself, said he was taking care of the cost and the tip today, so you're good to go," said the man at the desk.

"Yeah. I caught Alex on the way in," said Ashe.

"He's a good guy," said the man. "We get lots of work from him. And he's funny as hell."

Ashe smiled. She walked to the couch and took a seat. She picked up one of the tattoo catalogs and started to flip through it, looking at the different art work through the many pages. On one of the pages that she turned to, she saw an image of an angel that she found herself oddly drawn to. It was a single being, yet straight down the center of the body the being was divided. One side seemed to shine with ethereal glory; the full-feathered wings had a radiance that embodied everything you might believe an angel would have surrounding its being. The other half was a darker image, with cruelty in its eye and a large, bat-like, leathery wing and a clawed hand. Ashe was entranced by the image, and somewhat unsettled.

She moved on to another image, page after page, and listened to the music that played through the speakers, patiently waiting a little bit longer for her turn as the artists in the room, in each of their vastly decorated artist booths, tirelessly buzzed along.

CHAPTER NINE

Jake, Miranda, Gabriel and Lydia walked through the front door of The Sagittarian Sunrise new-age shop at almost the same moment that Ashe sat down and started flipping through the tattoo catalogs at the Angry Hamster Tattoo Parlor.

They had just pulled off of US-127 after the two-hour trip from Jake's house. It was an early start, and a relatively quiet morning. There was little small talk and an obvious awkwardness that filled the atmosphere around the tiny group that was heading into territories unknown.

The world had changed for all of them the day before. Revelations had been made. Perceptions about life and the world were altered in ways that had never before been imagined. And yet, these things in some ways seemed small and irrelevant to the emotional turbulence that was felt between friends old and new.

While Jake honored Miranda's wish to be left alone, he could not quite put a finger on what it was that he was feeling now. Lydia was relieved and happy to see her, but could not shake the sense that there was something deep and distant that had somehow changed in Miranda.

Miranda herself only pretended to sleep the night before they departed. She stared out at the distant stars through the window of Jake's bedroom, and she allowed her mind to wander without any real thought or direction. It was the closest way that she had to forgetting who and what she was. These were the brief moments that helped to calm the storm inside of her.

Jake made them breakfast. Eggs and bacon and English muffin toast. They ate in silence. Miranda ate as well, although she didn't have to eat, nor did she have a real inclination too. But the aromas that filled Jake's kitchen and little dining room of the home-cooked breakfast meal took her back to so many childhood mornings, especially weekend mornings, when her mother would cook a family breakfast before they would all go about their days playing and working around the house. Gabriel seemed overly eager to take in the meal. He had come to really appreciate eating, and loved exceptionally good home-cooked meals. They came few and far between for him, mostly eating in fast food joints as he traveled on the road.

Lydia had a bag with extra clothes that she always carried in her SUV. It was a good habit to get into living in Michigan whenever she traveled anywhere, especially in the winter months when there was always a chance that a storm could roll up out of nowhere and strand you in unfamiliar territory. There was a lot of room in the SUV, so she kept the bag tucked in the back, just in case. She came out of the guest room in blue jeans and a tee shirt, a far more natural feel for her than the pretty summer dress from the day before.

Gabriel traveled light. A few change of clothes, a couple

of books to pass the time, and some cash from odd jobs. He was thousands of years old, and when he was still an angel, he had looked since the beginning as if her were around 20 human years old. Now, he looked to be in his early to mid 40s. A handsome man for his 'age', and he kept himself strong, at least until his imprisonment by David Gale. But still, he new what he had to do to stay strong and fit, and he did so, with the exception of poor dietary choices in the fast-food industry, which was less a matter of choice than it was a matter of financial necessity.

Greta stepped into the retail floor of the shop from her back room. She was startled to see anyone in the store so early.

"Good morning," she said to the four of them. "I'm sorry, I wasn't expecting anyone here so early on a Saturday morning. I usually don't open the store until 10 a.m. Is there anything that I can help you with?"

Gabriel stepped up ahead of the rest, with Jake close behind.

"Are you Madame Racos?" asked Gabriel.

"Yes," she extended her hand to Gabriel, and he took it. "Greta Racos. I am owner, operator, and psychic-on-duty," she playfully said. "What can I do for you?"

"Are you a Racos of the old world Racos line," asked Jake.

Greta's eyes narrowed suspiciously at the question. Gabriel tried to suppress a sigh. He knew Jake was anxious, but he also knew that this was best left in his hands at this point of their journey.

"Yes, my family goes back several generations. What is this about?" she asked.

"We need your help to find something that is lost," Miranda spoke up from behind the two men that had taken charge. She looked to her right and saw a crystal that was long and pointed on the display rack. The crystal rose from the rack and slowly started to spin in a counter clockwise motion in the air next to where Greta and Gabriel stood. "I'd imagine it looked something like this, perhaps…maybe shinier."

Greta stepped back with a gasp. Gabriel quickly reached out and grabbed the crystal from the air and pushed it back down to the counter. He shot a sharply displeased look to Miranda, but the expression on her face revealed nothing about her action.

"I'm sorry, Miss Racos. We don't mean to frighten you. We desperately need your help to find an object, and we believe that someone with your family's history of the special gifts you possess may be the only way to find it. We will pay you for your services, and I assure you we are not here to bring you any harm," Gabriel told her.

Jake pulled Miranda aside as Gabriel spoke to Greta.

"What was that?" he whispered to her.

The stone-like expression she had as she looked at Gabriel moments before softened as Jake looked into her eyes.

"I'm…I'm sorry. I just thought it might speed things up a little," she whispered back to him.

"She was terrified, Miranda! The world…it's not ready for this. Maybe in some ways it needs it, but this isn't the way," he said. His stare softened as he looked into her eyes now.

Gabriel turned around and spoke to the others. Greta retreated back into the room where she does her readings.

"She said she would try to help us. I think she just wants us gone, but she is the only one that can do anything to help us find the sword shard," he said.

They followed Greta into the room.

Ashe sat herself in the chair in Felicia's tattoo booth. The booth was heavily decorated with drawings and trinkets of all sorts, and paintings on the walls done in acrylic and watercolor. There was a mask hanging on the post along one side of the booth of a jester, full of equal parts color and black, with the bells dangling from the corners of the mask that extended out from the face.

Ashe slipped her foot out of her flip-flip and rested it on a cushion as Felicia prepped her for the tattoo. Felicia was herself heavily tattooed all over her visible body. On the left side of her head her dark brown hair was buzz cut short and it revealed a mandala design, with the tips of the mandala extending almost to the edge of her cheek. There were so many different images across her body, and it fascinated Ashe. Her right hand – her tattooing hand – had an image of a moth with a skull on its back that covered most of the back of her hand.

"Did you do all of these paintings?" Ashe asked her.

"Yep. I did all of them. They're for sale too if you are interested," Felicia replied.

Ashe looked around at the paintings and saw a small one that closely resembled the moth on Felicia's hand. She saved some money by not having to pay for the tattoo today, so maybe she would pick up a little something extra for herself.

"Okay," Felicia said. She applied an ointment of some kind to Ashe's foot. She then took a small strip of paper with the image of the tulip reversed on it and gently laid it down on the top of her foot where she had applied the ointment. She pulled the paper away, and the image of the tulip was on Ashe's foot.

"I bet you wish that was it," Felicia said with a grin. "Wait. Is this your first tattoo?"

"Yes, it is," Ashe replied.

Felicia jumped up and ran to the front of the store. Ashe heard the clang of an iron bell ring through the tattoo parlor.

"VIRGIN!" echoed Felicia's voice through the parlor, followed by the bellowing of the rest of the tattoo artists working in the shop that day repeating the word *virgin* as Felicia ran back to her booth.

Ashe was laughing as Felicia got back to the booth.

"Now, I have to tell you," Felicia started as she took the tattoo gun in her hand. "I'm sure you have heard the horror stories about how painful it can be to get a tattoo. It's really not that bad. *However...* the top of the foot and the ribcage are some of the more sensitive areas to get them. Trust me, I've have it all done. But just hold tight. I promise I am gentle, and this will be done in no time!"

The buzzing of the gun seemed to be the only sound now that Ashe could hear. She gritted her teeth...and Felicia started.

Greta, Gabriel, Miranda, Jake and Lydia all sat around a round table in Greta's parlor. The room was adorned with a few paintings of birds in tranquil settings and long red and purple drapes that hung from the ceiling to the floor, letting little light in from the outside. In the corner there was a small electric fountain that was almost completely silent except for a trickle of water that was soothing and relaxing. Gabriel sat on the right side of Greta. To the left sat Lydia, followed by Jake and then Miranda.

Greta still had an air of agitation about her, but she was a professional and focused on the task at hand.

Miranda could still sense the tension as well. She realized fully the mistake that she had made in her rash attempt to speed things along.

"Madame Racos," she spoke up, drawing the slightly worried looks of her companions. "I should not have done what I did. We just really need your help. I thought if you saw, if you believed we are sincere in our intentions and why we need your help, that it might help you believe in your ability to help us. It was never meant to frighten you. Please forgive me."

Greta felt the sincerity in Miranda's words, and while it brought her some sense of comfort, there was an uneasiness that she found difficult to shake. Greta nodded her head to Miranda in acceptance as the others in the room came to realize they were holding their breath.

"What is it that you are trying to find?" asked Greta.

"It is a portion of an ancient relic. A piece of a sword," Gabriel told her.

"Have you seen this sword before?"

"I have, yes."

"Have you held it or ever touched it?"

"I have touched…a part of it," he told her, extending his hand with the scar across it.

Greta took his hand in hers and ran her fingers along the scar. She then released his hand and looked Gabriel in the eye.

"I have never truly embraced the idea that any of this, that my family was known for, as being real. My mother taught me as if it was the truth, but all of this around us…it's all for show. Everything that I have told people through the years, it's all been from my gut feelings. Intuition. What you people are after…I don't think I can help you with," she said as she looked around the table at each of them.

Gabriel gently took her hand in his once more. "I believe in you, and I believe what your mother told you and what she believed was true. Just try and believe in yourself. You may be the only one that can help us.

Greta nodded softly and turned Gabriel's hand over and once more ran her fingers along the scar…

The buzzing of the tattoo gun in itself was a bit unnerving, and Ashe certainly felt the pain. At first, it was what she would have described as a deep scratching feeling, then followed by an almost burning sensation. She did her best to keep still. She knew she couldn't back out now. She just tried to focus on different things around her.

Ashe concentrated on the paintings…the moth on Felicia's hand…the mask on the post. Somehow, her mind wandered back to the image she saw in the book while she waited for Felicia to finish her last job.

She remembered the drawing of the angel, split down the middle. And then…there was something different that began. The pain intensified in her foot. She looked down and Felicia was on the last little bit to do, but she had saved the most painful part for last. Ashe felt tears begin to well up in her eyes.

Then, through the tears she felt like she was floating. She was in her grandmother's shop and she saw four people walk through the door. An older man…a younger, cute man, maybe a few years older than she was, followed by a woman in a black jacket with dark eyes…very dark eyes…and another girl with short blonde hair. They spoke to Grandma. Suddenly she could see her Grandma's eyes…she could feel the fear in her heart. Ashe let out a scream and a slight full body spasm as Felicia finally pulled the needle away.

"Are you all right?" Felicia asked with genuine concern in her voice.

Ashe was breathing deep, trying to catch her breathe. "I...I don't know. I have to get home."

She jumped out of the chair, pulled a twenty out of her wallet and handed it to Felicia, and she quickly started for the door.

"Wait," Felicia called to her, and rushed over to Ashe at the door and handed her the aftercare instructions. "You need to follow these instructions and apply the ointment on a regular basis. If you have any questions or concerns, call me. My cell number is on the card."

"Thank you," Ashe said, still visibly shaken. She hurried out to her Jeep and gathered herself together as best she could.

"What the hell is happening to me...?"

She started the Jeep and sped off, heading for home.

"I'm sorry," Greta said to Gabriel. "I'm not getting anything. A haze. A few flashes, but nothing that forms any real image in my mind."

Gabriel sighed. Then, he looked to Miranda.

"Miranda, trade places with Lydia," he told her. They switched places, although Greta looked uncomfortable with the switch.

"Greta, please - take Miranda's hand. It's alright," Gabriel said assuringly.

Greta continued to touch the scar as she took Miranda's hand in her other hand. She closed her eyes, and concentrated. After a few minutes of silence, she spoke again.

"I'm sorry...I cannot see what you need me to see," she told them. She released both of their hands.

"She is sensitive," Miranda said. "I can feel it. There is something there, but it is not strong enough to reach beyond this room. She can feel much, but it is limited."

Greta was astounded with what Miranda said. She was thinking the very thoughts that Miranda was stating, but in her own words.

Miranda smiled at Greta. "Thank you for your help, Madam Racos." Miranda got up and was the first to leave the room, followed by the others. Gabriel thanked her as well, apologizing once more for the minor intrusion on her life, and found a fifty dollar bill in his wallet for her time. She took it, and smiled, stopping him behind the rest.

"I hope you find what it is that you are looking for. I really do," she told him. "I sense that there is a great urgency in it."

Gabriel smiled with a nod and he gently patted her hand in his.

Ashe pulled the Jeep into the driveway beside the building that housed both her home and her grandmother's new age shop. She was shaken and her vision slightly blurred from the tears in her eyes. The tattoo was still stinging fresh on her foot, and she also lost her flip-flop getting out of the Jeep.

She passed through the shop door as the people inside were walking out. She knew that she was a mess and didn't look up at the people as she squeezed by them in the doorway. Her hand brushed against another as she rushed by, and an eruption of sensations began to rage in her mind.

An overwhelming surge of emotions flooded Ashe's mind and heart. Fear. Loss. Anger. Hatred. Pain. Loneliness. A vision of fire and flames and lightning crashing through glass and shattering it to pieces and a man's bones breaking as his body was pressed into the glass…the pain of a family lost…of a woman being shot before her eyes.

Miranda turned and felt the same sudden rush…all of

the things that Ashe was feeling, and the pain of the tattoo on her own foot…the lost little girl who just found out her mother had died…the fear in her heart right now rising from the image of her grandmother's fear only minutes before.

Ashe turned to Miranda. Miranda to Ashe…and the world seemed to slip into slow motion as their eyes met…and they both collapsed to the ground.

CHAPTER TEN

Miranda opened her eyes and found herself lying on a couch in an unfamiliar place. Lydia was sitting beside her in a recliner chair. Voices could be heard coming from another room that was far more well lit than the one she was in now. The voices were low, but she could make out a few words. Angel. Lucifer. Words not often used in casual, everyday conversation. Gabriel was telling Greta the truth about everything.

"Hey," Lydia's soft voice spoke to Miranda. "You alright?"

Miranda pulled herself up. She still felt stunned, which was an odd feeling for her. She hadn't felt anything remotely like this since she had her nightmares. But she hadn't had a nightmare or a dream of any sort for that matter since before the night at the Stratusaint Tower.

"What happened? I remember a girl...who is she?" asked Miranda.

Ashe walked from a hallway into the room where she

121

came into view of both Miranda and the others in the lighted room.

"Ashley!" called out Greta as she came rushing to her granddaughter and embraced her. Ashe still looked as groggy as Miranda did, but once they saw each other they both found a sobering feeling come over them.

"Grandma, what's going on…who are…" she stopped, and then a realization came over her. "I saw you." She looked around at all of the strangers in her home. "I saw all of you as you walked into the shop."

"You mean as you walked into the shop," said Jake.

"No. I was at the tattoo parlor getting my tattoo," Ashe said, pushing her bare foot forward to show them the tulip tattoo on her foot. "I was in the chair and I saw you all walking into the shop. The three of you," she said, making a gesture with her hand towards Jake, Gabriel and Lydia, "and then you," she pointed to Miranda. "But your eyes…they were all black, like the blue had been swallowed up by the pupil."

Miranda stood up. "You are Ashe," she said. It wasn't a question. Somehow she knew Ashe was the girl's name.

"Miranda," Ashe said. "I'm sorry…about your parents…I…don't know how I know that you lost them. I lost mine, too."

"I know," Miranda said. "I'm sorry too."

Lydia looked back and forth between the two young women. Everyone else stood in a silent disbelief.

"I can't be the only one completely confused as to what is going on here, am I?" asked Lydia.

"Ashe, you say you saw us? Have you seen things before?" asked Gabriel.

"She knew that her mother had passed away before anyone ever told her she had," Greta responded.

Ashe looked to Greta with confusion in her face. "Grandma? What are you talking about? You came to the school that day. You told me she was in an accident."

"Yes, I did. But only after you were brought from the classroom. Before I had a chance to say anything, you told me first that your mother had died," Greta told her.

Ashe sat down on the edge of a chair that sat next to the hallway. She thought back to that day. And she remembered. She remembered the words coming from her lips. She remembered the feeling she had in her heart. She remembered…a kiss from her mother's lips on her cheek only moments before the principal came to the classroom door and called the teacher into the hallway.

Ashe took a sudden deep breath in and her eyes widened.

"What's going on? Why are you here?" she asked the strangers collectively.

Gabriel looked at Greta for a long moment, and Greta, with some reluctance, nodded her head in approval.

"Ashe," said Gabriel, "Perhaps you'd better sit down at the table with your grandmother and I. We have a lot of explaining to do."

Gabriel recounted the twist of tales that culminated into the bringing of the six of them together in that moment in time. Ashe listened with a quiet intensity. She had played the part in the store for her grandmother so long that despite the open mindedness she had for the mysteries of the great big world around her, she had not once ever really considered that she might somehow play a part in those mysteries that held her imagination captive so many nights reading the incredible fantasy stories of her childhood. Angels…strange powers…psychic ability…it was all real. And what else? There was so much more, so much possibility! She felt the rush of excitement, along with a similar rush of anxiety over the flood of feelings she got when her hand brushed along Miranda's.

"So," she started, looking to her grandmother, and then to Gabriel. "You think that I have an ability for these visions and feelings?"

"I think that goes without saying at this point," Jake spoke up. "You saw us coming, didn't you?"

Ashe smiled when Jake spoke. Another hapless victim of the boyish charm that Jake exuded naturally without even trying.

"Sometimes, like genetic traits, these abilities can skip a generation or simply not be as strong in some. My kind have observed this over the centuries," Gabriel said.

"Your kind meaning *angels*, right?" smiled Ashe.

"Yes," Gabriel said coyly. "My kind being angels. Your grandmother has the traits of a true psychic, but you show indications that you have an aptitude for these abilities that could be several times more powerful than what she possesses."

"So, what do you need me to do?" Ashe asked with enthusiasm.

Greta stood up. "I need to have a word with my granddaughter in private please." The words came with authority, and Gabriel stood up and nodded to Greta.

"Of course," he told her. Greta and Ashe moved down the hall into Greta's bedroom, and Greta firmly closed the door behind her.

"What's wrong, Grandma?" Ashe asked.

"Ashley, I can see it in your eyes, how eager you are to help these people. But we do not know them," Greta told her.

"Your 18 years old now, I know. You are an adult, and you can make your own decisions. I know that I did my best to raise you right. To be an independent thinker. But you also need to know that you don't have to do anything that you don't feel comfortable with."

Ashley saw sadness in Greta's eyes. She placed her hand on her grandmother's face and smiled. "I know this already, Grandma. It's because you did raise me right. But I also know that if anything of what they said is true, there is a lot more at stake here than just what's happening here and now. I have to try and help them."

Greta smiled at her with pride. "I know you do, sweetheart."

They all gathered once more in the private backroom parlor of Madame Racos. Greta locked the shop front door and put up a sign stating 'Closed for a personal affair'.

Ashe sat in the chair that Greta commonly sat in, with Gabriel to her right and Miranda to her left. There was an apprehension in both Miranda and Ashe about the two of them touching each other again, so they stayed aware of where they were in proximity to each other.

Gabriel extended her hand to Ashe, and she took his hand into hers.

"The scar," said Gabriel. "It wasn't made by the thing we are looking for, but another piece of it."

Ashe touched the scar with her thumb. Her eyes widened and she felt a jarring rush run through her. In her minds eye, she was no longer in the room with the others. She was on a small, rocky ledge with thick brush and dense forest surrounding her. There was a path leading away from the spot, much overgrown, but still a noticeable path that drew her in the direction in which it lead. She followed along the path and spoke aloud what she was seeing.

"I see rocks and trees and thick forest," she said. "I'm following a path through the trees."

As she followed along, she came to a deep cave. All she could see was blackness. She walked on and came to another cave, much like the first, engulfed in blackness. She could hear birds, and she could sense the little creatures of the forest frolicking about. But there was something else…something darker, something that she could not hear or see, but she could feel its presence.

"Caves. The path led to caves," she said.

"Caves and forest doesn't exactly narrow it down. That could be anywhere in the world," Jake whispered to Gabriel.

Gabriel nodded his head to Jake.

"Ashe," Gabriel spoke softly and calmly to Ashe, "I want you to try something. I want you to rise."

"Rise? What do you mean?" she asked him.

"You are in your mind, and your mind isn't constrained to the limitations of your body. Gravity isn't an issue. So try to rise, and see if you see anything else to indicate where in the world you might be. Any signs will help."

Okay, she thought to herself. Rise. *How the hell do I do that?*

She decided to just visualize herself moving up. Just when she thought that was a silly thing to do, she quickly realized that she wasn't on the ground anymore. First, she felt scared, but then she realized how cool it was. She was flying! Sort of, at least in her mind she was, but right now she couldn't tell the difference.

"I see something, hang on," she said to the group around the table.

Ashe pushed herself toward what she saw and let herself down slowly into a courtyard. She looked around herself and took it all in.

"I'm at a house," she said.

"What does it look like? Can you describe it to us?" asked Jake.

"Well…it's old, that's for sure. And it looks like it was burned up pretty bad," she said.

Gabriel's head quickly twisted in Miranda's direction, just as hers turned to him.

"Ashe," Miranda spoke to her. "Is there a fountain in front of the house?"

"Yes," she responded.

"Is there an angel kneeling in the fountain?" Miranda asked her.

"Yes, there is," she said. "Do you know where this is?"

"Ashe," Gabriel said to her. "You did a great job. You can come back now." He released her hand and she found herself back in the parlor with the rest of them.

"So, where is this place?" Lydia asked.

"It's the Gale House in Galestone," Miranda answered her. "The place where I was born. The place where my mother died. The place where all of this began."

Gabriel stood up and stepped to the window, his back to the rest of the group.

"What are you thinking?" Jake asked him.

At first he stood silent, lost deep in his thoughts. A wave of revelation came over him, something that he had not considered before that moment.

"The Gale's were among a line of believers that the prophecy could bring good from the return of Lucifer. But I don't think that it was a coincidence that of all the places in the world to travel to and settle down that they would land themselves in the one place that might hide an object that could possibly stop Lucifer if that part of the prophecy wasn't true. There has to be something more to it all," Gabriel mused.

"Well there is no way to know now what that was," Jake said. "David Gale was the last of the Gales. There is no one left to ask about it."

"There is one person left to ask. At least I think she still lives," Gabriel said.

Miranda narrowed her eyes at her father. "Who? Who is it that is still alive?"

"Victoria. Your grandmother. She was ill, and the last I knew, David set aside enough of his renewed fortune to take care of her and put her in a special home. He resented her, as he did Susanne, but he couldn't hate her. She may be the only one left alive to know what led the family to Galestone to begin with."

"So where is the home?" asked Lydia.

"Just outside of London," Gabriel said.

"London. Great," responded Jake. "If what you think Lucifer is up to is coming soon, we're already running out of time."

Jake turned and started out of the room, visibly frustrated. The old temper that followed him through his youth reared its ugly head on rare occasions, and this was one of them.

"Miranda can do it," Gabriel said.

Jake stopped. He turned around to face Gabriel. "Miranda can? How?"

"She still has abilities that she hasn't uncovered fully yet. I can teach her how to get there on her own, but it may take a little time and practice. Far less time though than one of us flying to London and back," Gabriel assured them.

"How can I help?" Ashe asked.

Greta was going to speak up, but she hesitated, remembering the conversation she had just had not long before with Ashe. *She has to find her own way*, Greta remembered.

Gabriel looked at Ashe. "I'd rather not have you mixed up any more in this than you already are. But, even if we find out why the Gales came to Galestone, we may still need help finding the sword shard, and you are the only person that can feel its pull." He looked to Greta. "With your blessing, of course, Miss Racos."

"Ashley is her own woman. She can choose her own path, and she has my blessing," Greta said to him.

Gabriel nodded. He turned to Ashe. "Okay, then. We will find a place to stay in town, and tomorrow morning we will come and pick you up."

Jake led the way out, followed by Miranda, and Lydia. As Gabriel followed, Greta stopped him.

"She has my blessing, but I expect you to take care of her, Gabriel," she told him sternly. "Be her guardian angel."

"I promise you I will do whatever it takes to keep her safe, Greta. I cannot be more grateful for all of your family's help."

Greta nodded, and they went their separate ways.

CHAPTER ELEVEN

The sun shone bright on the grounds of the well manicured outdoor churchyard as people walked about, taking photos and sitting scattered about in the long rows of pews that led up to the alter facing the northwest. Behind the alter stood a massive crucifix, the most sacred and holy symbol of Christianity. People around the world were drawn to this place to see the giant bronze statue on the cross built from the wood of a redwood tree. They came to pray. They came to worship. Many came to take selfies with the crucifix in the background, so they had something more than just the image that adorned post cards that were sent around the world.

Sitting in a center pew and staring at the face of the suspended Christ was the first angel of creation, the one called Lucifer. He could not put a finger on what emotions he was feeling the most in that very moment. The image before him was of the one being that Lucifer loved the most, in that being's moment of greatest suffering, at least in a physical form. But this was not Amanthus' greatest suffering. There was pain, and the pain of death, but there was greater pain in the loss of trust and faith in that of his first son. Lucifer found this to be true, although for some time, he could not have known the truth. Not until after he came back into the world, and saw what had truly become of it. Amanthus was gone, to where, no one knew, not even his great brothers and sisters who remained ever obedient, watching over the Infinite Lands and the worlds beyond.

Lucifer's mind wandered back to a night just before the Great Fall. Only Amanthus and Lucifer know what happened in the Garden of Gethsemane that night, so long ago…

Christ walked and mused. He knew what was coming the next day. It had been orchestrated long before, and he knew what it meant. It was not fear that he felt so much as guarded anticipation of the coming pain that would lead to a new way, a new salvation, for all that would come afterward. Being human had given a different perspective that a god alone cannot experience in the same fashion. But he did not foresee his first son coming to visit him on this occasion.

"Hello, my Lord," Lucifer said softly to his Father, and his Mother, and his Creator.

Amanthus turned to him, and he smiled and embraced his son. "It pleases me to have you in my company, Lucifer. However, I fear that your coming here is not for a pleasant purpose."

Lucifer dropped his head low. Amanthus took his hand and placed it upon Lucifer's chin, gently lifting Lucifer's eyes to his own.

"You know what I seek," Lucifer said to Amanthus. "I…I beg of you to grant me the same freedom that you have granted them."

"Lucifer, you have a much greater purpose to me by my side. I created you as my right hand. One simply cannot cut off their right hand and expect to be able to do the same great things with one hand that can only be done with both," Amanthus told him.

"I am more than a simple appendage, my Lord!" Lucifer blurted, immediately feeling shame for his outburst.

"I know you are...you are so much more, and I beseech you – do not do this thing you are planning to do."

Lucifer was taken aback by the admission that Amanthus knew of his plans to leave the Infinite Lands, even without his Creator's blessing.

"Who told you? Michael? Gabriel?" asked Lucifer.

"None told me. I may be in the restricted form of man as I walk in this world, but I know you, my son. Now it is I that begs of you. But you will do what you will do. Now, you must leave me." Amanthus began to walk back in the direction of the disciples. He was prepared for what was coming next. Lucifer stood frozen, with tears streaming down his cheeks.

"Father...please," Lucifer pleaded. Amanthus stopped walking. If there was ever a moment that Amanthus ever felt true temptation to move against his own will, it was in that moment, for the love of his son. With a step forward, followed by another, he moved on, and Lucifer was left in the garden and to his own fate.

Lucifer found the tracks of tears on his face once again as he reflected on the last time he spoke to Amanthus. He dried the tears, and felt a sudden rush of joy in what was to come. He was going to make Amanthus proud, and he would see him again. He pulled the literature he had collected from his pocket and smiled down at the flyer.

The flyer read "Conference of United Faith – the first ever of its kind, a live televised gathering of the leadership of the world religions, all in one place. This will be a summit of all of the most influential religious leaders of our time to help and bring a sense of unity and strength to a world that has become lost in religious conflict and the corruption of the ideals in which the several faiths are based upon. Christians, Islam, the

Jewish community, Buddhism, Hinduism - All faiths – One Place. Atlanta, Georgia."

The date of the event was only a few days away. This was more than Lucifer could have hoped for. He put the flyer back into his jacket pocket and smiled once again.

A man was taking a picture of his wife and daughter with a statue of St. Peter in the center of the pews where there was a small open space around the statue. He snapped the picture, and immediately realized there was a blonde man caught in the background of the picture. He looked to see where the man was now, trying to avoid catching him in the picture again. The man could not possibly have walked away so quickly, but he was no where to be seen. He checked the camera image again, and the man had definitely been there seconds before.

The man with the camera shrugged it off, and he took the picture again, this time, it was just the man's wife, daughter, and the saint. The mystery man had simply vanished.

CHAPTER TWELVE

Two rooms had been booked at the Mount Pleasant CentralMi Inn Suites. Lydia insisted that she put the rooms on her credit card. Jake protested, but it was to no avail.

"I have to feel like I am contributing something to this," she said to him.

"Trust me, you are just by being here," he told her. He meant it in both the sense that she was a good person to have your back and for the fact that out of the four of them traveling together, she was…a normal person. And in some small way, Jake hated himself for admitting that feeling. He had loved Miranda, and in some way he still loved Miranda. It didn't matter to him what she was. That would change nothing. But who she was now changed some of the feelings he had inside for her. He knew there was something different, and he wasn't entirely sure if it was the fact that she had changed…or if it was because he had changed.

Lydia got the room keys and they headed up to two adjacent rooms. Before they entered to settle in, Gabriel made a request that he was certain Jake was going to object to, but one he felt was necessary.

"I need to have time to work with Miranda – alone. I think that Jake and Lydia should take one room and that will give me time to teach Miranda what she needs to know to get to Victoria," Gabriel told them all before entering the rooms.

"I don't think that is a good idea," Jake said, just as Gabriel predicted. "I think we all should do this together."

Miranda spoke before Gabriel or Jake could escalate the argument. "Gabriel is right. I need to learn what I can, and I can more than take care of myself, Jake. Besides, I have a few things to work out with my father."

Jake stood silent and acknowledged Miranda's wishes. He could never stop her from doing what she wanted before, and he knew he sure as hell couldn't dissuade her now.

Jake looked to Lydia. "I can get a room of my own, it's fine," he told her.

Lydia slid the card in and out of the electronic lock, and the door opened.

"There is a couch. I'm sure it'll work out fine, if you are good with it," she said to him.

Jake looked into the room. "The couch it is."

Jake brought his bag into the room and so did Lydia. Gabriel and Miranda put away their things as well, but there were no words exchanged between them. The four of them opted to go and get a bite to eat, and they went to a pizza place not far from the hotel. They ate, with little small talk. Lydia commented on the fact that at one time she considered going to Central Michigan University, which was right there in Mount Pleasant where they were now. The conversation didn't really go anywhere after that, and everyone was eager to get back to the hotel and relax. The tension was unnerving, and while no one was willing to walk away from the task at hand, even in not knowing where it might possibly lead, they couldn't wait for it all to be over.

What normal life would be like after all of this, no one knew. All that could be focused on was one day – in all reality, one moment – at a time.

Once back at the hotel, Jake pulled out his laptop and he and Gabriel scoured the internet for any clues or signs of what Lucifer may be up to. It was almost impossible to determine what his endgame might be.

Lydia pulled Miranda aside and asked her to go for a walk with her. Miranda smiled and agreed; it would be good to get some fresh air alone with her friend.

"We're going for a walk," Lydia told the boys.

Jake was about to say something in protest, but Gabriel reached over and placed a hand on his arm.

"They'll be fine. Miranda can handle herself. Trust me on that," he said loud enough so only Jake could hear him.

Jake nodded, knowing Gabriel was right. "Have fun." He said it with a smile, but with guarded hesitation.

The sun was slowly lowering into the western sky. Mount Pleasant was a mostly wide open flat land, peppered with buildings and businesses and concrete in most directions, broken by the occasional grassy field and forest lands. They stopped for ice cream, a late night staple from the days when they were cramming for an exam the next day back in school.

"It's seems like a lifetime ago, doesn't it?" asked Lydia.

Miranda didn't immediately respond to her. She looked off absently into the distance, reflecting on the words.

"Yeah," she said, savoring the cold flavor of butter pecan. "A lifetime."

Lydia could no longer skate around the cloud hovering

above Miranda that was both ominous and obvious from the moment they were reunited the previous day. She stopped walking and stood face to face with her friend.

"Miranda," she started, unsure of what was going to come from her lips. It was not some deep wisdom that she was reaching for, but more a bridge to find an understanding to connect with the girl who had been both her roommate and who had become her best friend.

Miranda looked her up and down and could see the soft pleading in her eyes.

"What is it, Lyd?" she asked her. Whatever it was that she felt within her on most days was hard to bury, and even with her considerable power and abilities, human emotion at times seemed an almost insurmountable force.

Lydia went on. "I don't know what to say or even where to begin. I can't...I can't imagine what is going on inside of you. With both everything that you've lost coupled with all that you've found out about who you are...and who Gabriel is to you and...I swear, I cannot begin to know what this has done to you."

Miranda looked down to the cracked pavement. She said nothing in response to Lydia. She didn't know what to say. Lydia was right. There was absolutely no way for anyone to know what was happening deep within her. There was no one like her anywhere, and there weren't support groups for half-breed one of a kind angelic entities who have lost to madmen and the whim of celestial beings almost everything that they have ever cared about.

Lydia reached out her hand and gently touched Miranda's cheek. Miranda hinted an almost undetectable shudder when Lydia made contact with her, but recovered with a smile and gently placed her hand upon Lydia's.

"I'm okay, Lyd," Miranda assured her. She mustered all that she could inside to appear sincere. She didn't want to lie to Lydia any more than was necessary.

Lydia sighed, if only slightly, on the inside. The clouds were dark around Miranda, and Miranda rarely opened up about things even before everything that had happened that turned her world upside down. At least that was how it had been when they had first met. Miranda had been in a dorm room with a girl named Amanda when she first arrived at South Central Michigan College. Amanda was the consummate college party girl, and she liked to bring the party, and the guys that came with all of the partying, back to the dorm room quite frequently.

It was not a scene that Miranda took to at all. She had done the party thing, and while she wasn't opposed to having a good time now and again, it was not something that she wanted night after night after night. She found herself perusing the bulletin boards in the dorm and classroom building lobbies, checking postings for people off campus looking for roommates. Lydia had an English class with Miranda, and while she didn't know her, she had noticed as she passed by her in the classroom building hallway that Miranda had been checking day after day for a place to live.

One day she took a seat beside Miranda in the class. It was about ten minutes before class started when Lydia finally mustered the courage to speak to Miranda. She felt a slight bit of intimidation speaking to her. She didn't know if it was more the tough exterior with the battered leather jacket Miranda often wore, or the sleek natural beauty that seemed as uniquely complimenting to Miranda as the toughness that accompanied it. Miranda rarely spoke to anyone, and that fact didn't help the awkwardness that Lydia felt, but there was just something about the girl that drew Lydia to her, something that told her this was a good person and that maybe they might be able to help one another.

"Hi," Lydia finally said as others were slowly shuffling into the large auditorium classroom.

Miranda looked around her at first, wondering who it was that the blonde, pony-tailed, sweatpants-wearing girl sitting beside her was actually speaking to. She finally realized that this girl was looking directly at her.

"Hi…" Miranda responded in a slow, drawn out greeting.

Lydia extended her hand to her, and Miranda accepted the gesture. "I'm Lydia."

"Miranda."

Lydia smiled. "Hi, Miranda. I noticed that you've been checking the boards for off campus housing. I'm looking for a roommate. Someone to split the rent with. I'm quiet, I don't date…*too* much, and I don't bring home strays. I'm mostly a bookworm, to be honest. I don't spend a lot of time outside of the classroom and the gym when I'm not at home. And I love listening to music through my earbuds."

The class professor walked in to the classroom at that time.

"Good morning, people," the thick-bearded, grey-haired man in the pale grey suit said as he walked into the room. The chatter of the room from the gathering students halted almost immediately. The professor, Mr. Waverly, by his presence alone demanded a degree of respect that seemed to come quite naturally without prompting from more than just his appearance in the room. He came to the front of the room as the last students rushed in from the hallway and found their seats, adjusting his horn rimmed glasses as he reviewed his notes from the last class session.

Lydia leaned over and whispered to Miranda. "If you're interested, talk to me after class. We can work out the details.

When the class was over, Miranda was quick to leave the classroom and beat the rush. Lydia noticed her swift departure from the room and decided that Miranda must not be looking for what she had to offer. She gathered her things and walked into the hall after most of the class had already departed. Miranda was standing alone in the hallway away from the others that had left the classroom, leaning against the hallway wall and facing the classroom doorway. Lydia stopped in surprise when she saw Miranda in the hallway, apparently waiting for her.

Miranda smiled, the first time that Lydia had ever seen a smile on the often brooding girl's pretty face.

"I'm interested," she said to Lydia.

It all seemed so distant now. In her heart, Lydia knew how much she cared for Miranda. But somehow when she looked at her now, she could only see shadows of her friend as she stood before her. Lydia forced a false smile to her lips.

The two women walked on down the sidewalk, back in the direction of the hotel. There was much ahead of them that was to be done, and a great weight upon both of their hearts, though different weights indeed.

"You are having feelings for Jake," Miranda said, not the least in the way of a question, rather a flat statement. There was little, if any, emotion in her voice when she said it.

Lydia was shaken by the statement. She didn't know what to say in response. She walked on beside Miranda, the stride unwavering as they moved closer to the front entrance of the hotel.

"Lyd…it's alright. I'm not upset. Jake and I…we had

our time. He is and always will be one of the most important parts of my life. But what there was between us was a long time ago, and it is over now," Miranda said with assurance to Lydia, now standing and facing her eye to eye. There was a softness in her gaze and her smile that seemed far more sincere than any other relief that Miranda had to offer Lydia in their talk that day.

"Miranda, the only thing that I care about right now is helping you however I can to get through this. After that, whatever you need…all I want to do is be there for you however you may need me to be. Jake has been kind and been there for me when you were gone. I think that being there for each other was the one way that we could both feel closer to you. That's all," Lydia told her.

Miranda smiled at her friend. "He's a good man. A good person all around, Lydia. A far better person than I could ever be." She turned and walked through the door of the hotel, leaving Lydia standing on the sidewalk to ponder what she had just said to her.

Lydia followed close behind Miranda, but neither of them spoke the rest of the way back to the rooms.

The evening came, and Jake settled into his makeshift bed on the couch of the room that he shared with Lydia. Lydia had taken a shower and came out of the bathroom in a pair of sleeping shorts and a tank top. Try as he may, Jake found it hard not to stare at her for a brief moment. Without make-up she was just as pretty, if not more so, than with make-up on.

She noticed his gaze, and suddenly became self-conscious of herself.

"What? What's wrong?" she asked him, looking around the room.

"What? Oh, nothing…sorry. I was just…nothing," he said, shifting his attention to a paperback he found in a drawer in the hotel room.

"Did Miranda say something to you?" she asked him.

"No," he responded, swinging himself up to a sitting position on the couch. "About what?"

"Oh, nothing," she said, reaching to change the subject now herself. "The shower pressure is fantastic. You should try it out."

Jake took a quick sniff at his armpit, then to the other one. "Something you're trying to hint at?" he asked her with a grin.

She smiled back. "Nope. I just appreciate a kick-ass shower. That's all!"

Lydia slipped under her covers and pulled out a copy of a horror novel she brought along in her bag. Jake laid back down on the couch and found where he had left off on the book he was reading, a historical novel about Alexander Hamilton.

Jake was the first to doze off. As soon as he had fallen asleep, Lydia set her book down and curled herself up in a position where she could see him as she drifted off to sleep. She felt a certain comfort in knowing he was close by, and even in the midst of the uncertain hours and days ahead, she felt peaceful.

For a long time into the evening, Miranda stood alone on the small balcony that overlooked the town, staring off into the stars that she had become all too familiar with on her many nights on her own. Gabriel worked silently on the laptop, continuing his search for Lucifer long after Jake had retreated into the adjacent room. The tension in the room was as thick as a suffocating fog, and he knew that it could no longer be avoided.

Gabriel closed the laptop and rose from the chair. He walked to the sliding door of the balcony and stepped out through the door. There was a light breeze, although the air was still very warm. Miranda did not turn to face him, although she was aware that he was now standing beside her.

"It is hard, Miranda, to look at you and not see your mother's face," he said to her. She did not respond. "I know I have a lot to answer for…" he started before she suddenly turned to face him. Her eyes were sharp and her gaze was stern.

"You're goddamn right you do! What the hell kind of man – or angel - are you? Where were you? Why weren't you there?" she snapped at him.

"I had no choice, Miranda. I was forbidden to return after Suzanne became pregnant," said Gabriel. "I was stripped of my angelic glowen and I was warned never to have any contact with you or Suzanne."

"By who? Amanthus? You're precious creator?"

"No…no, no one has felt the presence of Amanthus since Lucifer was cast out. Michael was the only one left to lead the remaining angels after the fall. He did only what he believed Amanthus would have done," he said.

"And yet here you are. Now. Not when my mother and the rest of the Gales who had died were burning to death in that house. Not when my adoptive parents and brother were choking on their own vomit in their sleep. Why is there no consequence for you being here now?" asked Miranda.

"I don't know the answer to that. The host of Heaven does not any longer speak to me. I can only assume that something changed when you released Lucifer. The angels are forbidden to interfere with what happens on Earth. But I am no longer an angel, and you are not bound to the rules that they are. Perhaps they know, as I do, that you are the only thing that can possibly stop Lucifer's plans." Gabriel was looking off into the distance, turned away from Miranda as he spoke, looking beyond the lights of the small city. He turned to her after several seconds went by in silence and saw the tears streaming down her face. His heart sunk, and he moved toward Miranda to embrace her, but she stepped back and held up her hand to him. She moved backward through the sliding door and turned to walk back into the room. Gabriel followed behind her.

"Miranda, please. I am here for you now...", said Gabriel, but Miranda would not have it.

"No!" Miranda hissed, spinning toward him and clenching her fists. Her eyes had gone black. The small coffee pot on the room suddenly shattered and the thick glass of the sliding door made a loud snapping noise as cracks appeared up the entire length of the window. "You do not get to be here for me now. I don't need you now. We will do what we have to do to end this and then we will never see each other again."

Gabriel was shaken by the sudden outburst of power. He could almost feel the energy in the room. He raised his hands slowly and nodded to Miranda.

"Okay. Okay," he said in almost a whisper. "Then let's get started. I don't yet know what you can do. Have you ever tried moving from one place to another by your will?" he asked her, smoothly switching gears in the conversation to the business at hand.

Miranda's eyes slowly changed back to her natural blue hue, and Gabriel could see that she was finding calm once again. "What do you mean, 'by my will'?"

"When you saw my brother, he didn't just walk away, did he?" asked Gabriel.

"No…he spoke to me, and then he was just…gone," she said.

"As angels, we travel across not just places of material space but across the boundaries of worlds and planes. This obviously can't be done on foot or by taking the bus. Mankind at some point came to visualize us with wings because it was the only way it made sense to them that we could travel as we did, down from a cloud, so to speak. While gravity isn't really an obstacle to us, mostly we chose to move long distances through bending the structure of the physical plane through sheer will. I know it sounds complicated, but it's really a matter of visualizing where you want to be and willing yourself to slip through to that place."

"So, all I have to do is see the place in my mind, decide that I want to be there and I will be? What if I don't know what the place looks like that I want to be?" she asked.

"There are a few things that can be done. I have seen the house where she had been cared for. If she is still there, I can show it to you with my mind. That should be all you need. But first, try using this ability."

Miranda took a deep breath. She closed her eyes and she decided that small steps would be a good start. She pictured in her mind the other side of the room first, and in the same vision in her minds eye she saw the room from the new position she envisioned herself in.

She opened her eyes and she was there. She looked back to Gabriel and he smiled with a nod.

"Good. Now, try a little further away," he told her.

She closed her eyes once again and envisioned the view from the balcony. She pushed herself there and opened her eyes, and she immediately started to plummet down. She reached out and caught herself on the railing of the balcony.

Gabriel ran to her and grabbed her hand and began to pull her up, but she soon realized what he had meant when he said that gravity was not an obstacle for angel-kind. She didn't need his hand. She simply rose up and over the railing until her feet were firmly planted on the balcony once again.

"I guess I overshot that a little," she said to him.

"Just a little," he said back with a snicker. He had a sudden rush of panic when he realized what she had done, but inside he was still aware that she was never in any real danger of being hurt in a fall.

"Try again," he suggested.

She closed her eyes again and she thought and remembered, and then she was gone. She opened her eyes and stood on a dark street, lit only by a few streetlamps in a small suburban neighborhood. She was standing in front of the house that she had grown up on. The mailbox that had once had the name in bold, gold letter spelling STRATTON was now replaced with a new, heavy plastic mailbox with the name 'Randall' on it.

She looked all around her. Even in the darkness she could see very well, almost as if it were twilight time. But it was not the physical environment that she was seeing in her thoughts. It was the memories of growing up in this place.

She could see Lorri planting flowers in the flower beds that ran across the front of the house beneath the living room picture window. She could see Steven riding his bike up the driveway and down into the ditch past the culvert, trying to get enough speed to jump onto the road, but only ever managing to get the bike a few inches off the ground at best. And she could see her father coming home after work and she would remember how she used to run out to him and give him a big hug as he walked up to the front door.

Miranda stopped looking. She closed her eyes and willed herself back to the hotel room. When she opened her eyes, Gabriel was standing before her, and while the contempt had started to resurface again, she resisted the urge to lash out. She retained her cool and composure.

"Where did you go?" he asked cautiously.

"I think I am ready. When should I go?" she asked, ignoring his question and walking past him to grab her leather jacket.

"Morning. Before the others awaken. It's best that they not see you go. It is very early in London now. If we wait until five or six in the morning here, it'll be late morning there and hopefully Victoria will be awake and lucid," Gabriel answered.

Miranda nodded, and again stepped out to the balcony.

"Are you going to try and sleep?" asked Gabriel, knowing full well that she had no need for sleep.

Miranda didn't reply. She had something else on her mind, although she did hear Gabriel, she chose not to respond. Gabriel settled himself on the couch and before long he was fast asleep. Miranda came back into the room when she was sure he was out for the night.

When Gabriel had gripped her hand as she held to the railing, she had seen a flash of vision from his thoughts and memories. There was much that she needed to know, and there was little time to ask him, not that she wanted to have to ask him to begin with. She wanted to know what she was truly up against. She wanted to know where it all began – everything – and most importantly in her mind, she wanted to know everything she could about Amanthus. The most effective way to get what she wanted was to see it through Gabriel's eyes in his memories, everything that he could recall, all that he knew, all with a simple touch.

Miranda walked over to her sleeping father, the former archangel Gabriel. She sat on the floor beside the couch and watched him breathe deeply in and out, and she reached out her hand and placed it gently yet firmly upon his own hand. Her eyes went black, and she let out a quiet gasp…and she saw…

Rick Jurewicz

CHAPTER THIRTEEN

Darkness. Vast, unending darkness. A void of incomparable nature, impossible to truly describe. Devoid of substance. Devoid of any semblance of the visually conceivable. Devoid of even time, for time, like distance, can only be measured against something of substance. To measure either, there must be a place to start.

But there was something, indeed. There was a consciousness, and that consciousness, in the moment where all things including time itself began, became self-aware. And in the absence of everything, the self-aware entity's first act was an exercise of creation.

First, there was substance, and then, there was form. A face. A body. Arms and legs, and golden hair (although no one could have known what golden would mean yet, in the absence of light).

And then the Great Entity, wrapped in the same darkness that his first creation lie within, spoke the first word in the first language.

"Live," said the Entity.

The being opened its eyes. It was, by all means biologically understood, a male being, six-feet in height, floating in a void of absolute nothing except itself and the conscious unseen entity that allowed its presence to be felt by the newly created being. The Entity knew that its first creation was an exceptional being, created with an intelligence that rivaled its own. The Entity created the being well, perhaps too well, but the being did not know its purpose, although it knew how to seek knowledge.

"What am I?" asked the being.

"You are the first created," spoke the Entity. "You are the first of many and the first of all. You are loved. You are strong. You will lead many. You are called angel and archangel. You are higher than all but your Creator. You are called Lucifer. Lucifer who brings the light."

"Who are you?" asked Lucifer.

"I am called Amanthus. I am the beginning. I am always. I am the genesis. I am the structure by which things are created and held. I am order. I *am*..." Silence followed the last word. Lucifer waited for more, but nothing else came.

"You said I bring the light. What is this?" Lucifer asked.

"Hold out your hands," Amanthus told him.

Lucifer obeyed, and held his hands outstretched in front of him, with his palms held open and upward. He felt the weight within each hand, his right embracing the rounded handle of the item while the other hand caressed the razors edge. Lucifer gently ran his finger along the blade.

"This tool will harness your very will, Lucifer. Use it now. Strike at the darkness," Amanthus told him.

Lucifer raised his sword high above his head and brought down the blade, slashing at the darkness with a mighty force. The dark nothingness roared like the loudest thunderclap and ripped in two. In that instant, Lucifer knew light, blinding and powerful and overwhelmingly beautiful. Bright, white, pure and all-encompassing. He expected to see Amanthus, as he could still feel the presence of the Creator, but all he could see was the light.

"I need no form other than this, my son," explained Amanthus. "For as much as I and the light are the source of all life, those who want to find me need only to seek my presence."

Lucifer nodded in understanding. "Yes, my Lord."

Following the creation of Lucifer, the remaining of the nine archangels were created by Amanthus.

The first was Michael, second only in strength and power to Lucifer among the angels, with dark, raven black hair in stark contrast to the golden hair of Lucifer. He was imposing and strong, meant to stand beside Lucifer as equals, brothers-in-arms, and to serve the will of Amanthus unconditionally.

Next came the archangel Gabriel. Beautiful and strong with thick short hair, not quite so dark as Michael's. Gabriel would find his place in time as the chief overseer of man, when man finally came to be.

Metatron followed Gabriel, tall and thin and bald with starkly green eyes that felt as if they pierced through you if he stared at you, yet by contrast a gentle spirit through and through. Metatron was granted a special task by Amanthus. He was the great communicator: a connecting presence between all angelkind regardless of wherever they may be, and he could connect the thoughts and feelings of the angels that allowed their thoughts and presence to be known. Metatron acted as the emissary of the will of Amanthus to all of the angels. He was the recorder of all of the history of creation, documenting all that ever was. It was through him that the very first moments of the Creation – those from the very moment that Amanthus first enacted will – were shared with all of the angels that were later created as part of a communal consciousness and memory.

Following the first four came Raphael, who would come to be the archangel of plants and trees and all manner of vegetation and crops in the coming world. Then there was Veramlus, architect of the winds and storms and weather of every kind, followed by Uriel, the archangel of the sea and all water bodies, as well as the overseer of the life within them.

Finally, the first female archangel was created. She was called Ember, with long, deep red hair that suited the name of Ember long before there was a language that even reflected the meaning of the word. And what would eventually be deemed appropriate as well was that Ember was charged with the command and power over fire and heat, bending and forming the core of the world and harnessing the power of the sun. She had strength and ability to rival Michael and Gabriel, yet all were still overshadowed by the power of Lucifer. But her role along with Uriel and Raphael set the stage for the eventual prosperity of life in the coming world – the world which would be called by Amanthus *Eden*.

The final archangel, rounding out the Nine Great Archangels, was Kaborus. It would be his task to be caretaker and the architect of all things past. He would design decay itself, and the collapse of living organic matter. He would be the essence of the reaper of souls. Kaborus was the angel of death.

But before there was death, there had to be life, and like all life it would begin with a flicker of light, and Amanthus had

Lucifer spark that light, one that would grow greater and greater and burn brighter and hotter than any before it. Explosive and mighty in its bright and glorious fury, this is the light that became the sun. A thousand-million other suns followed around the expansive universe, but to those of Eden they would only be known as the stars.

Then Amanthus set forth a mass of solid matter, and commanded Ember to form the core, harnessing the powers granted within her to heat and form the core of Eden. The core grew and expanded from the seed planted by Amanthus and the immense and furious power of the fires of Ember. Amanthus set forth Uriel to bring forth the mighty ocean of Eden, the waters erupting in violent reaction to the molten infant world just coming to be.

When the steam finally settled, the world was a calm, silent ocean, its tranquility a peacefulness that would never be known again once the still waters were broken.

The world shook, and the land came piercing through the surface of the Great Ocean with a mighty wave that moved every drop of the waters of the ocean. It was one great mass of land, displacing nearly a third of the entire surface of the world called Eden. Once the land was settled and the turbulent waters calmed, Amanthus carved a winding canyon through the center of the land, and this canyon filled and flowed with the waters of the ocean. This great river, Atlantia, would flow with water fresh and pure, unlike the salted waters of the great ocean. It would offer a source of nourishment and life-giving sustenance to the coming inhabitants of Eden.

Now it would be Raphael's turn, bringing forth the seeds of vegetation that would make Eden lush and green, accented with the vibrant colors of the light spectrum within the image of the many beautiful flowers that grew across the lands.

Finally, Amanthus brought his archangels together to witness the next part of the plan for Eden. From out of the fertile soils of the land itself rose the first men and the first women of the world. The archangels knew the feeling of surprise for the first time when they saw that these men and women of Eden, while all unique and special in their own ways, were created in the very likeness of the angels. It was just not a single man and woman that was created, but hundreds of them at once, on both sides of the Great River. The east side of the river would be the home of the eastern tribe called Adam, and the west side was the home of the tribe called Eve. Amanthus told his archangels it was their job to serve their purpose under Amanthus; they themselves were to lead others to serve the will of their Lord. Amanthus then brought forth the legions of angels, more than 3000 more beings to serve under Amanthus and the archangels. They set out amongst mankind to teach them about their new world.

Mankind learned to farm and harvest from the land, but also to serve the land as well and preserve its nature and sanctity. The tribes formed societies and those societies worked and traded and helped one another to prosper and grow. The population of man grew more than three-fold over the first ten years after Eden came to be. The angels walked amongst man and freely interacted with the men and women of Eden, but they were strictly forbidden to engage in any act of physical relationship with mankind. The men and women of Adam and Eve knew that the angels were different from what they were. They recognized the angels as beings of great power, and came to know the names of Lucifer, Gabriel and Michael very well and the great emissaries of the powerful being they came to call God in their own slightly altered version of the first language of the angels, although few came to be familiar with God's first name of *Amanthus*.

Over time, things started to change, and the changes that were happening brought a keen awareness that even the angels hadn't realized at first.

The thoughts and ideas of man took a different direction. Some started to act in ways that presented a sense of self-interest rather than the interest of the greater population of Eden. Greed and lust reared their ugly faces for the first time, and others of the seven great sins followed suit. Gluttony and pride came to pass in the forms of excess indulgence in the fruits of the land and the glory of accomplishment in the self-serving wants of men and women all around.

The angels came forth to teach and correct the behaviors of those who had gone astray, but more and more as the desires of man became a dominant driving force of their actions, the more the angels were cast aside and ignored. A group amongst the Eve tribe broke away from the main tribe and moved to the regions of the northwest of the great river, no longer accepting the name and the tribal unity of the mother tribe, calling itself the tribe Cain. A similar group followed on the Adam side of the river, moving from the main tribe north and calling themselves Abel. In contrast to the rebellious nature of the Cain tribe, the Abel tribe wanted to be a self governing group of, sustaining themselves and living by a different set of rules from the main tribe. They would still come and trade with the Adam and Eve tribes, but the Cain tribe would not be heard from for some time.

The angels were puzzled by the actions of the tribes, and brought their concerns to Amanthus. While the angels knew and understood their function and place, they did not know how man was not punished for their rejection of the structure of Eden.

"The Tribes of Eden, in whatever course they take, are the subject of their own path. Their will is their own. While it is your great duty to guide and nurture their way, it is the choices that they make that will lead to their salvation or their destruction," Amanthus told the angels.

The concept seems alien to the angels. There was, for the first time, a feeling of dissension throughout the ranks of the angels. It was a feeling that, even in the subtlest of ways, ran as high as the greatest of the archangels. The question of *why* was first brought into play amongst the servants of Amanthus.

Why is it we were made to only serve?

Why has Amanthus granted these disobedient creatures the freedom of their will?

Even as the angels were starting to question the motivations of Amanthus, tensions grew between the tribes of Eden. The embrace of sin spread like an infection. Amanthus ordered the angels to leave the lands of Eden, but this action in itself was little noticed by the inhabitants of the land. The angels watched from afar with mixed feelings as to the course that man was taking, abusing the great gifts bestowed upon them.

The gift of life.

The gift of plentitude.

And the gift that was suddenly so coveted by a great many of the angels of Amanthus - the gift of freedom.

The final blow came swiftly to the heart of Amanthus and the angels when the long lost tribe of Cain made their presence known in furious fashion as they stormed the shores of the Great River north of Adam in the land of Abel and slaughtered the Abel tribe out of existence.

The Abel tribe was a tribe of farmers, not warriors. Up until that point, in the land of Eden, there was not such a need for a thing called warriors. The Cain tribe found themselves unsuccessful in drawing sustenance from the soils of the land itself, and they had hunted the local lands clean of game for meat. They took all that remained of the salvageable crops of the Abel tribe after the massacre, and with the newfound success of the actions they took, they moved south with the intent to take all that they could from the Eve and Adam tribes.

When word spread to the southern tribes about the fate of the Abel tribe, the two original tribes created weapons of their own and moved forth to meet the coming Cain tribe. The battle erupted into what would be the first – and final – full scale world war of the fledgling world called Eden.

As the people of Eden shed the blood of one another across the land, the angels watched in horror. Some wanted to reach out and put an end to it all, but Amanthus would not allow it. Amanthus watched as well, with a sad fury growing inside. Brother killed brother, fathers fought sons and mothers, daughters, and sisters clashed all the same. For they were all born one another's siblings in the young new world, and now they lashed out at each other in fear, vengeance and greed.

And then came the roar from the Heavens. Some might say it was a scream of anger, while others a cry of despair. Either way, the fighting stopped and the Nine Archangels descended upon the land of Eden.

By the command of Amanthus, five of the archangels lined the banks of the Great River on the west side, while the other four found their places on the banks of the east side, spanning the entire distance from the northernmost point to the southernmost point.

Their fingers dug deep into the rocks, mud and clay

along the banks of the river and with a mighty force, the archangels tore the land of Eden in two, dragging the lands farther and farther apart by thousands of miles. The act itself shook the lands so greatly that most of the structures and homes built by the guidance of the angels through the hands of man were reduced to rubble. What wasn't destroyed by the quaking land was mostly washed away by the resulting great flood that overtook the entirety of the two great continental land masses that now existed in the place of what was once the great land of Eden.

Most of the existing life that once flourished on Eden had been wiped out, save for a handful of the humankind and many of the species of animals that had been given a reprieve from the devastation of the flood. The existence of man had been decimated to only a few, and all that had been gained and learned from the world before was now lost to the waters that washed them clean. Man would have to start over, and this time, they would be on their own, with no help or guidance from the angels.

Amanthus vowed to not turn a back to mankind, but all that had been known, learned or remembered about the existence of Amanthus and the angels had now become a matter of rumor, myth and legend. Upon the whispers of God were built rituals and systems of belief, some based on archaic design while others a more spiritualistic set of beliefs. They gave God a gender, calling him their Holy Father, and for those who sought him out, he would listen, if not always answer.

Cultures came into being and flourished on both sides of the new great ocean, and vague memories of Eden became the subject of scripture and religious practice. New tribes and empires rose and fell, and history came to know the rest. Through the wars and the epic struggles of life and death, the world now known as Earth was born, and the paradise that was once Eden perished on the very ground beneath the feet of the inhabitants of Earth, echoing everything that once was and all that could have been.

It was a new struggle now, and it would last to a time without end.

The angels were given the charge to watch over – but never reveal themselves to – the world of man. They were not to interfere in the challenges and triumphs of mankind, only to observe, leaving mankind to its own tragedies and accomplishments. The souls of mankind were in their own hands, and it was now a matter of faith, either in God, or in the goodness and righteousness within them – that would determine their fate beyond the shackles of life. These things were entirely interchangeable, for neither offered any certainty. There was only the intention that man could choose to do the right things in life regardless of the lack of certainty in the promises of rewards everlasting. And what that meant, no one could know.

But for the angels, there was a seed planted in the shadow of the misdeeds of mankind that questioned the authority of Amanthus and a craving of free will beyond the servitude of God. It was these events that would lead to a day where even the most loyal servants of Amanthus would face trials that challenged their devotion to the sanctity of their place among their own kind, and an even deeper challenge of carrying the weight of their own hearts…

Miranda gasped loudly and fell back from Gabriel, striking her head on the table on the floor beside her. Gabriel's eyes were open and he was watching her, as he had been for the few minutes since she had first set her fingertips on his hand. He was a light sleeper, and no sooner had she touched him did he awaken to see her sitting there, eyes black as the night. He knew what she was doing, and he could see everything that she saw, although while it seemed like a long period of time had passed to Miranda, it had only been a few minutes in the waking world.

Gabriel didn't even flinch when Miranda fell back. He knew she was obviously fine. He sat up slowly and leaned forward with his elbows upon his knees, hands clasped in a matter-of-fact pose looking down on her. She pulled herself up on her elbow and looked up at him, feeling uncharacteristically disheveled.

Gabriel did not have any definable expression on his face.

"Did you find what you were looking for?" he asked her, a flat tone in his voice.

"Yeah," she said, pulling herself up from the ground.

"Next time you want to know something, just ask," he said to her. He laid back down on the couch and pulled the blanket over him, and he went back to sleep.

CHAPTER FOURTEEN

Early the next morning after a quick stop for breakfast, Lydia picked up Ashe from the apartment above Greta's shop.

Jake, Miranda, Lydia, Ashe and Gabriel gathered in the room that he and Miranda had stayed in the night before. Gabriel locked the door and pulled the shades shut on the patio. While prying eyes didn't seem like they would be a problem, he wasn't taking any chances.

"Miranda, this may seem like it is much more difficult than what you did last night, but the difference is only in your mind. Moving the distance between the room and the patio is no different than moving across the ocean. It is only a matter of visualizing where it is you want to be," Gabriel told her.

The others took seats around the room, Jake and Lydia beside one another on the couch, Ashe sitting on the edge of the bed that no one had slept in the night before.

"How will I know what to visualize?" asked Miranda.

"I've been to the house where David arranged for her to be cared for. Just from afar. I wasn't permitted to make direct contact with anyone in the family. I kept my distance, but I still chose to follow my duty to observe the family. Unfortunately I failed at staying hidden and was taken by David's men after I had been noticed hanging around the grounds," Gabriel said.

"Okay," Miranda said, taking a step toward Gabriel and reaching out her hand. "Show me what I need to know."

Jake sprung up from the couch. "Are you sure you are ready for this?" he asked Miranda.

She looked at him with a straight and determined face. "Yes. I'm ready."

Jake nodded to her and sat back down. He knew better than to present any argument when Miranda had that look in her eye.

Gabriel lifted his hand and took Miranda's. "I will picture the house in my mind. Focus on what you see and when you are ready…"

Before Gabriel could even finish his thought, Miranda was no longer with them in the room. Jake and Lydia jumped up from the couch.

"Where is she? What happened to her?" demanded Jake.

"She's a fast learner," Gabriel remarked. "She's on her own…in England."

Miranda found herself standing on a well-kept grassy lawn of a pristinely maintained two-story home. The air was fresh and the sun was much higher in the sky than it had been around 8 a.m. in Michigan. The grass had been freshly mowed. The smell of fresh cut grass always took her back to happier times in her childhood. She thought of how her father Robert would walk back and forth, again and again, across the large picture window that faced the front yard on Saturday mornings while she and Steven, who was only a toddler at the time, watched videos on the television as the roar of the mower passed by. Robert would often make faces at them and stick his tongue out as he moved past when he was closest to the window. Miranda would laugh the hardest at Steven's laughs at his daddy, smacking the window with his little hands and sometimes falling back on his butt as he did.

It brought a smile to Miranda's face for a moment as she let the memory bring her a brief glimmer of joy - an emotion she forbid herself for quite some time as a form of self-punishment for the guilt she carried inside her.

She looked the house over. It was on a private, wooded lot, far away from any other homes down the lane. There was no flaking paint, no rust on the iron gates that stood open at the end of the driveway. Everything seemed flawless, suggesting that despite the feelings he held for his mother, David held true to his commitment to her care and the environment in which she would be cared for.

There were two cars in the driveway. Miranda had not worn her leather jacket before she departed the rest of the group. She stood between the gates in blue jeans and one of her v-neck plain tees, assessing her surroundings.

She walked up to the house and peeked in the windows. This was more out of the habit of living as a human being for most of her life before the discovery of whatever it was that she was now. If she did not want to be noticed, she would not be. There was a woman in the kitchen preparing a meal of mostly broth soup and a glass of water with a straw in the glass. In a smaller dish beside the water was a variety of pills.

Miranda entered the house through the front door and watched the woman walk past her with the tray and up the

stairs to the second floor. The woman took no notice of
Miranda as she went past. Miranda could hear whispering from
the second floor between two people.

"How did she seem this morning?" asked one of the
voices.

"She's slept pretty much through the morning," said the
other.

"I heated this up for her, just in case," said the first
voice.

"I don't think she is going to have it," said the other
voice once more.

There was a period of silence after the second voice had
said this. Miranda noticed that there were elevator doors in the
living room. The house had been modified around the care of
Victoria Gale. David had spared no expense for the care of his
mother. Miranda's disdain for David moved her to believe that
there could only have been selfish reasons why so much care
was given to the well being of his mother. He could so brutally
remove or manipulate anyone that would stand in the way of
his darker intentions, so why so much expense and attention to
Victoria's care? Miranda refused to allow herself to think that
David Gale had even a glimmer of decency within his cold
heart.

The two nurses charged with the day-shift care of
Miranda's grandmother followed one another down the stairs
and past where Miranda was standing. Miranda moved on up
the stairs and down the hall that led to the room where she
would find Victoria.

The room was large, taking up most of the second
floor. There were large windows that could have let the warm
sunshine in, but the shades were drawn as Victoria slept. Her
breaths seemed shallow, and her frame seemed small to

Miranda. Her hair was almost white-grey, cut short, and Miranda felt a great deal of pity for the woman in the bed. She could remember only bits and pieces, like most of the memories from the time before her life as Miranda Stratton. There were only flickering flashes of images now.

What she could recall of what she saw of Victoria Gale in her own minds eye, from her memories as a very young toddler, was the image of a woman that seemed larger than life. Strong and firm, an elegant and proper woman, but also deeply caring and full of love. Miranda couldn't even imagine how she would know these things, but she believed them and trusted her feelings none the less.

Miranda turned to look around the room. The walls were devoid of any decorations, but there was a large dresser on the wall across from the bed that was covered with framed pictures. From the research that she had done when she was digging into her own past, she recognized a portrait of Thomas Gale, her grandfather and Victoria's husband. There was another picture, much older that the portrait, of what looked to be the wedding photo of Thomas and Victoria. Beside that photo was a picture of Miranda's mother Suzanne, which Miranda guessed was a year or two before she was born. The young boy with the dark eyes and heartless smile in the next framed photo was her uncle, David Gale.

Miranda picked up the framed picture and looked at his eyes with deep contempt, and while the impulses within her wanted to throw the photo against the wall, she forced herself to gently lay the photo face down on the top of the dresser.

"My...my lord...Suzanne...my sweet, sweet girl...it's time."

Miranda turned around as she heard the frail and cracking voice coming from the shell of the person lying in the hospital bed against the far wall. Victoria's eyes, once a bright blue like her own and her mother Suzanne's, were now a pale and cloudy grey. The whites were yellowed – a sign of a slow surrendering of her liver functions – and she had a quiver in her lips when she spoke. She had aged physically far beyond that of a woman in her seventies should have aged. The life she had lived, and the losses that mounted because of that life, had taken their toll on Victoria.

Miranda walked over to the door of the room and quietly shut it so that she and Victoria would not be heard by the nurses below. She then walked to the edge of the bed and looked down at her grandmother.

"Suzanne…is it time?" whispered Victoria, reaching out for the young woman standing before her that she believed was her daughter.

Miranda took her hand, being sure not to let her power overtake her mind at that moment.

"No Grandma," Miranda said to her in a gentle tone. "It's Miranda. Your granddaughter."

Victoria's eyes widened and her quivering lips went still, her mouth opening a little wider than it had been. It was as if suddenly there was a newfound strength in the older woman, and Victoria tightened her grip on Miranda's hand.

"Miranda." Victoria said her name as clear as can be, and tears came streaming from her eyes. She pulled her tightly down to her and Miranda let her frail grandmother embrace her.

"How…how are you here? How did you find me?" asked Victoria.

"My father found me. He told me you were alive, and he told me where to find you," Miranda told her.

"Your…father? Gabe? I don't understand…he

abandoned you and your mother. How could he have found you?" asked Victoria.

"He didn't...he didn't have a choice. I'm sorry...there is too much to explain. I'm here now, that's all that matters. I need to know some things, and I am hoping you can help me."

Victoria pulled her close again and her voice turned firm and strong. "Miranda, you need to get as far away from here as you can. Forget the Gales. Forget...forget me. I love you...you need to be free of all of this. If David finds you..."

"David is dead. I'm sorry to tell you...like this," said Miranda.

Victoria eased her grip on Miranda's hand, but she did not let go completely. She laid her head back and looked up at the ceiling.

"My son is dead? How did it happen?" she asked Miranda.

Miranda felt a lump form in her throat. She owed Victoria the truth, regardless of the ugliness of it all.

"David...he murdered my family. He tried to hurt me and my friends. He took...he took everything from me. I...I didn't have a choice. I killed him."

Almost the entire truth. She always had a choice.

Victoria looked back at Miranda. "You killed him?"

Miranda nodded her head. Victoria looked back at the ceiling once again.

"Thank God," she said. "There was something horrid in his soul. I can feel peace now that I don't have to worry what kind of suffering he is causing in the world. But my dear, I am so sorry for what he has done to you. *Why?* Why did he do this to you?"

"I don't know how to explain this...I still don't understand it fully myself. I am the one in the prophecy. And

I…I let Lucifer out. He is free, and I have to stop him. I need to know why my great-grandfather chose where to build the Gale house. Why Galestone? I think there is something there that we need to find."

Victoria sat in silent astonishment at what Miranda revealed to her.

"After all these years…after all this time. It's all true after all," Victoria muttered. She looked Miranda in the eye. "There is one thing that I can offer you. But there is one thing in return that I ask…a favor. You don't have to…I owe you so much…but perhaps you will."

"What is it?" asked Miranda. "Anything I can, I will help you."

Victoria smiled. She pointed to the dresser. "Top drawer, where I left it the last time that I saw it. Go. Look."

Miranda walked to the dresser and pulled open the top drawer. There was a leather photo album on the right side of the drawer, and on the left side there were stockings, underwear, and a jewelry box. Under the glass frame of the jewelry box was a picture of Suzanne and Miranda standing in front of the fountain at the Gale house.

"Beneath the photo album is what you are looking for," Victoria said, her voice growing weaker and more tired again.

Miranda moved the album and beneath it was a leather-bound book, wrapped and tied with brown leather straps. She pulled the book from the dresser and closed the drawer. She took it back to Victoria's bedside.

"What is this?" asked Miranda.

"It is the journal of your great-grandfather, Francis Gale. It has been years since I looked through it, although it was never mine to look through. It was given to my husband, Thomas, after Francis passed. Francis chronicled many things over the years about the Gale family history, but much of that was lost in the fire. This somehow survived, and it details a journey that Francis and his father, Charles Gale, took many years ago. They were searching for something…just in case the prophecy about Lucifer wasn't all that it was supposed to be. You may find…what you are looking for…in here…"

Victoria's consciousness was slipping. Miranda took her hand once more, and closed her eyes. She was attempting to transfer some small bit of energy to her grandmother, and it was to some degree working, but Victoria was too weak to hold on for long.

"Grandmother…what did you want me to do for you?" asked Miranda, her heart feeling heavy for the poor old woman.

Victoria smiled, the quivering in her lips returning with the smile. "I was going to ask you to help me die…but I think I'm not going to need that after all," she said, just as her hand slipped out of Miranda's and her last breath came from her lips. Her head fell gently to its right side, facing the window that was shaded from the sun.

Miranda took her hand and softly closed Victoria's eyes. She was overcome with the empty feeling that she had in recent years become all too familiar with. She walked over to the window and pulled the shade aside, letting the room flood with sunshine that washed over her grandmother's frail and empty body.

"Miranda."

Miranda turned and saw, standing in the corner of the room, a much younger and profoundly vibrant and beautiful Victoria. She had a bright smile on her face, and she wore a dress that looked similar to the dress she had seen in a newspaper image from long ago. Miranda walked over to where the ghost of Victoria Gale stood.

"I don't have much time," said Victoria. "I feel the pull…but there is one thing that I have to tell you before I go."

"Tell me," said Miranda. "Please…"

"The mines. They weren't closed because of safety issues with the mines themselves. There were a number of animal attacks. The deeper they mined, whatever it was they were looking for, the attacks grew stronger and more vicious. But the men…what they reported had attacked them, it didn't seem in any way *natural*."

"What do you mean?" asked Miranda, but Victoria was fading from her sight, although she could still hear her voice as her visual form faded.

"They were beasts, Miranda…they were not creatures born of the natural world…" Victoria's voice faded into the distance, and she was gone. Miranda was alone once again. She could hear footsteps coming up the stairs, and so she took her leave just as the door to the bedroom opened.

The nurse was surprised to see the sunlight flooding the room, overlooking the fact that the bedroom door had been closed. She walked around the bed and closed the shade once again, and then turned to see the face of her charge. She immediately knew when she saw her face that Victoria was gone.

She walked over and gently touched Victoria's cheek, having found a true affection for the feisty and beautiful woman over the many years that she was in her care. The nurse sat down in the chair beside the bed. She held her hand and she wept for Victoria Gale.

Miranda stood on the balcony of the room where she had left from only an hour before, clutching the journal that Victoria had given her. Several minutes had gone by before she stepped in from the balcony, her immediate presence startling everyone in the room except Ashe, who had fallen asleep reading on the bed. She woke when the others had made a sudden gasping sound as Miranda entered the room, and sat up in a groggy haze.

Gabriel was the first to come over to her. He saw a look of distress in her eyes.

"Are you alright?" he asked her.

"She gave me this," Miranda said, handing over the journal to Gabriel. Gabriel took it from her and opened it, fingering through the pages.

"Francis Gale's journal. I've seen this at the Gale house before, although I had never paid any real attention to it. This may help greatly," he said. "And Victoria is…"

"She's dead. She passed after we talked. And we spoke again briefly after she passed."

Ashe looked around at everyone else in the room to see if they had the same confused look she had. The expressions of the others had not changed, so she suppressed her obvious confusion as to how Miranda spoke to Victoria after she had already passed. Ashe assumed the weirdness level would get more commonplace as time went on, but another part of her didn't truly believe that.

"I'm sorry Miranda," Gabriel said to her with a real sincerity. Miranda didn't respond to his gesture. She continued talking as if he had said nothing at all

"She told me the real reason that the mines closed was because there were attacks. The deeper they dug and the closer they got to whatever was in those mines, the more frequently the attacks were happening. She said they were described as unnatural creatures."

"Nolamids," Gabriel said.

"Nolamids?" asked Jake. "What the hell are Nolamids?"

"Beasts that live in hiding all over your world. Abominations created experimentally by many of the renegade angels that fell with Lucifer in the time when Amanthus walked the Earth as a man. The angels were beyond his sight, so the renegades that wanted the same freedom as man did what they pleased, and sometimes that meant abusing their powers of creation. These creatures are often drawn to objects and places of power. They desire to feed off of it, and they are not kind to those that stand in their way. We will need weapons when we go to retrieve the shard."

"I can supply some firepower. My family's hunting cabin is on the way to Galestone in the U.P. Shotguns, high-powered hunting rifles, and a few smaller arms," Jake told the group.

Gabriel nodded. "That will help. But these things are not going to be like taking down a bear or a deer. They are faster and stronger and harder to find. They blend in naturally. It's why they are only looked at as a matter of myth and folklore."

"Like Bigfoot?" asked Lydia.

"Exactly like Bigfoot," Gabriel nodded.

Lydia and Ashe both had looks of astonishment on their faces.

"Just when I thought the day wasn't going to get weirder, I find out that Bigfoot is real now, too," Ashe muttered to herself.

"But before we go to the mines, I need to find out whatever we can about where we are going and what we are looking for. Let's pack up and start north. I can read in the vehicle. Hopefully by the time that we get to the hunting cabin, we'll know all that we need to before we start out for

Galestone," Gabriel said.

"Agreed," said Jake, as Lydia headed out to get the rest of her things from the room she and Jake stayed in the night before. Jake looked at Miranda, who seemed distracted as she blankly stared out the patio door at the blinding sunlight bursting through the glass.

"Miranda? What is it?" Jake asked. Gabriel was packing up the laptop and gathering his other belongings.

"It's nothing. I'm good. Let's go," she said, walking past him out the motel room door.

CHAPTER FIFTEEN

The Journal of Francis Gale
An excerpt…

23rd – October, 1923 – I can almost not contain the excitement that I am feeling accompanying father on this journey to one of the darkest and most mysterious places in all of Europe! I recall as it takes me back to the thrill I had hiding beneath the covers of my bed at only twelve years old reading for the first of many readings the tale of Jonathan Harker's journey to the castle of Count Dracula across the wilds of Germany, Hungary and eventually into the heart of the Carpathian Mountains where we are now traveling!

I do know and understand the serious nature of this trek, so I contain this enthusiasm in the presence of my father Charles Gale and exude it only in my writings. It was a surprise to say the least that father called me away from my studies at Oxford University to have me come with him by railway to this far off destination, but it was even greater the surprise that he had done it three months prior to tell me the secrets of which the Gale family has been custodian to for centuries.

Perhaps it was the fantastical nature by which my imagination was privy to that he had for so long kept these tales from me, or perhaps it was the fact that he did not think I was ready for the truth of these dark secrets, but now a time had come…he said it came to him with a dream…that these need be shared with the next generation of the Gale line and the necessity of the coming journey (that which we are on now) became greatly evident.

When I first came home, father seemed oddly detached as I had not seen him before. The first few days back I rarely saw him, and I must be honest, I felt slightly annoyed as to the sudden urgency for which I needed to return. Then, late one evening just after sunset I was called into his private study. The day servants had been sent away, and mother and my sister Julianne had settled in for the evening. Julianne is such a reader! She and mother spend hours every week reading and talking of the books they have read. I told them they should gather a group together and discuss the things that they have read, but they still choose to keep to themselves, engrossing themselves in novels written in both English and Italian. Julianne is far more talented in her Italian, both speaking and writing, while I, fair enough in my Italian, have excelled in my German and French. During the Great War, I felt for certain that I would be called to the front lines because of my German and Italian fluency. I was just eighteen and I was ready to go and fight against the Kaiser for the good of all nations, but suddenly the war had ended and all that was left was the rebuilding of a war torn continent. My studies at Oxford were delayed by more than a year as I helped, alongside father, through our family's many business channels ship goods and supplies to many different parts of the European continent that were affected by the atrocities of the war. In these ways, my language skills became a great asset…but, my apologies, I digress…

Father locked the door behind me as I entered his study, and without a word he walked over to his private wall safe. Just before he opened it, he turned to me and beckoned me to his side. That was the day that he shared with me the combination to the safe, which was something that he had not even ever shared with my mother. I remember his words all too well, as there was a sadness in them that I had never before that day heard.

He said, "A time has come, Francis, that I had hoped never would, that which a family legacy begins its journey into your hands."

I did not know what this was to mean at the time, as I thought family legacy was something to take on with pride and honor. But this was to be explained soon after, as father removed from the safe the documents of the Caducus Oraclum and I was first told about the Order of Sanctity.

Our Gale family was the last of a line of families that had been caretakers of the Caducus Oraclum, a tale and a prophecy regarding the fall of the archangel Lucifer from the grace of God, and the prophecy spoke of the possibility of hope and enlightenment through the grace of God by Lucifer himself with the coming of one who could release him from the bounds of Hell itself...

I must confess, at first, I thought father was playing some strange game with me, testing my gullibility and even more so my sensibilities. It was not until I saw the tears upon his face that I knew for certain that he truly believed what he was telling me, and it shook me to my very core. Never had I seen Charles Gale weep, not even at the loss of his own parents years before, but this was something deeply different, and behind those tears there was a great fear of an unknowable future.

As father explained the history of the Order and the Oraclum itself, he confessed his own doubts of the authenticity of the entire tale. It was the deeply held belief, after the split of the Order in the 1700s, that the custodians of the Oraclum held a responsibility to be watchful for the return of Lucifer so that we may receive his great knowledge and that God would finally, through his first son, grant mankind wisdom and enlightenment. But father did not believe as deeply and the generations before him, and he intended to let go of the legacy. He had made the decision only days before he sent message to me at Oxford to return home immediately.

Ah...we are now arriving in Budapest. Father has some other business dealings to attend to here, as it is now early morning. Tonight, we will leave Budapest for the remainder of our rail journey to Brasov, deep in the heart of the Carpathians. I will certainly need rest for the travels beyond that point, but I will continue my tale then.

24th – October, 1923 – The train was delayed for several hours before we finally could depart Budapest. It is now thirty minutes past midnight, and it was going to take the entire night and several of the morning hours to reach our initial destination in Brasov, Romania.

Father had me join him in his business dealings in the afternoon hours. It was not actually a deal in which Gale Holdings was directly a part of, merely a favor of Father's for associates to help broker a transaction of wheat exports from Hungary to other foreign nations. Wheat is one of Hungary's greatest export strengths after the war, and an important part of their recovering economy after the defeat the country faced after the Great War. The difficulties of a nation that lost nearly two-thirds of its land at the restructuring of the Eastern European map seemed by and far overwhelming. Father wanted to try and help, feeling a sense of sympathy for all that were affected by the war. "The egos and atrocities of a nation's governing powers are not always the fault of the good citizens of those nations, Francis," he told me before the meeting. He is truly a man of the people.

Now, back to where I left off – Father's decision to put the line of custody of the Caducus Oraclum to rest.

My father has always been a man of strong faith. He attended church with my mother on a regular basis, and as children, Julianne and I were always brought along until an age when, out of character for our community, we were allowed to make a choice as to how we wanted to have a relationship of our own with God, aside from the teachings of the church. I never quite understood this...at least until that night in the study.

On the very night that Father had decided to forever close the door on the Oraclum, he was plagued by a vivid dream. He told me the dream brought him two very different visions of the future regarding the Oraclum. The first was a vision of the great Lightbringer, Lucifer, a ushering in a new age of peace, prosperity and freedom. A utopian world, where Lucifer's knowledge brought about a return to the days of Eden.

And then, he said the vision changed. It grew dark and he saw a world burning beneath the wrath of Lucifer, once the bringer of light, and now, the bringer of darkness and vengeance upon the lands. My father saw suffering and death, and the only light that remained was that of the fires that burned the cities and forests alike, a cloud of ashen darkness that blocked out the light of the sun. There was a whisper through the burning embers of the walls of the once great city of London through which Father walked in the dream. The voice said, "Be prepared. Seek the seer in the east. Belnair… the Gypsy Racos."

That night, Father awoke in a cold sweat. He came to realize that there was no escaping the destiny of our family. The Caducus Oraclum must be preserved. But if the prophecy were to be fulfilled, what horrors might it release? This was the true purpose of our long trip to a region steeping with myth and superstition. Within the ring of shadows cast by the Carpathian Mountains there were secrets that could only be revealed from treading upon the very soils where stood those who guarded them.

It took research and correspondence from associates that frequented the region to reveal where to find the Gypsy Racos. Belnair was a small woodland village northwest of Brasov, Romania. It was not on any maps outside of the central region that was once Transylvania before the war. Father's good friend and German associate Frederick Kemp traveled to the region often and through his own investigation found the location and a map to the village. He warned though that the locals were very cautious of sharing information about that place. Fear and superstition, despite our modern age, were still very powerful forces in such places so cut off from the rest of the world. Still afraid of Dracula, I suppose…although in truth, the potential for monsters in reality was not a far cry, indeed, for what monster could be potentially greater than that of the Devil himself?

I must get rest. Today was long, and I fear tomorrow will be all that much more. For who knows what we may find on the road from Brasov.

24th – October, 1923 – continued…
Father and I both had a restless sleep through the night. We awoke and had breakfast on the train, and arrived at the Brasov station at 11:38 a.m. local time. Father had arranged a car to pick us up at the station, and we immediately were driven to a house on the northeast border of the city of Brasov. The car was left for us to return to the train station when we were to depart on our return journey. The house was arranged for us by Herr Kemp, a place he frequently stayed when visiting the area. We changed out of our traveling clothes and dressed more appropriately for the next step to Belnair. The road to the village was not a road that our car could take, as it was a narrow road up a mountain pass, so Herr Kemp secured a supply carriage that transported food and other village supplies to Belnair.

Herr Kemp did not share with anyone the information as to the purpose of our travels, although most he did not know, he was aware of the name of the village and the name of the gypsy we sought out. The transport would not be available until the following morning, as Herr Kemp had planned accordingly, knowing that the train schedules across the European continent did not always run on time. As things were, the post-war recovery was still an ongoing effort, even a few years after the war had ended. And of course given the course of the railways, there was always the potential for rockslides and other obstacles along the way.

We will rest now, have a proper dinner and a proper nights sleep and will head out in the morning's first light. I will not write again until after the true purpose of our mission is complete.

26th – October, 1923 – Our return to London has begun.

I fear that from this point on in my life, things will never be the same again. A new course must be taken, and a great responsibility lies in my hands. The very fate of mankind is what is at stake. The Gale legacy has taken a turn, and only uncertainty paves the road ahead.

After reviewing my notes and certain transcriptions made of our encounters, I am now prepared to chronicle the events of the few hours that my father, Charles Gale, and I, Francis Ernest Gale, spent in the company of the Gypsy woman Elena Racos.

The carriage was ready to depart at seven o'clock in the morning, and Father and I were ready and prompt. There was the driver and his eleven year old son, several supplies and just barely enough room for the two of us in the carriage. The driver had to leave some items behind to make room for us, but Father made sure that the driver would be well compensated for any lost profits from the trip.

The trip itself was slow going, as the road was as rough as was to be expected along the mountain pass. The driver's son held on to a rifle all the way along the path. He and the driver both spoke German, and I asked him what the need was for the rifle at the ready. He told me there are two things to worry about on the mountain passes at any time. The lesser of the two were bandits, especially along the pass we were traveling. There was far too much superstition for bandits to dare compromise the transport of supplies to a gypsy village. But the second, and more problematic obstacle, was wolves.

I took heed of this information and kept a watchful eye myself for any sign of a wolf, but there were no signs of any along our way.

When we reached the village, I found that the word village was not the best to describe what was actually a community of tent homes. There were fire pits burning all around the place, with kettles suspended above them cooking meals. Along the outskirts of the village there were animals strung up and being cleaned for food. It was like taking a step back in time, and this was the way this group liked it.

As we came to a stop, the driver said something in Romanian to a young woman who met him. She nodded and went to a tent near the center of the village. The driver asked us to please wait until the woman returned, and we complied with his request. A short time later, several men came and unloaded the rest of the wagon. Their form of dress was much like the working class of anywhere else in the country that we had already seen, aside from the silver jewelry that they wore. There were pendants and earrings and rings upon their fingers, and many were in the shape of the cross. Silver was, as one described to me later, a symbol of purity and protection, and it caused me to recall the stories from my childhood about werewolves and the such.

The young woman finally came back and nodded to the driver, who dismounted from the carriage along with his son, who left the rifle on the seat of the carriage. The boy told me that the wolves don't come here, so there was no need for the rifle within the boundaries of the village.

The woman (a very pretty Roma girl named Valencia) came to us and spoke in very clear German. She beckoned us to follow her, which we did. She led us to the tent that she had just returned from.

She said, "You have come seeking the council of the lady Elena Racos. I will take you inside to see my grandmother. She will see you now."

I find it important to note that no one in the village was made aware that we were coming to the village, or what our intentions were in coming there. This made what Valencia said both amazing and, I shall admit, somewhat troubling.

She led us into the tent and Elena sat on the edge of a bed across the large tent. The tent was one of the largest in the entire village, and there was a fire built within the walls of the tent that kept it warm at all times, with a chimney constructed through the walls in a way that would not cause damage to the tent material itself.

Elena was a very old woman, although I could not say for certain how old. Her hair was very long and straight and grey, reaching far down her back and resting on the surface of the bed. Her eyes were both deep and *dark, and the skin of her face deeply wrinkled. But the old woman had a wisdom in her gaze that held me from the moment I stepped into the tent.*

Valencia sat beside her grandmother and said something to her in Romanian. Elena replied in Romanian to her granddaughter.

"My grandmother speaks many languages. English is not one of them," Valencia said to us in German. As I was very fluent in German, my father was not. He knew a little, so I would have to translate to him the words to old woman spoke, and in turn, his words of English to her. The following is a rough transcription of the conversation between them:

Charles: My greetings to you, Madam Racos. I am grateful that you have allowed us to see you.

Elena: (nods silently to my father)

Charles: Did someone make you aware of our coming to see you?

Elena: I have known since you had your dream, Mr. Gale. I too had a dream much the same.

Charles: So I would hazard to say you know well what I have come for?

Elena: You seek a means to defeat the Lightbringer. In the case that he is indeed the devil we fear. Since the day I foresaw your coming, I have meditated on this, and I have found a possible way. Have you brought the Caducus Oraclum, Mr. Gale?

At this point, my father looked to me, at which I nodded and removed the documents from my leather satchel and handed them to Elena Racos. Elena gasped when her fingers made first contact with the parchment pages. This startled Valencia, who placed her hand on her grandmother's shoulder and spoke in a worried tone to her more words in Romanian.

Elena: (in German) I am alright, sweet girl. Do not worry.

Elena sat in silence for several minutes running her long fingers across the pages in her hands. She made no attempt to read the text. We sat in silence as well, until finally, Elena opened her eyes. And she said the words in Latin that I had only recently heard for the first time myself.

Elena: Cadere Gladii.

Charles: Yes. This is the place where the Oraclum was first discovered. What of it?

Elena: Charles, it is more than just the name of a place. It was an event. You have read the translations of the text in the Oraclum. It tells a story, but most get so lost in the greater implications of the tale that is being told that the fine details…slip by them. What does it mean?

Charles: It is Latin. It means 'the fall of the sword'.

Elena: Lucifer's sword. It is right there in the tale. The archangel Michael struck the final blow to end the war in Heaven by shattering Lucifer's sword across Heaven and Earth. These pages were found in one of the places that a piece of Lucifer's sword landed. But the one near this place is on sacred land out of my sight. More are beyond my sight. But there is one. Valencia dear, bring me the…what did you call it?

Valencia: It is called a globe, Grandmother.

Valencia brought Elena a globe that had detailed map drawings of the entire known world. The writing on the globe was in German as well, and Elena closed her eyes as she let the globe slowly turn beneath her fingertips.

Elena: I can feel it. It is deep. It had fallen hard, as did Lucifer. It is deep in the iron of the Earth. You must…dig deep.

Elena's fingers stopped the turning globe and her forefinger held a spot on the northern peninsula of the U.S. State of Michigan.

Elena: Here. Valencia, bring me a quill and ink, and paper. I will make you a map to the location at which you must dig. Give me one hour.

Charles: Madam, pardon my ignorance, but what will one piece of a sword do against an archangel of God?

Elena: It was his sword, the first to cut through the darkness and bring light into the universe. It is a tiny fragment of his power, and with the slightest scratch will turn even the most powerful angel into a mortal being.

Charles: How do you know this?

Elena sat in silence for almost a full minute before finally telling my father that he had to have faith.

We left Elena for an hour. Valencia showed us to a place where we would be fed, and we ate well and thanked the patron gypsies, and gave them silver coins that my father had brought in a pouch that I was unaware of until that very moment.

The hour went by, and Valencia came out of the tent and walked over to where we sat waiting. We stood up and she handed me the paper that she had brought blank to her grandmother. There were intricate details in the drawing and names of places nearby written in English. It was astounding how precise it was.

Valencia told us that her grandmother was resting now. We asked her what we could do to thank her for all she has done for us. She told us her grandmother said to tell us one thing – "Come what may, do not fail. Where ever there is light, one can always find shadow, and just as the like, where there is shadow, one can often find the light."

My father gave Valencia the rest of the bag of silver coin, which I can only guess was a significant amount of money for payment. I never knew how much was in the pouch, but it was not a light in weight.

And now, we travel home. I believe, with this map in our possession, plans will be made to follow a new destiny in America. I will make it my life's mission to find this item, and if ever the prophecy is fulfilled, we will be ready in case the bringer of light is truly the devil we have come to know of myth and legend.

End excerpt.

Rick Jurewicz

CHAPTER SIXTEEN

Gabriel read and re-read the journal entry regarding Francis and Charles Gale's trip to the gypsy. Miranda read through it quickly as well, as her ability to absorb the information at a phenomenal speed was one of the lesser known talents that came with her extraordinary abilities. Despite filling in a few blanks as to exactly how the Gale family came to end up in Galestone, it did in fact reveal a few details that had not been known to them before.

"Ashe, what do you know about your family history before your grandmother came to America?" Gabriel asked her.

"Umm...not much." Ashe replied. "I mean, my grandmother was born here. She said her mother and father were the first to come from Romania right around the end of World War II. Why?"

"Do you happen to know your great-grandmother's name?" Gabriel asked.

"Her name was Valencia. Grandma told me it was from her mother she learned about what she called the 'old ways' and our gypsy heritage," Ashe said. "I never met her. She died many years before I was born. She was nearly forty years old when she had Grandma."

Gabriel looked to Miranda.

"She kept the name," said Miranda. Gabriel nodded.

Ashe looked back and forth between them. Jake was driving the SUV and listening to the conversation while Lydia had dozed off in the back seat beside Ashe.

"Grandma said that. Yes, when they came to America, they chose to register there name as my great-grandmother's family name. She insisted on it, but Grandma Greta never knew why. How do you know that?" asked Ashe.

"I believe that your great-grandmother did that for one reason," said Gabriel. "I believe it was so that we would find you, Ashe. And I don't think it is mere coincidence that she came to Michigan from Romania. According to Francis Gale's journal, Francis and his father met both your great-grandmother Valencia and her grandmother Elena. I believe Elena foresaw a great darkness coming and knew it was her family's destiny to try and help stop it. Your family's destiny has been tied to the Gale's family destiny for almost a century."

Ashe took it all in slowly. Two days ago, she was a normal 18 year old girl excited about getting her first tattoo. Today, she was being referenced by a former angel and his daughter as being a part of some great world-saving destiny.

Miranda looked back over her shoulder at Ashe, straight-faced.

"I know how you must be feeling. It's not something you get used to."

Gabriel frowned but said nothing to either of them regarding Miranda's comment. He knew the truth behind Miranda's words. And he knew the guilt those words carried.

The group had just crossed the Mackinac Bridge and Jake passed the freeway exit for US-2 that would take them in the direction of Galestone.

"Jake, wasn't that our exit?" asked Gabriel.

"The cabin is near Hessel off of M-134. It's not exactly on the way, but only another 25 minutes out of the way. We need the guns, right?" asked Jake.

"Yes," Gabriel said with a sigh. He was anxious, and he was still unsure of Lucifer's grand plan. But there was a feeling in his gut that time was running short. Something was coming soon, and he had to find out what that was before it was too late.

Exit 359 on Interstate 75 came up fast. Just beyond the exit sign Miranda noticed a large green sign on the side of the interstate. It read 'PRISON AREA – Next 50 miles, DO NOT PICK UP HITCHHIKERS'. Jake took the exit ramp just before the sign and within ten minutes they were at the hunting cabin.

The 'cabin' was a two-story log built building with three bedrooms on the lower level and one large open loft bedroom on the upper level that looked out over the living and dining areas of the lower level. There was a large covered and screened-in porch at the front entrance, and the living area was accented with a massive stone fireplace. Jake's grandfather built the cabin in the mid-seventies not long after he moved from Ann Arbor to start his own branch of the manufacturing company he worked for back then.

When they first stepped into the cabin, Jake glanced a sideways glance at Miranda. For a moment, he almost thought he saw a smile come to her face, although the moment was fleeting. She knew what he was thinking with the look. The two of them had a few good parties at the cabin back in the day, which to Miranda seemed like another lifetime ago. And then there were the other times that it was just the two of them, sneaking away to be alone and hidden from the rest of the world. There was also their shared memory of the time Jake's dad caught them there. He came in, and although he knew Miranda had to be there with Jake in the loft, he pretended to not notice and left as quickly as he had arrived. Miranda had never seen Jake's face so red.

Finally, she allowed herself a smile and looked down at the floor, recalling her slight embarrassment. Jake saw, but he pretended not to notice himself.

"So, Weapons?" Gabriel seemed shorter than his usual impatient self.

"This way," Jake motioned toward the main bedroom on the lower level. He went to the closet and opened both of the folding doors.

The closet had a pair of hunting boots on the floor and camo bibs on a hanger. Otherwise, it was empty.

"Great," said Gabriel, visibly frustrated and waving his hands in the air.

"You know, for an angel that has been around since the dawn of creation, you are one of the most impatient individuals that I have ever met," Jake said to Gabriel.

Jake walked over to the phone on the table beside the bed in the room. He picked up the receiver and dialed 6-1-1-3, and hung up the receiver. The back wall of the closet started to lower into the floor revealing a huge steel safe behind the lowering wall. Jake stepped past Gabriel, Lydia and Ashe, who looked on in awe at the cool, secret agent like contraption. He entered the combination into the keypad on the safe and the door opened to reveal more than thirty different guns and dozens of boxes of ammunition.

Gabriel stood up from the bed and looked intently at the small arsenal.

"My apologies, Jake." Gabriel smiled at Jake. Jake returned the smile.

Jake reached into the safe and pulled out the first long gun case. He unzipped the case and tossed it onto the bed in the room, and held the gun out to Gabriel. Gabriel took the gun into his hands and looked it up and down.

"In all the years that I have watched over mankind, I have seen the horrors that have been wrought by these things. Yet, there is a craftsmanship and beauty in their design and function. Harnessing the power of fire and flame and steel in a frame formed with such care and design," Gabriel mused. Jake was quietly surprised by Gabriel's fascination with the gun. He thought it was remarkable that a being that watched the formation of the sun and the stars and the Earth could be so impressed by a simple creation of mankind, especially one with such a history of violence and chaos.

"This is my father's Remington 30/06 rifle," Jake told Gabriel, handing him a box of shells from a stack in the base of the safe. "One-hundred fifty grain rounds, with a capacity of five rounds per load. You don't usually need more than five rounds to take down a deer or a bear, so it's best to take the box and practice reloading. Out back we have a target range for practice and sighting in scopes and sights. We can take the guns and get familiar with them before we head out the rest of the way to Galestone."

Gabriel nodded and loaded the gun back into the case. Jake looked to Lydia next.

"Are you familiar with firearms?" he asked her, fully expecting a swiftly negative response.

"I've been around guns since I was four years old. My dad and uncle were on the board of our local sportsmen's club. Every Sunday until I was fourteen was spent at the range," she told him.

"What happened at fourteen?" Jake asked her.

"Boys happened," she replied. "It turned out that a girl who knew more about guns than they did intimidated them. So, I just pretended I was like the other girls…for a while."

"Aren't you just full of surprises," Jake smirked. "So. Do you have a preference?"

Lydia approached the safe and picked up a few of the handguns.

"The .44 is way too much power for me, although it would take down bear. I think I'll go for the .38 revolver." She picked up the .38 in its holster and Jake pulled out the box of .38 rounds. She took the box and stood beside Gabriel. Ashe stepped up next.

"Which one do I get?" Ashe asked enthusiastically.

Jake smiled, reached into the safe and pulled out a cylindrical canister that was inserted into a nylon holster. He handed the canister to Ashe.

Ashe slid the can up out of the holster and read the side of the can.

"Bear Pepper Spray." She looked at Jake quizzically. "Why do they get guns? What am I going to do with this?"

"Listen. No offense, but you don't exactly look like an outdoorsy kinda girl," Jake said to her.

"Well, neither does she," Ashe responded, pointing toward Lydia. Lydia looked down at the floor, trying to conceal an involuntary grin. Jake just cocked his head to the side and looked at Ashe.

"Have you ever fired a gun, Ashe?" he asked her

pointedly. Ashe bowed her own head.

"No. I haven't," she sheepishly replied.

"I promise you, this stuff may not put down a bear permanently, but if you spray this in the face of anything that comes at you, it will turn tail and run in the opposite direction. This is not a pleasant thing to get in your eyes. Trust me. When I was a kid and my grandpa first taught me how to use one of these, I got some on my fingers and accidentally touched my eye later on. I was crying for a week after that."

Ashe nodded her head, finally realizing it was a better idea to have stinging eyes than to accidentally shoot herself in the foot.

"Besides, we'll all be right beside you. We need to keep you safe, not just because you're the only one that can find what we're looking for, but because I'm more afraid of what you grandmother would do to us if anything were to happen to you," Jake said.

"So what will you have?" Ashe asked Jake.

Jake pulled out a Ruger 9mm pistol from a lower shelf in the safe. He popped the clip and looked it up and down. He slid the clip back in and laid the gun on the bed. He then reached back into the safe and pulled out a 12 gauge pump shotgun.

"I'm taking the 9mm with the thirteen round clip as back-up. The 12 gauge has a five round capacity. Since we don't know what might be waiting for us, I'm going with nickel-plated buckshot rotated with slugs. The shot should take down most things, but at the very least should slow something down before the slug puts it down permanently."

The area beyond the main yard behind the cabin was swampy and open, with a target area set up at different distances going several hundred feet back. There was a firepit in the back about 50 feet off of the covered back porch, and just beyond the pit was a long bench-like table that was built upon two posts that brought the surface area of the table up to about the height of Jake's elbows. The table itself was a large section of a cut log, sanded smooth and stained and clear coated to withstand the elements.

Gabriel, Lydia and Ashe followed behind Jake as he led them out to the table, with Miranda slowly trailing behind. They all carried their weapons, with the exception of Miranda who was in fact a weapon all to herself. There was no need for her to fire a gun, although in days past she had in this very spot fired lighter guns alongside Jake when they had made one of their weekend trips up to the cabin. It was not something that she had much interest in, but being in those days that her interest was Jake, she humored him with the momentary curiosity in firearms.

Gabriel was the first to load the 30/06 rifle. He aimed and fired the first round, hitting the target to the left. The next shot was dead-on, impressing Jake, and was followed by the next three shots that were near center of the target. Gabriel quickly reloaded and chose a target further from the spot from where he was firing the gun, and the rounds found the target fast and well.

Lydia stood up to the table next and loaded the .38. Jake lent her ear protection muffs and she found her stance and raised the pistol. She fired the first round with a light recoil. Although she had experience with guns in her early teens, it had been a great many years since she actually fired one. She recovered quickly, took her stance again, and emptied the rest of the cylinder into the target about 15 yards away, keeping a fairly tight grouping on the target.

Everyone watching was visibly impressed by Lydia's

accuracy, Miranda included. But Miranda's mind was preoccupied with a nagging thought that she had been carrying since they had been on the interstate. She wandered back away from the group as they all stood and watched Jake practice with the Ruger.

Miranda hadn't had a cell phone since before the events at the Stratusaint Tower. She slipped into the cabin and found Lydia's phone and brought up an internet browser, and typed 'OTIS' into the search engine. Miranda new of OTIS, or the Michigan *Offender Tracking Information System*, from discussions in her journalism classes in college. She clicked on the first website to come up which brought her to a Michigan Department of Corrections disclaimer webpage. At the bottom of the page she clicked on to the next page which brought her to a page of search fields. In the LAST NAME field, she entered 'Grimes', FIRST NAME 'Daryl'. She pressed SEARCH.

The name appeared in a single line on the search results. 'Grimes, Daryl. D.O.B. 12/18/1949. Sentence – LIFE. Location – Eastern Upper Peninsula Correctional Facility."

Miranda didn't notice at that moment that her hand was visibly shaking. The 'Prison Area' sign triggered the wave of awareness that the man who started all of the chaos in her life was only a short distance from where she was now standing. She also was not aware that Lydia had walked into the room and was now standing behind her.

"Miri? Are you alright?" asked Lydia. The sudden awareness of Lydia's voice startled Miranda, who dropped the phone onto the couch in front of her. Miranda quickly picked up the phone and closed the browser window.

"Lydia…I have to do something," Miranda said.

"Okay, I'll help you. What do you need?" replied Lydia.

"No, there is something that I need to do, and I need to do it alone. I need you to tell the others to go on to Galestone and I will meet them there."

"Miri, I don't think now is a good time to go off on your own. We all need to stick together right now," Lydia pleaded.

"I have to do this alone. Please, Lyd, try and understand…"

"I don't understand any of this, Miri! I am here for one reason and one reason only. I lost you once and I don't want to lose you again. There are…there are things happening here that I have no understanding of. Psychics and angels and wild monster things and the Devil and a whole entire world of shit that suddenly exists in the real world and apparently always has existed that I was probably a lot better off not knowing about, but the only thing that matters now is that we all stick together and get though this. Please, Miranda…"

Miranda turned away from her. She could feel the tears begin to well in her eyes. She closed them for a moment, and when she opened them once again, out of the sight of Lydia, her blue eyes had once again become a solid black. Lydia softly put her hand on Miranda's shoulder.

"I'm sorry, Lydia," Miranda said, almost coldly. "Tell the others. I'll meet you in Galestone." And she was gone, vanishing right before Lydia's eyes. Lydia's hand dropped to her side.

Jake and the others came walking into the cabin through the back door. Lydia stood with her back to them as they entered into the main room. She turned around and looked at Jake. He knew from the look on her face that something wasn't right, and his eyes darted around the room looking for Miranda.

"Where's Miranda?" Jake asked her.

"She's gone," Lydia said. "She asked me to tell you that she will meet us in Galestone."

"Gone? Did she say where she was going?" asked Gabriel.

"No," she replied, her head sunk down. "She said she had something to do, alone."

Everyone stood silently for several seconds before Gabriel finally broke the silence.

"Let's get moving," he told the group, and started to gather the guns and other items that they were taking with them.

"We can't just leave," Jake said, casting a sharp look at Gabriel. "We need to find her."

"She will have no trouble getting to us now that she knows how to use her ability to move from place to place with her power. We have no idea where she has gone and she clearly didn't want us to know, and if she doesn't want to be found, we won't find her. And we still have to get the piece of the sword no matter what else, and we aren't going to get to Galestone before nightfall at this point, when it will be far too dangerous for a myriad of reasons to go looking for the shard. We have to wait until morning to search, and as it is, I feel we might be running out of time. So, we stay on point. We know our jobs, and we will do them," Gabriel said with the authoritative tone of being the ancient devoted soldier that he was created to be.

Jake looked on at Gabriel, and while he didn't want to accept the fact that they were leaving without Miranda being with them, he respected the fact that Gabriel was right. Gabriel stood still and looked for a response from Jake, and Jake nodded to him without a word. Jake looked to Lydia and Ashe, standing off to the side quietly anxious.

"Let's go then," he said to them. "Miranda will find us."

CHAPTER SEVENTEEN

The Great Cathedral of the Lord Christ on High in Atlanta, Georgia, was ground zero for the organization of the coming Conference of United Faith, which was being held at the Marshalldome Center on the western outskirts of the Atlanta area beyond the city limits.

The Marshalldome was the completed dream of the late billionaire Peter Marshall. Construction originally started years before by the now disgraced evangelist and exposed human trafficker Delaney Christopher. The dome was meant to be the hub of his multi-million dollar ministry, but Christopher's arrest and the scandal that surrounded him halted the construction efforts of the football stadium sized facility. Some years after Christopher was sentenced to prison, Marshall bought the property and started renovation after a failed United States Presidential run in 2008, running as an independent. He wanted to take something that was created with ill-intent and make something great of it. Marshall dedicated his life to two things - his devotion toward helping the less fortunate, and his faith.

It was in the spring of 2015 that Peter Marshall first met the man responsible for the overall conception and organization of the Conference of United Faith - His Most Reverend Excellency, Roman Catholic Archbishop Martin Marseille. The meeting of the two men seemed like divine providence to both of them. Marshall had found his place and purpose in the final years of his life. To fully realize Marseille's dream for the Conference, it became Marshall's mission to complete the massive structure that would come to hold over 65,000 people, with its marble floors and domed, crystal-like heavy glass roof. The Marshalldome Center would become the dedicated home of what Marshall and Marseille believed to be the most important religious event since the time Christ himself walked the Earth.

Unfortunately, Peter Marshall would not ultimately live to see the Conference come to fruition, dying from a stroke and brain bleed at the age of 92, only months before the Conference. But his estate made it clear that Marseille would receive all of the support he needed to make the event happen, and the Marshalldome would be in trust of the Archdiocese of Atlanta, governed by an elected board of trustees.

Martin Marseille had served as a priest for many years in a southwestern Georgia diocese and developed a close relationship with the local bishop, His Most Reverend Excellency William Blanchard. They became good friends, and when Blanchard fell ill in the early 2000s, Blanchard expressed his wishes to the Holy Church and his colleagues that he wished Marseille to take his place as bishop. Upon Blanchard's death, and with a recommendation to the church, the offer from the Pope came and Marseille accepted the offer. He served as bishop for nearly 12 years and was greatly revered by his fellow bishops and the priests that served under him, although at times his ways seems too progressive for the tastes of many Catholic traditionalists.

When the Archbishop of the Atlanta Archdiocese died unexpectedly in a plane crash in 2015, Marseille was offered the position of the Atlanta Archbishop, and he accepted.

The Conference of United Faith was an idea Marseille had dreamed about for years. He was a man that couldn't even turn on the television news anymore. Crime and violence of every sort was sad and commonplace enough. Starvation and suffering and abuse of all kinds were a plague upon all nations since the beginning of time, but now more than ever, on a global scale and fueled by a world where nothing escaped the camera, God was put on trial on every single stage that mankind could see. There was so much blood and tyranny at every turn, in God's holy name, and by every name that he was called by. And they all truly believed they were in the right – every group, every faction, and every nation. Even now the Christian faiths that had stood for hundreds of years were fracturing more and more every day.

Marseille believed that there was an answer. And he believed that answer may lie in a unified declaration of peace by all of the major and minor branches of faith in the world. His God was a God of peace and love, and he believed that the true souls of all of the faiths believed this. Would it make a difference if they all stood together before the entire world? He believed so. And he made it his life's mission to bring it all together, and what better place to do it than right here in Atlanta.

Here, he could oversee everything. And there was much to oversee. The planning for tens of thousands people making the pilgrimage to this incredible event. There was the coordination of lodging and transportation for the leadership and emissaries from the world's oldest religious faiths. And, of course, the security.

With less than 24 hours until the start of the conference, the security issue was by and far the most complex undertaking of the whole affair. The Holy Church, as well as the other faiths that were already arriving for their attendance, put forth an investment of millions of dollars for the security of the event itself. Marseille had been in contact with city, state and local law enforcement agencies for months prior to the event. When the full scope of what the Conference would entail and who would be in attendance clearly came into perspective in view of the U.S. government, it suddenly became an issue of federal security as well. All anti-terror efforts went into full alert and the Conference became a priority-one security issue on all fronts.

At one point the White House and Pentagon affairs representatives had tried to persuade Archbishop Marseille to not go through with the event. His response was very simple and straightforward.

"This is the will of God. The Conference of United Faith will go on as planned."

The feds knew they had the power, as it being a huge national security risk, to stop the Conference from happening. They also knew how it would appear if they chose to directly interfere with a religious summit of this magnitude. The decision was made to proceed with extreme vigilance.

So, with the event in all respects just hours away, and security being at its very peak, there was a significant question at the forefront of Archbishop Marseille's mind:

Who is this man sitting in the armchair in the corner of my office, and how did he get in here past all of the security?

The Archbishop reached for the telephone on his desk

as Lucifer rose from the armchair. With a wave of his hand, the Archbishop found it impossible to lift the phone receiver from the desk.

"I assure you, good sir, there is no need to call for any assistance whatsoever. In fact, I am the only assistance you will ever need," Lucifer said to Marseille with a grin from ear to ear.

Marseille was deeply startled by the fact that his hand was unable to lift the phone. He said nothing at first, and stared a long time at the face of the man standing before him in his very secure and private office.

"Please, Martin. I am here with only one purpose and intention. I want peace. I want forgiveness. I seek redemption as does the whole of mankind. I want to help give that to them. And I want you to help me do that," Lucifer told him, reaching out his hand toward Marseille as if he were offering to help the stunned man up from his chair.

Marseille looked at Lucifer's hand but did not reach out to him. Lucifer drew back his hand. He could tell Marseille was not quite ready yet for any sort of personal contact. He often found it quite peculiar that those who have noted themselves so close to the power and majesty of God, in all of God's wonder and glory, were always the greatest skeptics when faced with a miraculous show of that power.

"Who…who are you?" The words trickled out of Marseille's trembling lips as he sat behind his large desk in front of the expansive picture window the looked out on the garden square of the Great Cathedral.

Lucifer noted the gathering crowds already filling the square. Not everyone would be able to attend the Conference at the Marshalldome, so large screens were being set up on the grounds of the Great Cathedral and other places of worship spanning the different denominations and faiths across the city, as well as other public venues. People were bringing tents and coolers and food supplies. It was like what he had witnessed at the wondrous music festivals that he had visited in his travels around the world after Miranda had released him. He'd become quite fond of the many different forms of music that he had experienced in his travels, and found awe in the amount of adoration that was shown for these talented musicians.

Awe, and a feeling of deep disappointment. Once, a long, long time ago, he had seen this kind of love shown for Amanthus. He did not blame the musicians themselves for being loved and worshiped. He felt sympathy for so many that had lost there way.

Now, he was starting to fully realize the power that this event truly held – and why it was the perfect place for him to make himself known to the world.

Lucifer stepped back away from the Archbishop's desk. He held his arms outstretched to his sides and lowered his gaze to Marseille. The thick, heavy drapes that hung on the heavy iron rod over the great window overlooking the square shut tight behind Marseille. Lucifer felt Marseille's fear as he sat almost cowering behind the heavy desk. He regretted the fear he was causing in the man, but he knew this man needed to understand with whatever theatrics it may take what he truly was.

The room grew dark, the only light coming from the many holy candles around the room that simultaneously lit at once. Lucifer rose a few feet off the floor and hovered before Marseille. His eyes went full dark and a great light shone from behind him, filling the rest of the office with blinding light and leaving the form of Lucifer as little more than a silhouette. Marseille dropped to his knees, his eyes glassy and teary, and he made the sign of the cross before clasping his hands together.

Marseille began the Lord's Prayer. "Our Father, who art in Heaven, hallowed be thy Name…"

Lucifer spoke in a comforting, yet echoing voice. "Archbishop Martin Marseille, do not fear me. I am an angel of the Lord God. I am here with a message to bring to all of mankind. You have done a great service to the Lord in bringing together all of the men and women who speak and act in the name of God. Will you help me in bringing the message to all?"

The bright light dissipated, and Marseille opened his eyes and once again saw the man standing before him, solid on his own two feet, smiling with an outreached hand toward him.

Marseille slowly stood and reached out both of his hands. There was a slight trembling in his motions as his arms stretched out in front of him. Before he touched Lucifer's hands he pulled away and rushed around the desk, dropping to his knees once again before Lucifer. He took Lucifer's hand with both of his and kissed it. Lucifer felt humbled and unworthy of such honors, but he understood Marseille's heart. He loved his God, and Lucifer's proclamation had made him the direct emissary of the Lord.

"It was you, wasn't it? In the river in New York, days ago. You saved those people…you are sent from the Lord," Marseille said to him, staring up at Lucifer with sincere adoration.

Lucifer gave him a single nod of his head.

"Please…Martin. Rise before me," Lucifer beckoned with an outstretched hand.

Marseille obeyed and stood before Lucifer.

"I will do whatever you need me to, in the name of my Lord."

CHAPTER EIGHTEEN

Miranda stood outside of the gates of the Eastern Upper Peninsula Correctional Facility, which would have been less than an hour's drive from the spot where she had been standing in only moments before. She looked at the fence that stretched out around the facility with the razor wire spirals catching the glint of the sunlight as it was slowly starting to sink toward the western skyline. She had an uneasy feeling within her, but she was not certain where it was coming from.

She had nothing to fear being in this place – or anywhere, for that matter – yet she could almost feel a tremor coming from her very core. She stepped toward the front entrance gate to the prison. Most people drove up to this point as far as she could tell, but she was obviously on foot. If it raised a red flag, she would deal with it however she could.

The corrections officer at the gate was a black woman with short hair and stern eyes. Miranda approached the gatehouse and stood at the window, waiting for the woman to acknowledge her. The woman saw Miranda standing and looked around the area for a vehicle, but there were no vehicles around in the visible area. The woman pressed a button to speak through a speaker mounted in the glass.

"Can I help you?" asked the officer. She had the name 'Plummer' on her I.D. badge.

"Hi. I'm here to visit an inmate," replied Miranda to C.O. Plummer.

Plummer looked at a computer screen for a moment. "It is getting close to the cut-off time for visitation. I assume you have a scheduled appointment?" asked Plummer.

"Yes. I do," lied Miranda. She knew this would take some of the special talents that she had been honing in her travels around the world over the past year.

"Inmate number?" asked Plummer, although it sounded more like a demand.

Miranda searched her memory back to when she had looked up Grimes name on Lydia's phone. She recalled the number and gave it to Plummer. Plummer typed it into the computer.

"There are no scheduled visitors for the inmate number that you gave me today. Are you certain it is the right number?" asked Plummer.

"Yes, I am certain. The visitation is scheduled. It is there, on your screen. For Daryl Grimes to be visited by," she paused, considering carefully before continuing. "Melissa Gabriel."

Plummer looked at the screen again. She sat in silence for a moment as she seemed to be struggling with something before regaining her composure. She smiled and turned toward Miranda.

"I'm sorry. There you are, Miss Gabriel," she said, pressing a button that opened the gate. "Just walk up to the visitation entrance for processing."

"Thank you," smiled Miranda. She walked up to the building entrance door where she was met by another guard. She went through a similar process with the guard at the door, who then walked her to another station where she presented additional identification and where she was searched with a pat down and metal detectors. The guards saw the name 'Melissa Gabriel' on the driver's license that she presented to them, but Miranda new that the name on the license was clearly Miranda Stratton. Each time a new guard she encountered validated the scheduled visitation with Daryl Grimes, they saw that it was legitimate – although there was no place that actually said any of it. Miranda 'pushed' what she wanted them to see into their heads, just as she did when she lived above the bookstore months after the Stratusaint Tower incident.

The guard at the final security checkpoint radioed to personnel within the prison to prepare Grimes for his visitor.

"Grimes hasn't had a visitor since I first started working at this prison 11 years ago," said the guard, whose badge read 'Miller'. "Hasn't said a word to anyone as far as I know."

"Maybe that will change today," said Miranda under her breath.

"When the light turns green, you can turn the handle and take a seat at any open table. An officer will bring Grimes into the room. All other visitors have already left for the day, so you'll have the room, with the exception of the guard in the room. Mandatory, I'm afraid. Once again, no touching the inmate, do not hand him anything, and if there is any indication of emotional, physical or mental distress, the visitation session will be terminated. Understood?"

"Yes, Officer Miller. Thank you," said Miranda. The

guard nodded and pressed the door lock button. The light turned green and Miranda entered the room.

The room itself was a large room with several half-moon shaped tables spaced evenly around the room. There was only one other door into the room where the inmates are brought in through, and there were four vending machines against the wall beside the door in which Miranda had entered. Miranda slowly walked to the half-moon table in the center of the room and took a seat at the moons rounded crest. The flat side of the table was for the inmate, and the rounded side of the table was for visitors. Each table had three chairs for multiple visitors at one time.

Usually the set-up for visiting a prisoner was a process of the inmate setting up a visitation list with only so many visitors allowed on the list, mostly family members or close friends upon approval. Miranda was none of these things to Daryl Grimes. He had no list, and no one had come to see him for most of the years that he had spent as a lifetime resident of Eastern Upper Peninsula Correctional Facility. A court appointed attorney had visited him in the first years, and a psychologist had been brought in to talk to him a few times, but since the moment he had been taken into custody, found on the rocky hillside overlooking the burning shell that was once the Gale home, he had not spoken a single word to anyone. Not since the moment he had heard the faint and distant cries of the young child trapped within the confines of the home being consumed by the flames he brought to life on that night all those years ago.

Miranda's thoughts had drifted off in the moments after she sat down. Her mind was fluttering with images that she had not ever before seen but could only imagine. Moments of a desperate mother she'd never know and the cries of a grandfather and an uncle and a cousin, burning to death in the flames or choking on the thick black smoke flowing from the old wood and the crumbling walls of the Gale estate. Her hands had become fists on the table in front of her and her fingernails, although short as they were, dug into the skin of her palms. So lost in her thoughts, she had not yet noticed that the inmate entrance door had opened.

Daryl Grimes was lead into the room by the guard. He seemed small to Miranda, his eyes sunken and his face gaunt. His hair, at least what remained of his hair, was stone grey and buzzed short, and he had a short disheveled grey beard. He was wearing prison orange pants and a short-sleeved top that looked like scrubs with his prisoner number on the upper right side of the chest. As he stepped into the room he stopped and narrowed his eyes at Miranda, but was nudged by the guard to continue on toward the table.

The guard pulled out the chair for Grimes, and Grimes sat down across from Miranda. The guard then continued over to the corner of the room and stood almost at attention as he would often do when he was assigned to watch over inmate interactions during visitations. Miranda was certain that he was still well within earshot, and she wanted no interference while she confronted Grimes.

"Miranda whispered the words, "Do not hear us." The guard made no indication that he could hear anything being said in the room. Grimes stared at Miranda with a deeply confused look on his face. Miranda turned her eyes directly on Grimes for the first time since he entered the room, her eyes firmly fixed on his.

"Do you know who I am?" Miranda asked Grimes.

Grimes held on to his look of confusion, shaking his head side to side ever so slightly.

"You don't recognize me at all? I don't look like anyone you remember?" she asked him again.

Grimes stared at her blankly, almost as if he didn't understand what she was asking, and certainly not why. His vision wasn't what it once had been, and his memories were cloudy as well, although he knew why he was where he was. That was something that his nightmares never let him lose hold of.

"Let me try and help you remember," Miranda said, extending her hand toward his. Grimes pulled his hands back, the sudden movement catching the eye of the guard in the corner.

"No touching," the guard stated from across the room. Miranda looked at the guard with a sharp glare, a growing coldness in her voice.

"Do not see us," she said aloud, well above the whisper she spoke before.

She turned back to Grimes, whose lower lip began to quiver slightly. He looked back over his shoulder to see if another guard was coming into the room, but no one was coming in. Miranda noticed the cameras in the room, but they would not make out her face if anyone were to look at them later.

Grimes found his hands, as if by some invisible force, pulled down to the surface of the table. They moved, quite involuntarily, away from his side of the table and stretched out toward Miranda. Miranda rested her fingertips upon the leathery backside of Grimes' hand.

A flood of vision came between both of them. The grim memory of the night Grimes spread the gasoline around the wraparound porch of the Gale home. The flick of the cigarette that ignited the flames. The sight of the fire climbing the old dry walls of the Victorian home. And the cries of the girl in the upstairs room. And then, there was another startling vision, far more subtle yet painfully clear and by far the most disruptive to the old man's fragile psyche. It was the memory of the little girl and her beautiful mother on the streets of downtown Galestone.

Her smile was like sunshine, he thought in that moment in time, back on the street of his old town. *A true reflection of her mother's radiant beauty.*

Grimes gasped and slide back in his chair. Miranda pulled her hand away at the same time, herself feeling overtaken by Grimes' wave of emotions. His eyes were wide now, fixed on Miranda in much the same way she had been fixed on him.

He opened his mouth. At first, it was only raspy sound, not much more than the sound of a whisper. His vocal chords seemed to have atrophied from their lack of use over the many years, but he found himself forcing the words to leave his lips.

"You're...the...g-girl," he started. "You're the o-one from...G-Galesstone," he muttered. M...M...Mira...".

"Miranda Gale," she said, her voice wrapped within an icy veil. "Why did you murder my family?"

"I...I'm s-so sorry...I ha-had to make it stop," he said, tears starting to well up in his eyes. He was shaking, not so much a convulsing as much as a mild trembling throughout his entire body.

"What did you have to make stop? Tell me," Miranda demanded.

"The voices!" he exclaimed in the clearest words yet. "It was th-the voices. They t-told me to burn them. *To b-burn you.*"

"Burn me? Why?! Who told you to do it?"

Grimes looked back at the door once again, hoping that someone would burst through the door. The guard in the corner had seemed to have broken free of the suggestion that Miranda had directed toward him and saw the distress that Grimes was in. He lunged toward Miranda, who was now on her feet. Miranda gave a simple hand gesture which caused the guard to be hurled against the corner where he had been standing before, knocking him out cold. She looked toward the inmate entrance door and then at the door through which she had first entered the room. She knew more guards were on their way. Seconds later a lockdown alarm was going off throughout the entire prison. She saw two guards trying to run a security card through the slot to open the inmate door. She spread her hands in both directions toward the doors and the steel in the walls melted to the heavy-duty steel deadbolts in the door locks. No one was getting in – or out.

Miranda turned back and faced Grimes once again, who was now on his feet backed up against the far wall of the room. She brought her hands out to each side of her as if she were pushing aside heavy curtains, and as she made the motion all of the tables and chairs suddenly flew to either side of the room, many of them smashing and breaking upon impact against the walls. Her blue eyes were now a solid black, much like the night that she confronted her vicious uncle, David Gale, at the top of the Stratusaint Tower.

She stepped toward Grimes with her right hand outstretched in front of her, and Grimes' back slammed against the wall behind him. His feet lost contact with the floor below him as he slid nearly a foot off of the ground. The guards at both doors were desperately trying to find a way into the room. They could clearly see everything that was happening. As they tried to break through the door, the guards watched helplessly in terror at what was taking place.

When Miranda reached Grimes, she held her hand to his throat.

"Tell me who told you to kill my family! Was it Lucifer? Who?! Why did you kill my mother? Do you have any idea what you started?" Miranda screamed at Grimes, who, try as he may, could not form a single word, be it the physical inability to with her hand firmly grasping his frail throat, or the sheer horror of the moment that prevented him from speaking.

"You don't need to tell me. I will rip it from your mind myself," she hissed. She was outside of herself, with all traces of humanity deeply buried inside of her. She reached out with her thoughts, the physical connection with Grimes bridging the deepest gaps between their two minds. She dove deep into his thoughts and his memories, to the night of the fire and all of the nights before it when he felt the torments that haunted him to the point that he would commit the vicious act of murdering almost an entire family.

She searched as the overwhelming fear and pain returned within Grimes and consumed him from the inside out. Miranda was aware of all of it, but if she cared at all she didn't react to it at all, only digging deeper, looking and listening for the voice that she was certain would be revealed to be Lucifer's hand in all of it. Finally, just as she felt she was close to what she was trying to find, there was an incredibly overwhelming backfire of power that not only blew Miranda out of Grimes' mind, but also sent her flying across the room and into the far wall with enough force to indent the shape of her body deeply into and almost through the solid block wall.

Miranda was shaken deeply by the impact and the backlash of energy. Something buried deep within Grimes did not want to be seen or heard. She slowly got her bearings and painstakingly pushed herself out of the hole in the wall. She was covered in fragments of block and dust, her hair tattered with bits of grey concrete and chips of white and blue paint from the walls of visitor room.

She looked over at the far door and made direct eye contact with a younger guard who was staring in disbelief at the scene in the room, while a superior officer was making little progress trying to pry the door open with a large crowbar. She then turned her eyes to Grimes.

Grimes' back was against the wall in the spot where Miranda had held him. His legs were apart and sprawled out in front of him, and his head was cocked to his left side as his torso leaned slightly to the left. Blood had been running from both of his eyes, as well as his nose and the left side of his mouth. His eyes themselves looked as if they had burst. The blood flow had already stopped. Miranda listened across the room for his breath, but she didn't really need to. She could see that the aura she had come to recognize in living creatures was no longer surrounding Daryl Grimes. Grimes was dead.

Miranda found herself feeling nothing about his death. There was no satisfaction, no remorse, no sense of anything except the frustration of not finding any reason or answer regarding the deaths of her birth family, her adoptive family, or her mother's good friend Aimsley Carter.

The inmate entrance door suddenly burst open and ten guards immediately flooded the room. But Miranda wasn't there. The only people left in the room were the unconscious guard and the lifeless body of Daryl Grimes. The other door was still sealed, yet there was no sign that another person had ever been in the room.

The young woman, who went by a name that no one in the prison could later remember and no security cameras ever got a clear picture of, had simply vanished.

CHAPTER NINETEEN

Nearly six-million people live and work in the metropolitan area of Atlanta, Georgia on a day to day basis, but on the eve before the Conference of United Faith the city's population had increased by thousands. The city had not seen such an influx of people since the 1996 Summer Olympic Games, which was largely overshadowed by the events surrounding the Centennial Olympic Park bombing. The memory of the bombing and the ever-looming shadow of the tragedy of September 11th, 2001 were both driving forces in the increased local and federal vigilance in security throughout and surrounding the city.

The Conference had become a pilgrimage for individuals of all faiths. Some believed that it somehow had been prophesized as a great beginning – a genesis for a new era of peace and prosperity throughout all faiths and nations. Others, even those of uncertain faith, felt the draw of a great energy in this place at this time. Indefinable in its nature, yet undeniable was the feeling surrounding the advent of the

Conference as if it was a vibration in the earth itself and in the air that surrounded the Marshalldome.

For the event itself it was agreed upon between the Archdiocese, the governing board of the Marshalldome, the City of Atlanta, and the State of Georgia that there would be a ticket fee to cover overall costs and expenses of hosting the event and to offset the cost of security surrounding the event. Marseille was not in favor of the idea of a fee, but he understood the practicality of it. The Marshalldome had a large multi-level parking structure that would satisfy most of the parking for the attendees that would be coming in for the single day event. Surrounding the structure of the parking facility and the Marshalldome itself were acres and acres of land that consisted of flat open areas of grass with clusters of wooded land interspersed throughout.

For days people had come to the property and set up camps in between rows of vehicles and campers. It had become a gathering of festival-like proportions. People played music and sang together, and they laughed and joined together in prayer and worship. What was all the more fascinating was the coming together of the people of many different faiths that attended. Boundaries seemed to dissolve as the people of the many different faiths – Christians, Muslim, Jewish, and so many more – found themselves brought together to speak and laugh and share common pleasantries with one another, brought together by a longing sense of peace and the belief in something greater than themselves.

As the sun began to set on the day of the eve of the conference, bonfires were built and people from all of the different backgrounds, religions and races were invited to share in the joy that had brought them all together.

Lucifer, looking like any one of them in blue jeans and

a black, button-down shirt, blonde hair pulled back in a pony tail, walked among them and observed the revelry amongst those gathered for what would truly become a miraculous happening in the several hours ahead.

He felt something in his heart that moved him to his very core, a feeling that he hadn't felt in a long, long time. He felt hope for the whole of mankind, and it was a feeling that was born in this place on this day. As his eyes looked over the crowds as they laughed and sang, he found dispersed through the masses of those that had gathered together for the event many others that had come searching for hope as well.

He came upon the family of a young girl, no older than eight years old by the look of it. The girl was strapped into a motorized wheelchair with a portable oxygen tank secured to the back of it. There was a machine alongside of the tank that pulsed with a steady stream of fresh oxygen to a tube that led up to the girl's nostrils.

Lucifer approached the family, but had only allowed himself to be 'seen' by the young girl.

"Hello there," he said to the girl.

"Hi," she whispered back, almost inaudibly.

"What is your name?" asked Lucifer.

"Sara," she said back to him. "Sara Waters. What's yours?"

"My name is...well, you can call me Lu." He cast her a bright and vibrant smile. Sara smiled back at him, although it took a greater effort on her part. "What is ailing you, Sara?"

"What...?" she replied, confused by his wording.

Lucifer smiled again. "I'm sorry, Sara. You are ill. What is it that is making you sick?"

"I have cancer. Leukemia. My mom and dad wanted to bring me here. They hope...they hope God will come back.

Mom prays every night…she cries, begging God for help…but he doesn't come to help."

Lucifer softly touched Sara's hand. He could see the doctors speaking to Sara's parents. She can hear what they say, outside of the hospital room door, but she was not conscious enough to understand the depth of the meaning of what was being said. They cannot keep her in remission. They have exhausted all of their options. The best they can hope for is to take her home and make her comfortable.

He moved his hand away from Sara's.

"This place is a special place, Sara. You are not alone here. There are many like you here. Their hearts are hurting for people that they love, and for themselves. I assure you that something special will happen here. But for you, my young friend, I have a gift. But you can't tell anyone. Can you keep a secret?"

Sara mustered a slight nod up and down of her head. Lucifer laid his hand down upon Sara's head and a soft, warm glow appeared from his palm and seemed to slowly seep through her small, frail body.

Her eyes had a spark of new life in them. She still felt weak, but there was something different within her.

"Shhh," he whispered to her. "It will still be a few days, but I promise you, you will get better." He held the warm smile on his face as he stared into her sharpening green eyes.

"Th-thank you," whispered Sara. "Are you…are you an angel?"

"Once upon a time, little one. Hopefully someday again," he said to her, standing up before her. He sensed something strange around him. He searched the crowds with his eyes, but saw nothing. He looked back down once more to Sara.

"I must go now. Take care, Sara." And he was gone, swiftly moving away through the crowds. His sharp eyes searched hard, piercing through the revelry and the excitement. And then he saw a familiar aura, deep in a swarm of people gathered around one of the fires. And then another, farther off to the right of the first. It was the aura of his brethren, and there were more.

He recognized them all. The angel Camille, a stunning beauty with long, white hair. And there was his brother Devos, one of those who stood against him alongside of…he felt it then…the strongest feeling he had felt yet in that moment.

He turned around to look behind where he stood, and there he was, only a few feet away from him. "Hello, Michael."

Michael stood before his brother, face to face for the first time since the moment the two brothers clashed swords in the Infinite Lands more than two millennia ago. The last time Lucifer had looked into Michael's eyes, he had only seen a storm of raging emotions, filled with both winds of sadness and anger. Lucifer was taken by surprise more at Michael's appearance than by his presence here on the grounds surrounding the Marshalldome.

Michael's black hair was buzz-cut short. Like Lucifer, he was wearing blue jeans to blend in, although just as Lucifer could, he could have seemed invisible to the crowds that surrounded them. He wore a white shirt and a dark blue denim jacket. He held his hands in the pockets of the jacket. His face wore a close cut goatee beard and mustache, very short like that of his buzzed head of hair. Lucifer had never imagined Michael like this. Always the long black locks and a clean shaven face. Of course, a lot can change in two-thousand years.

"Hello Lucifer. It is…good to see you," Michael told him. His voice was sincere, as were his words, as Lucifer knew they were. He felt the very same.

Lucifer stepped toward Michael and Michael removed his hands from his pockets. The two angels stopped inches from each other, face to face. There was a moment of pause between them before a brotherly embrace, thousands of years overdue. As they released each other, Lucifer placed his hands on Michael's shoulders.

"I did what I had to do, brother. And I cannot say that I wouldn't do it again. But it has pained me for the past two millennium," Michael told him.

"I know, my brother," replied Lucifer. "I know. As I did what I felt I had to." Lucifer glanced around them at the other angels present, still far off in the distance. "Why do they stay away? Did you anticipate that our reunion would not go so well?"

"Some of them feel as I do. Some of them took your departure in other ways. Many did not want me to come to you alone," Michael replied.

"And what of you, Michael? Did you at all fear what would happen coming to face me?" asked Lucifer.

"No. I did not at all. I only fear that you may not listen to reason," Michael said.

"And what reason do you want me to hear? How did you find me?" asked Lucifer.

"Reason itself was enough to lead me to find you here, in this place. And do not think Gabriel will not realize this as well. We cannot interfere in what you are doing here, nor can we assist Gabriel in any way. It is forbidden, and our sacred oath to Amanthus will be held to at all costs. You know better than anyone the price to pay for defying him," Michael told Lucifer.

"Him? You are starting to sound like *them*, Michael."

Lucifer hinted surprise in his tone. *Had Amanthus claimed a gender in the past 2000 years?,* he wondered.

"Them? Is it contempt for them that you pursue this foolhardy venture, Lucifer? Have you any thought of the consequence of your actions?" Urgency sounded in Michael words. "Amanthus is our Lord. And as our Lord, to some, *he* is a father. To others, a mother. To many he is a warm glowing light in a world of darkness and despair. But to all in this world, he is a mystery that was never meant to be solved by simply showing the world the extent of his glory and power. He wants to be found, yes! But it has to be through their hearts. Not through a fear of the consequence in knowing he exists and defying his will and rejecting him. It is faith, brother! Faith in themselves even more importantly than faith in Amanthus. Faith to do what is good and right in their hearts," Michael pleaded with him.

Lucifer mused on Michael's words for a moment.

"He wants to be found? Then where is he, Michael? Where has he gone? You cannot know that this is not what he wants. They need to be reminded of his greatness. This happening has come to fruition for a reason. They are reaching out from all of the different systems of belief because they want to find their God again. They are desperate. They are *losing* their faith. I need to make things right…"

"You need to? Is this what it is all truly about, Lucifer. Getting Amanthus to see you, to forgive you? Do you not realize what you have done? You hurt him. And in hurting him, you have left us all in darkness. The Crystalline Tower has gone dim since the moment he cast you and the others out. We have not heard his voice or felt his glow since that moment, Lucifer. We have all paid for your defiance," Michael said bitterly.

Lucifer turned away from him. He let his shoulders

drop, his head bowing toward the ground. He spoke, his voice weakened by the shame he felt from Michael's words.

"That is all the more reason why I must do this. I must…make things right," he said.

Michael bowed his head and approached Lucifer, placing his own right hand on his brother's shoulder.

"They…the people of this world…carry the greatest of burdens, Lucifer. If you take that away…if you could only see, then perhaps you can be forgiven for what has been wrought," Michael said to him.

Lucifer turned back to Michael. "What do you mean?"

One by one the other angels in the crowd vanished into the air around them, leaving only Michael and Lucifer.

"I cannot stop what may come, Lucifer. It is your choice, and the consequence lies in your hands. But I can leave you with a warning," said Michael.

"What warning? You have already said you cannot stand against me," replied Lucifer.

"It is not us that you should fear. The girl. She is far more dangerous than you may realize. Her power is strong…but there is more. I wish I could say more, but we must remain outside of the situation. I offer you my final plea, Lucifer. Stop this, before it is too late." Michael was gone. Lucifer was left in the shadow of Michael's plea and warning.

He walked on through the crowds and off into the darkening trees as the night began to fall over the Georgia landscape, pondering his brother's words, wandering and wondering. He stopped, and looked toward the clear night sky, noting not just the thousands of stars visible to the human eye, but the billions that could be seen by his own eyes.

"Miranda," he whispered to himself. For the first time since he stepped out from his Hell onto the dusty earth in the pit the day Miranda set him free, he felt an overwhelming sense of unease.

"What have you done?"

CHAPTER TWENTY

Gabriel emerged from a veil of darkness into blinding light. The towering buildings that were surrounding him were slowly coming into focus. As the sharpness of his vision returned, he scanned the area around him to try and figure out where he was, and even more so, how he got to wherever it was that he now stood. It didn't take him long to discover that he was in a familiar place, one that he had been to many times as an angel, and one time as a man walking the Earth. Times Square, New York City.

There was one distinct aspect of the situation, outside of the obvious question of how he had arrived in Times Square, that stood out and added profoundly to his confusion regarding that particular moment. There was not a single person in sight anywhere.

Not one person, not one vehicle on the streets, not a single sound outside of the electric hum of the giant video screens that lined almost every building in the square. The sounds of car engines, honking horns, the scuffs and steps of a million individuals in constant motion of every race, religion, age and gender were starkly absent from the city; a city that is one of the beating hearts of not only America, but the entire world.

He walked on deeper into the square and glanced toward the risers that were commonly filled with tourists, and felt a draw to climb them. He took a seat looking out over the open area that was usually filled with visitors from all over the world; people taking photographs of the magic and majesty of Times Square, as well as the many costumed characters that crowded the square who were very willing to take a picture with the passing tourist – for a small fee. As he sat and pondered the quiet emptiness around him, it occurred to Gabriel that he was in fact not in Times Square at all. He was dreaming, and although he had been human for the past 23 years, he had been an angel for thousands of years before that. Dreaming was still, by angelic standards, a relatively new experience. Angels did not as a rule have dreams. In the occasions when Gabriel found himself dreaming, there was usually a period of adjustment between the initial confusion of the moment and the realization that it was a dream.

But what of this dream? He didn't subscribe to the human theories and ideas that dreams were hidden psychic signs coming from somewhere beyond themselves of future events. He knew that dreams can be a conduit for certain psychic events, but not a way of fortune telling or prophecy. He also knew that dreams had somehow become a way for those fallen angels cast into Hell to peer into the living world. It was more of a compounded punishment than anything else. They could see not exactly into the world itself but into the dreams that were reflections and aberrations of the true world. Some were fantasies, some were the manifestations of the pains and fears that mankind carried within them.

Was someone looking at this dream?, he wondered.

Something was coming, or *someone*. He watched the shape of a person form in the hazy distance far down 7th Avenue. He stared for a long while as the person approached, and when the person was within a distance at which he could clearly make them out, Gabriel rose to his feet with his heart racing.

Suzanne…he thought. *But this…this is a dream.* This was a fact that again became obvious when he found that he could not move from the spot where he stood on the risers.

Suzanne moved closer to where he was, but she didn't step onto the risers. She stopped, and looked up at Gabriel, who could do nothing more than look down at her.

"Suzanne…I'm so sorry." The fact that Gabriel knew he was in his own dream didn't matter. He knew it was not Suzanne standing in front of him, yet his heart was reaching out in ways it had wanted to for more than two decades. Those two decades felt longer than the whole rest of his existence. The guilt that he carried for her death – and for not being there for her and Miranda – was an almost unbearable weight to carry. There was sadness in her eyes, yet she said nothing to him in return.

Suzanne's physical form began to almost flicker. She began to fade, and her body became semi-transparent. Suddenly, more and more semi-transparent forms of men, women and children began to appear all throughout the square. The more that appeared, the faster more would follow, coming out of thin air. It was not long before the entire square was filled with as many people as one might see on some of the busiest days of the year in New York City.

But it did not stop there. The people kept coming,

appearing beside Gabriel and around him. The crowding of the faded people thickened, leaving almost no space between one another.

"Suzanne! What's happening?" Gabriel called to her, but the silence had been broken as well, a sound like the gushing of air squeezing through the growing crowd.

Suzanne looked around, and then turned her despairing eyes back to Gabriel.

"No...where...to...go." Suzanne's voice, once so sweet to his listening ears, sounded like the same wind that rushed through the crowds, but twisted into words by her lips. *"Not...without...faith."*

The beings in the square started to fade into each other. They would keep running over and through one another, and as long as mankind continued to live and die, it would go on and on. This was the fate of mankind if Gabriel and the others with him failed. They had to, at all costs, stop Lucifer from revealing himself. This was not what Amanthus wanted. But Amanthus holds the universe together by abiding to his own structure and rules. He would not intercede. Everything was in the hands of a half-angel, a former angel, and three brave human beings.

Gabriel felt a strange sensation unlike any that he had felt since he realized he was in a dream. He looked back to Suzanne, but she was no longer in the crowd of people, at least not that he could see. The crowd had started to become such a congestion of souls that he could no longer discern individual faces. He looked around him in every direction. He felt eyes upon him – a searing, seething stare from some unknown entity. But this new sensation didn't feel like a dream. This felt like something *real*.

Gabriel searched the buildings that surrounded him,

turning to every window for some sign of who or what was watching him. And then he saw, high atop the One Times Square building, a vague shadowy form of a being with pinpoints of red in the place of eyes, staring directly at him. No sooner had Gabriel found the mysterious force that was staring him down, the strange force pushed back against him.

Gabriel was knocked out of the dreaming world and jarred to waking in the real one. He let out a loud gasp that startled everyone else in Lydia's vehicle. Jake was driving, while Lydia rode along in the passenger seat. Ashe had been sleeping as well, but while Gabriel's gasp had shaken Jake and Lydia, it only disrupted Ashe enough to rouse her awake.

"Are you alright man?" Jake asked, peering into the rear view mirror.

"Yeah. Sorry." Gabriel cupped his face in his hands. "Nightmare. I'm good."

"Where are we?" Ashe was groggy, waking into a state where the time of day held only enough light left in the sky to be able to confuse dusk with dawn if you didn't know which direction was east or west. The darkness would fall soon over the woodlands of the Upper Peninsula of Michigan.

"We are making the final turn toward Galestone. Just another twenty or so minutes. Lydia called ahead to a B-and-B Miranda told her she had stayed at when she first came up here. They are expecting us. Guns stay locked in the car. We don't want to give the wrong impression," Jake instructed them.

Gabriel nodded, turning his face to look out the window. He remembered this road like it was yesterday. Some things, especially in areas like this, changed very little at first glance. But deep beneath the surface, everything had changed.

Lydia's SUV pulled up to the Wellman House Bed and Breakfast. Jake, Lydia Gabriel and Ashe stepped out of the vehicle and all stretched after the long drive. The twilight time of the evening was close to passing into the dark of the night. A tall man in his late 50s appeared at the screened front door across the large porch.

"Evenin'," said the man at the screen. He opened the door and stepped out onto the porch. He smiled and looked over the four guests standing on the gravel near the base of the steps. "Tom Wellman – owner, operator and host, alongside my beautiful wife Bev, who I'm afraid is in the shower at this very moment, so the greeting of you folks is all my pleasure!"

Jake stepped up the steps and extended his hand to Tom. "Jake Neilson. This is Lydia and Ashe, and the grumpy guy grabbing our bags is Gabriel."

"Nice to meet you all. Miss," he directed his attention to Lydia, "Lydia? I believe my wife spoke to you on the phone."

"Yes, I called on the way up here. Sorry for the short notice," Lydia told him.

"It's not a problem at all. The season's been a buggy one. Not a lot of people coming around here lately. We're glad to offer you an opportunity to check our place out. Just staying the one night?"

"I believe so," Lydia said, "but if that changes, we will let you know – if that's alright."

"That'll be fine young lady," Tom reassured her. "Nothing booked for another four days, so if you folks need to stay another day or two, it'll be alright."

Jake nodded. "Thank you." He grabbed a couple of the bags Gabriel had unloaded from the SUV and led the group up the steps and through the screen door into the house.

There was a large stone fireplace in the main entrance room that used to be the living room area of the house. Above the mantle over the fireplace was a 50 inch television with the volume turned all the way down. At first, no one was really paying any attention to the TV. Lydia found herself transfixed on the stonework of the fireplace and the large oak mantelpiece that was stained in a natural finish, smooth and glossy and very knotty.

Ashe looked around the room and stepped over to a four-foot wide by six-foot high curio cabinet filled with all shapes and sizes of sad clown figurines. She found the vast array of statues and also a few painted plates on stands depicting the frowning and droopy-eyed clowns both fascinating and a little somber. It seemed like such a contradiction to her, all the sadness from something that was supposed to be symbolically a figure of happiness and joy. It almost started to make her feel a little sad herself.

"This one is a painting of Emmett Kelly." A woman entered the room from a side hallway and approached Ashe as she stood looking over the clowns behind the glass. Ashe shuddered from the sudden appearance of the woman pointing at the painted plate farthest to the right. "He was one of the greatest and most well known circus clowns of the early 20th century. I apologize if I startled you, dear. I'm Bev. I see you've already met my charming husband."

"Hi. It's okay," Ashe said, reaching out to shake Bev's already extended hand. "I'm Ashe."

Lydia, Jake and Gabriel followed suit in the introductions. Bev turned her attention back to Ashe, who had turned back to the glass cabinet.

"I bet you're wondering what kind of person would like to collect so many sad looking things." Bev smiled at Ashe, who wasn't sure how to respond. She didn't want to say anything to offend their hosts. "It's okay, I understand."

"They all just seem like…I feel lonely looking at them," Ashe told Bev.

"When I was young, but still a couple of years older than you, I'd guess…how old are you?" asked Bev.

"I just turned 18 yesterday," Ashe responded.

"Well then, yes. I was in my mid-twenties when I first had a panic attack. I called my older sister in the middle of the night and she came to my apartment to pick me up and bring me to her house. She knew that I was scared, and she had dealt with the same types of attacks herself, but hers had started at an age even younger than mine. She collected these, although she only had a few at the time. She would have times when she would teeter between anxiety and depression. One day during one of her down periods, a good friend of hers brought her the first one, this little guy right here." Bev opened the cabinet and took out a small ceramic statue, no larger than four inches high. It was a sad little clown wearing a derby hat with a daisy on the dome. The clown was sitting on a stump with a sad puppy curled up beside him, staring up at the clown.

Bev handed Ashe the statue to look at closer. She was trying to imagine what both the clown and the puppy were thinking about as they stared at each other. Ashe handed the statue back to Bev, who placed it precisely back in the same spot it had been, where there was a small dust outline on the glass shelf.

"It was my sister's friend's way of letting her know that even in your darkest moments of sadness you are never truly alone, even though at times you may feel like it."

"That's a very beautiful thought," Lydia told her, listening from a few feet away. "Your sister must be a very special person to have such wonderful people in her life."

Bev held her smile strong, but her eyes turned glassy.

"Yes. She truly was. But alas, it was too much for her. She took her own life when she was only 36."

"I'm sorry," said Ashe, feeling terrible for even looking at the clowns to lead them to this moment.

Bev placed a hand on Ashe's shoulder. "No no no! Don't fret about that, dear. It was a sad thing, losing my sister, but this gift that she gave me has guided me through some of the darkest days of my life! I look at these baubles and sad bunglers and I remember her, and I remember the meaning behind the one that started it all, and when I have had my own bad days I would make it a mission to find a new one to add to the collection, and the spirit of overcoming my own demons goes on and on, for me, and for my sister."

Ashe smiled at the thought of this. Lydia did as well, nodding her head.

"Now," Bev said, reaching out to each of the girls and guiding them by their shoulders, "Let me show you two to your room. It is a nice room upstairs with a little terrace to walk out onto and look over the stream that flows through the little valley below. It's a relaxing and peaceful view – if you can stand the mosquitoes and the black flies that have been unrelenting this year. Thankfully, there are a few Pic coils in the room as part of the complimentary package."

Bev led the girls up the stairs to their room. Tom was left with Jake and Gabriel in the living area.

"Well, looks like the job of leading you boys to your room is up to me," Tom remarked with his ever present grin.

"Thank you," said Jake. "We really appreciate your hospitality."

"It's all my pleasure. You boys will have to take the room with the driveway view, I'm afraid. No walk-out, but hey, you've got a microwave with free popcorn, not to mention satellite TV!" Tom said enthusiastically.

The mention of the TV drew Gabriel's eyes to the television over the fireplace. He froze in his steps and dropped the bags he was holding on the floor.

Jake turned back to him when he heard the bags drop. He looked at Gabriel's face and immediately could tell something had hit him hard. Jake turned to the television screen, and then back to Gabriel.

"What is it?" Jake asked, his concern growing with every passing second.

"Can I turn up the volume?" Gabriel asked Tom.

"Uh...yeah, sure. That remote right there on the arm of the couch," Tom responded.

Gabriel turned the volume up on the television. Jake stepped beside Gabriel and watched the events unfold on the screen in front of them. A news reporter stood in front of a large crowd outside of the Great Cathedral of the Lord Christ on High in Atlanta, Georgia. As the volume rose, it cut into the dialogue of the reporter as she spoke.

"...never before a gathering of this magnitude in modern history, and as I understand it, perhaps ever before. As you can see behind me, there is a train of heavily escorted leaders from the many different faiths around the globe, all arriving to take their places and represent the religious communities that follow them and the God that they believe has brought them all together for the first ever Conference of United Faith, which will take place starting tomorrow afternoon at the Marshalldome Center just outside of Atlanta.

"This event was the dream of Atlanta's Roman Catholic Archbishop Martin Marseille and the late billionaire Peter Marshall, who passed away just months ago. Although Marshall knew that he might not see the conference come to be, he dedicated the last years of his life to making it happen. Now, be it Muslims, Hindus, leaders of the Jewish community and many of the different branches of modern Christianity, all have been brought together in this very special place and time to celebrate their united faith and love in a greater being."

"That's been on every news channel the last few days," Tom said. "Heck, I thought everyone knew about it by now. I heard they are going to broadcast it worldwide on all the big networks."

Gabriel looked ill, to the point that his color had gone from his body. Jake was starting to feel a great deal of concern for him. He stood alongside of him and waited to see if he was going to say something. Then, the color returned slowly as the blood in his veins flowed a cold and steady stream.

Gabriel continued to stay fixed on the screen. "I can't believe I didn't see it before."

"You couldn't have known. The New York thing, it was a distraction that got you focused on finding Miranda. You were following me, and then we've been chasing this thing with the sword. He just needed enough time to keep us distracted," Jake told Gabriel.

The girls came back down from upstairs.

"You guys need to see what the brook outside looks like in the moonlight," Ashe told them excitedly. Lydia took notice of the looks on the faces of the two men.

"What is it? What happened?" she asked.

Jake motioned to the television. The words 'Conference of United Faith' were large and bold across the lower portion of the screen.

Tom felt a strange tension in the room. He felt there was an underlying personal issue that was best not to be a part of. "I'll leave you folks to yourselves. If you need anything else,

241

Bev and I will be in our personal quarters in the back. Just press the button on the wall near the kitchen door if you need anything at all. Have a good night."

Lydia looked at him and forced a smile to her face, thanking him for everything. He smiled back and nodded his good-nights.

"This is how my brother will have his ultimate audience, before the faces of the leaders of every major religious group." Gabriel dropped down onto the couch behind him, and rested his head in his hands.

Ashe was already looking up anything that she could find about the conference on her phone. "It's says on the official website for the conference that the main introduction and welcome speech from the Archbishop isn't until 2 p.m. in the afternoon. Before that there will be coverage of the arrival of the religious leaders and introductions."

Jake looked to Gabriel. "That will give us time. If we leave at first light, we will have time to find the piece of the sword."

"Which will be useless if we don't have Miranda!" Gabriel cut Jake off in mid-sentence. "She is the only one that can get to Atlanta and get close enough to Lucifer to stop him in time."

"Well we can't just give up!" replied Jake sharply. "We keep going, and we fight whatever comes our way. You are the one that told us how important this whole thing is, and what can happen if we fail. Well, I'm not about to just turn over and give up." He looked at Lydia. "There is too much at stake, and I've got too much to fight for."

Gabriel looked up at Jake. He stood up from the couch and came face to face with him, and then Gabriel nodded his head in approval. "I can see now why my daughter was drawn to you, Jake Neilson. You've got a fire in you. A good heart and a strong soul. Okay then. You're right. Please accept my apology. At first light then."

Jake nodded back to Gabriel, who then picked up his bag and took his leave up to their shared room. Ashe followed him up and returned to the room she shared with Lydia, leaving Jake and Lydia behind in the main room. Jake clicked the TV remote, shutting off the TV. He heard the front screen door of the Wellman House open and shut behind him, turning to see that Lydia had stepped out onto the front porch. He followed her outside and found her standing in silence at the top edge of the steps leading down to the driveway.

Jake walked up behind her and stood still and silent for more than a minute, listening to the chirping of the crickets hiding in the shadows and the distant song of a whippoorwill echoing through the northern wilderness.

"I'm scared, Jake." Lydia finally broke through the calm quiet as she revealed her fears. Jake put his hands on her shoulders from behind her.

"I know. I am too," he told her.

"The funny thing is," she said without turning around, "that I don't know what it is that I am scared of. There is…something. I don't know what it is. I'm not psychic like Ashe, but I have this terrible, terrible feeling that there is something else not right about all of this."

"Everything that we've had to take in over the past few days is enough to make anyone feel like that. I know that I am barely keeping things together myself. Running around with an angel and trying to save the souls of mankind from some unknown fate if we don't stop the devil – who is not really a devil at all, just a messed-up angel with parental issues – is, to say the least, fucked up."

Lydia turned toward Jake. She could finally let a smile come to her face, and it made Jake think of the bright smile she had, just a couple of days before, when he saw her in the pub in her cute summer dress. He couldn't help but smile in return.

"You have a good way to put a bad situation in perspective," she told him. "I guess God and his own kids have just as screwed up a relationship as any of the rest of us."

Jake chuckled and looked down at his feet for a moment. His eyes came back up and met Lydia's, and time seemed to stop in that very moment. He leaned toward her, and she to him, and their lips met each others for the first time. The moment seemed to go on and on, a moment that neither of them wanted to end. Finally, the kiss broke and the two of them looked at each other until Lydia finally broke free from the trance-like gaze.

"I'm...I'm sorry," she stumbled awkwardly back from Jake.

Jake's confusion was obvious. "'What's wrong?"

"Everything feels wrong right now, Jake. And there is you and Miranda. I know that you still have feelings for her. I could see it when she first showed up the other day."

Jake sat down on the top step of the porch. "Lydia. Yes, I still care about Miranda. I can't *not* care about her. But so much has changed. I've changed. And it's pretty obvious that she has too. I will always care about her. We've been through a lot, and we've both lost a lot in our own ways. She has lost her family and so much more, and I...I've lost a sense of the world that I thought I had a grip on." He stood back up and turned to Lydia. She was staring off into the distance at the trees that ran along the edge of the yard, dark and dense and deadly silent.

"What I'm trying to say is that there may not be a lot of things that I feel like I have a firm hold on right now. But you…" he stopped, gently touching Lydia's chin and leading her face to look him in the eye, "you've given me something to hold on to. Something to push harder to come out the other end of this thing on top. That is something *real*."

She leaned into him once again and kissed him, and then buried her head in his chest for the next few minutes.

"We should probably get some sleep. Tomorrow is going to be…honestly, I have no idea. We just need to be as ready for it as we can be," Jake told her.

Lydia nodded her head and Jake led her back into the Wellman House, shutting and locking the door behind them.

Out in the darkness that Lydia had been staring into were a pair of eyes that were undetectable to any human staring back.

Miranda had stood watching and listening to her friend and her former boyfriend share their feelings for one another. She reached deep down into herself and searched for a discernable emotion, something tangible that she thought she should have been feeling. She had been telling herself for quite some time now that her feelings for Jake were a part of her past. On some level she hadn't been sure if she was being truthful to herself, or just trying to ease within herself the burden of pain that she carried of having had to turn him away for his own good.

Finally, she felt something, but it was like the double edge of a dagger. She felt a sense of relief, the kind that came with realizing that the truth was she knew that she and Jake were truly no more than friends, and that is all that they would ever be. The other side was that she felt little connection or sense of feeling for anyone from her past any longer. It unsettled her, but she chose not to dwell on it. She needed to be free, and finding such a sense of detachment made it that much easier.

She pushed all other thoughts out of her mind as she stepped out from the dense foliage and came to the steps of the Wellman House porch. She sat down, and escaped into the solace she so often found staring at the stars and pretending that she didn't know the secrets that lie behind them.

Miranda had her task at hand, and that was all that mattered. Finish this, and put it behind all of them.

CHAPTER TWENTY-ONE

Gabriel was the first to come down the stairs that morning. He'd taken a long, hot shower after waking, and it was well needed. It wasn't so much about the need for hygiene and cleanliness as much as it was the need for the escape and feel of the hot water pounding down over his body to clear his head. There was no aspect of today that he was looking forward to. He didn't want to fight his brother. He in fact cared very deeply for his brother and his plight.

The truth was, since his time as a mortal on Earth, he had found a great deal of sympathy for Lucifer that he hadn't allowed himself to see before. It was meeting Suzanne that started him along this path of self-actualization. In the many millennia before Suzanne, Gabriel had met and gotten to know many human beings. Never once did he ever have any desire to do anything but faithfully serve Amanthus. While he felt a deep sadness when the rebel angels fell, he believed deeply in his devotion to the rest of the legion of angels and to Amanthus. But with Suzanne, it became something far different.

Love does that. It makes you abandon all rationale. If you have a foolish corner of your heart, no matter how deep it may be buried, love will shine a bright and burning light on that little lost corner and bring it to the surface. But acting on love doesn't make you a fool. No, acting on love becomes you. It helps you discover who you really are and what it is you are willing to sacrifice to allow yourself into love's grasp.

For Gabriel, it was a willingness to sacrifice everything. For as much as he loved Amanthus, there was no one on any plane of existence that captured his heart like Suzanne did. He knew both love and desire, and although not quite the same thing, he understood that Lucifer had found a sense of desire as well. It was his desire to be free, free to make his own choices and carve his own destiny aside from Amanthus' wishes for him. It was a hard choice for both the father and the son, but the choices were made and the dues were paid by all.

Now Gabriel knew – Lucifer was no different than he had been. He was willing to sacrifice everything on a chance at embracing all that he desired. And they had both lost - dearly.

Coming down the stairs, Gabriel immediately smelled bacon, followed by the delicious aroma of coffee and the scent of frying eggs. He stepped into the dining room.

"Good morning!" bellowed an exuberant Tom Wellman. "Coffee?"

"Love some." Gabriel smiled as Tom reached out to hand him a steaming hot mug.

Tom stopped short before giving him the mug. "Or do you prefer decaf?"

Gabriel waved his hand at Tom. "No, no. Fully caffeinated for me, thanks."

Tom's smile widened. "Good man! Fully leaded." Gabriel took the cup and poured a bit of sugar into the cup.

"Everyone else on the way down?" asked Tom, looking past Gabriel toward the stairs.

"They shouldn't be too far behind, especially once they get a smell of Bev's delicious cooking," Gabriel replied. "While we're waiting, I'm just going to step outside for some of that fresh northern air."

"Go right ahead," said Tom. "Shouldn't be more than a few minutes, and I think I hear some rumbling around upstairs. I think they got a whiff!"

Gabriel nodded with a smile and stepped to the front door. He opened the door and found Miranda sitting where she had been all night, waiting for the others.

"Miranda," he said, closing the door tight behind him. "Where did you go? What happened?"

Miranda stood up from the steps. He saw something in her eyes, an uncharacteristic coldness. It was the first time that he had looked at her and lost sight of the reflection of Suzanne that he had so often seen in her.

"We both need to stop pretending that you are anything of a father to me. You don't have that right, nor do you have the right to question me." Icy defiance emanated from her words.

Gabriel knew nothing he could say in that moment would have any affect on Miranda's current emotional state. He held in the deep concern he was feeling, not only for Miranda herself, but for how whatever it was that Miranda was going through was going to affect the outcome of the perilous day ahead of them all. If she was off her game, it could mean disaster not only for the little group entering the mines today, but for billions of people around the world, and all future generations to follow.

He turned away from her and started to head back into

the house just as Lydia was stepping outside with a cup of coffee as well. Gabriel hurried past Lydia without saying a word. Lydia saw Miranda and quickly set her coffee down on a small table next to a wicker rocker on the porch and walked over to Miranda, stopping short of hugging her. Miranda could see the concerned look on Lydia's face.

"I'm alright, Lyd," Miranda told her. "I just had to clear my head. We're all going through this together. I'm fine."

Miranda said what she knew Lydia wanted to hear. She held the expression of someone carrying a great weight like Lydia understood she must be carrying with all that was happening now. But Lydia couldn't shake the uneasiness she felt that something was *missing* behind the words Miranda had spoken. She knew something wasn't right. But she also knew that she needed to go along with it – for now.

Jake was the next to come outside, and it was his first instinct as well to rush over to Miranda and question her about where she had been and if she was alright. Lydia intercepted him on this, trying desperately to convey a look to Jake that told him to *lay off.*

"Hey," Lydia said, stepping between Jake and Miranda and meeting Jake's eyes. "Miranda needed to clear her head on some things. Happens to us all. I'm just glad she's back." Lydia forced a smile. Jake looked beyond her at Miranda. He took a deep, silent breath.

"You're good?" he asked Miranda across Lydia's shoulder.

Miranda smiled and nodded to Jake. "I'm good."

Jake nodded back to her and glanced to the side at Lydia. "There's a wonderful breakfast in there. We need a good meal, and I'd hate to disappoint our hosts." He turned directly to Miranda. "You should come and eat too. I know you don't have to, but it might seem strange if you didn't. And it smells too good to pass up."

"And there's coffee!" Lydia smiled, holding up her cup.

Against all desire to, Miranda brought up a grin to her lips and stepped forward. "Well, when you are selling it like that, how can I refuse?"

Lydia locked her arm in Miranda's and they walked through the door together, following Jake.

Bev and Tom were thrilled to see Miranda. They remembered everything about her stay with them, even though it was only a few months short of almost two years since she had visited them that October – the week that her life had changed forever. There really wasn't all that much to recall about her visit, aside from the story they had heard about the wolf Miranda encountered on her walk back from the Buckshot Tavern. Bev commented how she was thankful Dean Humphrey was leaving near the same time as Miranda, otherwise it might have been a far different outcome.

Miranda knew better though. The wolf had become far more afraid of her than she was of it – she just didn't know at the time why that was. The wolf was far more sensitive to the danger that she was than the people around her. The wolf didn't have any darker intention than she felt Dean Humphrey did as he followed her out of the tavern that night.

After breakfast they loaded their belongings into the SUV, thanked their hosts for the wonderful meal and told them how much they all loved the bed and breakfast. Ashe waved out the window as they pulled away and turned toward the direction of the Gale Estate.

Before the turn-off road to the estate, they came by the Buckshot Tavern. Miranda looked out from the backseat window of the SUV as they passed by. A man had just stepped out of his pick-up truck and looked up as the unfamiliar vehicle moved past him. Miranda recognized Dean Humphrey, the man from the night with the wolf, as he made eye contact with her as the SUV passed by. Miranda quickly looked away as the SUV continued up the road and took the turn off to the former Gale property.

"What the hell?" Dean remembered Miranda as well, not so much for the incident with the wolf – wolves were just another part of living in the deep backwoods of the Upper Peninsula. He remembered her for the grief that Miranda had somehow caused his friends Ken and Mary Ann, the owners of the Buckshot Tavern. He was there that night and saw the whole incident. Mary Ann would never speak of why the girl looked so hatefully at her and brought her to a weeping mess of tears. But he always suspected that it had something to do with the Gales.

Dean got back into his truck and waited until the SUV was far up the road. He then started the engine and followed a safe distance behind them.

Both Gabriel and Miranda felt anxious coming up the path to the Gale Estate property. The gate that was normally locked before was broken down and left hanging on its hinges. After the death of David Gale, the corporations under his control spun into chaos. An old, abandoned mining property in the Upper Peninsula of Michigan was the least of anyone's concerns. No one was any longer being paid to oversee the estate and mining property, so it didn't take long before kids from Arlo and other sightseers caused it all to fall into a chaos of its own.

"I…I recognize this place," Ashe stated, watching out the windows as they drove past the gate. "Not from this view.

It was when I was…flying." It sounded strange for her to say it, but they all knew what she meant.

There came a point in the road where it veered to the right and continued on to the Gale house. They weren't going to the Gale house though. Gabriel directed Jake to follow the road straight, which led to the heart of the mining operation. It would be about another half-mile up the road. As they made their way down the road, Gabriel glanced to the right, up at an overgrown and narrow two-track that no longer looked like a two-track at all due to twenty-plus years of small tree growth and other various vegetation obscuring the path. But he was well aware of its existence, even when no other person passing by would even take notice of anything being there.

The path that was once there was long forgotten by all others who may have ever known it was there, but not to Gabriel. Never Gabriel. It was a place that he and Suzanne would sneak away to on so many evenings, meeting in a small clearing near an old natural cave formation. It was a safer place than in the Gale gardens late at night, a place where they could truly be alone. A place where they could be intimate.

Gabriel looked away, but the troubled expression on his face did not escape Miranda's attention. Very little did anymore. She was finding herself more and more keenly aware of the sensations and vibrations of the world around her, as subtle as they may be.

The densely wooded hillside rose steeply on the last quarter mile stretch of the road. It felt as if they were now in a deep valley that was about to open into a large and wide open area. From this point, upon leaving the eerily darkened valley, the road diverged into many different directions.

"Follow this road here to the right." Gabriel pointed off in the direction that ran along the base of the steep hillside.

There were many sets of railway tracks that led in differing directions.

"Where do all of these tracks run to? Are they all just for mine carts that ran into the mines?" asked Lydia.

"Many of them were for that, yes," Gabriel replied. "Some of the larger tracks there and there," he pointed out, "were for the full-sized rail cars that hauled the ore to places in the western U.P. and into Wisconsin. This was at one time a very lucrative operation. Jake – stop the car."

Jake stopped and Gabriel got out of the front passenger seat. There were a set of tracks that led to a pile of collapsed rubble and large pieces of timber and twisted steel tracks. The others all got out of the SUV and looked around the area. All that could be seen in the open distance to the west were piles of old rotting wood and stone scattered about across the abandoned tracks and roads that seemed to lead to nowhere at all. It was like a ghost town of sorts, but one where nothing seemed like a discernable structure of any sort. There were no buildings or structures left standing. All of the equipment had been taken down and hauled away, while all of the remaining buildings were left for ruin.

"What happened here?" Ashe asked.

"Uncle David happened," Miranda said, almost under her breath. She looked to Gabriel. "Didn't he?"

"David gutted the property for anything of value when he took control of the Gale holdings. Anything that could have any remaining value was sold and the rest for scrap value. The rest he left, and time and vandalism did the rest." Gabriel turned his attention back to the tracks that led into the pile of rubble at the base of the hillside. "This is our real problem. This was the main entrance to the mine. I knew the mine had been sealed, but I didn't know to what extent. This is much more than I had anticipated."

Jake looked incredulously at the entrance of the mine. "What was your plan for getting into the mine if it was sealed? We don't have the equipment or machinery to bust through anything."

"We have Miranda," Gabriel stated flatly. He looked to his daughter. "How well can you control your ability to move objects with your will?"

Miranda looked at Gabriel for a moment and then turned to the entrance to the mine. She stepped over to an area about forty feet from the collapsed debris and stared at the pile with powerful intensity. The smaller stones and broken timber pieces began to vibrate and move away from the main pile as if they were pieces of ash being scattered about by a light wind. Suddenly the walls of the outer structure surrounding the entrance of the cave began to groan fiercely. The rest of the group, along with Miranda, could feel the earth begin to shake beneath their feet.

"Careful, Miranda," Gabriel cautioned. But Miranda was letting her contempt for whatever obstacles that came before them get the best of her better judgment. She pushed harder, with the ensuing surge almost knocking Ashe off balance.

"Miranda! What's happening?" Jake urgently tried to get her to back down. Suddenly, rock fragments and debris, along with a cloud of dust and sand shot out in several directions from the blocked mine entrance. Miranda stopped her efforts to force the mine entrance open.

Lydia and Ashe had taken cover behind the SUV. They looked over the hood of the vehicle after the dust cloud had settled.

"What happened?" asked Lydia.

Miranda's head was down. She brushed off the little bit of dust that had landed on her leather jacket.

"From the sounds of it," Gabriel said, "it was collapsed deeper than we thought."

"And now it is even more," Miranda bitterly remarked. "I'm sorry."

"How many entrances are there into the mines?" asked Jake.

"Originally there were three main entrances. But they would have all been closed up in the same way to make sure no one could go snooping around inside the mines," Gabriel said.

Ashe closed her eyes and opened her mind in nearly the same way that she did in her grandmother's apartment. But she didn't allow herself to fly this time in her mind. She looked, in a deepened state of concentration, far into the rocky hill.

"It's here," she said aloud. "I can see it...it's like a source of light almost. A flicker...far inside the hill from here."

"Great." Jake sat on the ground with his arms rested on his knees. "Perfect planning. You know, for an angel, you really haven't thought this through."

Gabriel walked a few paces away and stared off into the distant western sky. Then he turned back around in a swift movement and rushed over to Ashe, startling her in the process.

"You said it was distant from here...you saw a flicker? Was it back in the direction that we came in from?"

"Yes," she said to him. "I think so. Deep inside the hill..."

"Deep from *here*...but perhaps not as deep from another spot!" he said excitedly.

"What are you thinking?" Jake asked.

"There was an old service road that we passed on the

way here about halfway back to the turnoff to the house. It is overgrown, and it was mostly overgrown back when the Gales still lived here because it wasn't used for anything. There is a natural cave there. I should have realized it before. The cave is fairly small but it went deep. It had been explored some by the mining crews, but the location didn't make it an ideal drilling site, so it was mostly ignored and forgotten by most."

"So you think it might be a way in?" asked Lydia.

"Yes, possibly," said Gabriel. "But more than that. When I was sent to retrieve the first shard at Cadere Gladii, it was in a cave formation much like this particular cave. It seemed almost unnaturally formed. When Lucifer's sword was destroyed, the destructive force was something that didn't abide by any laws of physics that you know of. It was an explosion of cosmic devastation that sent pieces across all of reality with incredible force. The initial blast itself leveled the entire host of angelkind to the ground, scattering us about the Infinite Lands for miles. When we recovered, the third of our kind that stood with Lucifer were already gone, banished to Hell. That's it!"

"That's where the sword fragment tore into the Earth," Miranda said nodding. "Okay. Let's go get it."

The five piled back into the SUV and Jake turned it around rather abruptly, apologizing to Lydia as he spun the vehicle around. She only smiled at his coyness. Jake slowed down at the old service road and carefully made his way through the high grass and small tree growth.

"This might scratch the hell out of your car," he remarked to Lydia.

"Not the top of our list of problems right now," she said back to him.

The road went about a quarter mile back and then came to a small clearing at the base of the hill. He stopped, and they all got out. Jake opened the hatch in the back and started pulling out the guns, handing each of them their assigned weapons, including the can of bear pepper spray for Ashe.

The cave looked as if it had been undisturbed for a very long time. There was a lot of shrub and plant growth disguising its entrance. The group stepped up to the mouth of the cave. It was wide enough for two of them to enter at a time. Jake gave everyone LED flashlights and he and Gabriel wore the headlamps to make it easier to handle the 30/06 and the shotgun if they needed to inside the cave.

"We have to be very cautious with the guns in the cave. Controlled dynamite blasts were one thing for professional miners. An uncontrolled blast could be dangerous for the possibility of a cave in, especially with portions of the mine destabilized from previous blasts," Gabriel warned.

Miranda knew part of that statement was regarding her effort to clear the main mine entrance, but she didn't respond to it at all.

"Jake and Lydia can lead in, guided by Ashe right behind, and Miranda and I can follow. Whenever you are ready Ashe," Gabriel told her.

Ashe closed her eyes once more, finding it easier each time she tried to find the focus to visualize the direction of the shard.

"It's much closer now," she said with her eyes still shut. "Go ahead." She reached forward and pinched the back of Lydia's shirt. Jake started ahead slowly. The cave walls were rough and in some places jagged, and in the distance they could hear a steady and distance howl like air was moving somewhere deep within the hillside.

Before Miranda and Gabriel followed them in, Miranda stopped him.

"I saw you looking up this road when we first came past it up the main road. What is it that you were remembering?" she asked him.

Gabriel looked her in the eye and stood in silence for several seconds before finally telling her. "You were conceived right here," he said, looking down at the very spot they were standing at the mouth of the cave. He moved on into the cave behind the others, leaving Miranda to look down awkwardly at the spot where she was standing before following behind Gabriel into the cave.

Dean Humphrey had slowly made his way up the old mine road in his pickup truck, creeping along the side of the road tightly, as the branches from the trees alongside scraped against the right side of the truck.

The truck was a beater, but it was his pride and joy, along with the Winchester rifle that was hanging across the back of the cab of the truck. He had already been past the turnoff road to the cave when he noticed that Lydia's SUV was already coming back down the road, so he threw the truck into reverse and started to back up quickly in the direction that he had just come from until there was an area where the trees had thinned out enough for him to back the truck deep into the cover of the brush well off of the road. He shut the engine off and waited for the SUV to pass by, but it never came past him.

Dean got out of the truck and listened. In the distance, not so far off through the trees, he heard the engine of the vehicle stop and voices from the people that were inside of it. He remembered that there was an area that looked like it might have at one time been a path off the road, and decided that was where they must have gone. This made him wonder even more what it was they were up to.

He quietly opened his truck door and reached into the back and grabbed the rifle from the harness that secured it to the back of the cab. He opened the glove box and grabbed a handful of rounds for the rifle and loaded them into the gun, putting the spare rounds into his left vest pocket. Dean pushed the door shut and began to creep through the woods with the silence of an experienced hunter.

It didn't take him long to get within a distance that he could see the last two people in the group outside of the cave. The last man outside went into the cave, leaving Miranda standing for a moment looking down at the ground outside of the cave before following the man inside.

Dean knelt down for a moment and stared in the direction of the cave.

"What in the fuck are these people up to?" he said to himself.

There was a rustling in the brush up the rocky hillside about 100 to 150 feet from where he stood. Dean whipped his head in the direction he had heard the noise, but the sound stopped when his eyes turned in that direction. He brought his gun to the ready in both of his hands and raised the scope to his right eye and searched the side of the hill for whatever it might have been that made the sound. He saw nothing at first, and then caught in the crosshairs what looked like an ear of an animal sticking up above the top edge of a fallen tree.

Dean held the ear steady in the sight and watched to see what the animal was. The head slowly raised and was looking in Dean's direction. He wasn't sure what he was seeing. *Was it a fox?* he thought. The head looked similar to a fox, but there was something wrong with the eyes. They were larger than a foxes eyes, and the animal was very dark in color, darker than any fox he'd seen in the area before. *Wolf, maybe?*

No. It was definitely not a wolf. Dean knew wolves. He

had illegally shot his share of then and sold the hides and teeth and claws to black market traders. *What the hell is that thing?*

The animal moved its head as if it was now purposefully staring Dean down, and that was when Dean saw the most disturbing thing yet about the thing. It had another set of eyes above and between the larger set of eyes, slightly smaller but certainly there.

Dean's heart began to beat faster, and he pulled back the slide to chamber the round. As he did this, the creature stood up from behind the fallen tree and its height rose to almost Dean's height on four long and thin legs. Dean involuntarily lowered the barrel of the gun and stared at the thing. The creature opened its mouth full of sharp teeth and let out a screeching scream, leaping over the tree it had ducked behind with ease, with speed unlike anything Dean had ever encountered in these woods. It moved like a four-legged spider through the brush, and while Dean's first instinct was to run, he kept his head about him enough to raise the barrel of the rifle once again and tried to fix the creature in his sight.

The underbody of the thing was covered in thick fur like the head, but the back seemed smooth and leathery, yet just as dark as the fur. He held the sight on the center of the underbody and squeezed the trigger, firing off a shot that found its target, knocking the thing back about ten feet. It landed at the base of the hill.

Dean froze for several seconds, just trying to catch his breath as his heart continued to race. He took a few steps in the direction of the thing, but stopped himself. He wanted to know in the worst way what the thing was, but at the same time he felt an overwhelming sense of fear rising from the pit of his stomach that was telling him to get the hell away from it.

Neither option was going to happen. The thing raised

its head from the ground first, and then with two of its four legs, it pushed itself up from the ground and landed on all four. Dean chambered another round, but the sound caught the attention of the thing. It shook its head back and forth, lowered itself into a crouching position on its front two legs and let out another screech as it once again eyed Dean. Then, it pushed itself upward into the air and the brown leathery backside of the thing spread apart to either side of the creature into wide, bat-like wings. It lunged at Dean, who on instinct and nothing else raised the gun once again and fired off a shot, but the round came nowhere close to hitting the thing.

Dean turned and started running back toward his truck. He kept looking behind him as he ran, hearing the horrible screech the thing made and the sounds of the leaves and branches in the trees above being knocked about, but unable to tell exactly where the thing was at. He kept running, and saw his truck not far ahead through the trees.

A quick stop and a glance around did not help him in locating where the thing was. He took a moment to chamber another round in the gun, and continued running in the direction of the truck.

The sun was bright and beating down on Dean and the truck, and when he looked up once again when he was only a few feet away from the truck, he almost blinded himself as he looked right up into the sun. He saw for a moment a shadow move across the hood of the truck, and he fired absently into the sky above the truck, hoping against hope that he hit something. He threw the gun into the bed of the truck and grabbed the handle of the door. From seemingly out of nowhere, the thing grabbed Dean with raven-like claws at the ends of its two front legs. Dean screamed and thrashed about trying to strike the thing's face as the creature pulled him up from the ground toward the sky above, but the creature's legs held Dean far enough away that he could not reach it. Once they were at the top of the trees, the thing stopped its upward movement and opened its mouth for one final screech at Dean before lunging forward with its razor teeth, tearing into Dean's neck.

It held Dean there at the tree line, flapping its huge leathery wings as it continued to rip into his body with its teeth. Dean stopped thrashing and slumped in its claws as a steady flow of blood rained down on the windshield of Dean's beloved pickup truck.

The thing flew off with the remains of Dean Humphrey. His body would never be found, and it would be weeks before searchers found his blood-spattered truck. Most would say it was a bear that got him. But the residents of Galestone that knew the history of the town and the Gale family would always believe in the back of their heads that it was something far more sinister that was responsible for the disappearance and sad, mysterious end of Dean Humphrey.

Jake was in the lead about 75 feet into the cave. It had started to get a bit narrower in spots, but there were some areas that widened out again. The path ahead was abruptly cut short. There was rubble and stone pushed out and scattered in the path directly in front of him. Gabriel stepped up beside Jake to assess the blocked path.

"I'm not a cave exploring expert," Jake said, "but this doesn't look right."

"Dammit!" Gabriel said in almost a whisper. "It's the mine. When they were blasting their way through the hill digging one of the shafts they cut right through the cave."

Jake looked back at Lydia. She looked worried. Ashe

waited to see who was going to come up with what they were going to do next, but no one was saying a word. The moment felt empty. Jake looked to Miranda, who was staring ahead at the pile of rubble with sunken eyes.

"Miranda. The mineshaft is just beyond this pile of rock," Jake told her. "I know you can get us through there. Don't think of it as blasting through a barrier. Think of it as playing pick-up sticks like we all did as kids. Carefully feel your way through a little bit at a time."

Jake looked to Gabriel, who stood still for a moment before nodding in agreement to Jake. He turned toward Miranda. "He's right. You can do this."

Miranda looked at Lydia and Ashe, who both nodded to her.

"You got this, Miri," Lydia reassured her.

Miranda looked at the pile of rock and debris ahead of her. "Step way back," she directed the others. They moved several steps behind her. Miranda planted her feet firmly on the floor of the cave and lifted her hands to the level of her hips, palms up, and she closed her eyes.

The first rocks were small ones, rolling off to either side of Miranda. The smaller bits of stone and pebbles along with the pulverized, sand-like stone began to flow away from the blockade like a running river of rock. There was a groan in the cave wall ahead that momentarily startled Miranda. She stopped for a moment, not feeling fear for herself, but instead for her friends standing not far behind her. She took a deep breath and began again.

The largest rocks began to move, and as she pulled at them with her mind she remembered when she was a little girl playing another game with her father when she was seven or eight years old. It was a game of stacked blocks, where you take a block out of the middle or bottom of the stack and place it on the top. The next person would then take a turn and do the same thing, trying to not knock the stack down while continuing to build the stack up higher and higher.

She wasn't very good at the game, and she would sometimes get so frustrated she would lose her temper and knock the entire stack down on purpose. Each time that would happen, her father would make her stack them back up and try again. She would rebuild the stack, and it would start all over again.

"Miranda," her father finally told her. "You need to try something different. Take deep breaths, and count each breath you take very slowly to yourself. It will calm you and focus you. Try it."

So Miranda did, and she found that she got better and better at sliding the blocks out and stacking them up. Soon, she was winning more and more games against her father and almost anyone she played it with. She was winning so often that she finally stopped playing the game altogether because it wasn't a challenge for her anymore.

Now, Miranda looked at the larger rocks still blocking the way. She closed her eyes once again and took the first deep breath.

One. The first of the big rocks pulled away from the path and rolled slowly to the side of the cave. There was a rush of air that flowed through the small opening it made into the mineshaft.

Two. The next larger rock pulled away from the small hole into the mineshaft. Miranda drew it down and pushed it with her mind over beside the first rock. The hole was larger, but still not enough so that they could fit through to the mineshaft.

Three, she counted to herself with another long breath, and moved the final of the largest rocks away from the mineshaft and opened up the way with more than enough room to get through.

She let out a sigh of relief. Lydia came up from behind her and put her hand on her shoulder. Miranda looked up at her and Lydia hugged her. Miranda hugged her back. It was a moment of relief in Miranda, and Miranda had for a moment let her emotional guard down. She let go of Lydia and looked at her for a moment. Lydia once again could see the distance in Miranda's eyes, and the smile she had for a brief second flickered away.

"Good job, Miranda," Gabriel told her. Miranda didn't respond to him. The moment of relief at her success in clearing the path was past almost as quickly as it came.

Jake led the way into the mineshaft and assessed the area. The old steel mine rails led straight through in both directions. The original cave was once again blocked by the same collapse on the opposite wall of the mine. That was the direction they needed to go.

Gabriel turned to Ashe. "Can you tell how much further the shard is?"

Ashe closed her eyes and turned in the direction of the collapsed wall ahead. "I see it…I'm not sure how far. Maybe…only about 50 feet more. But there is another way to get close to it." She turned her head to the right without opening her eyes. "This is so weird," she said, speaking mostly to herself.

"What is it?" Jake asked her.

"Sorry…just, doing this. What I can see. There is another shaft that runs alongside this one - I think they are about 20 feet apart. There is a…a path that was made that connects the two shafts a few hundred feet down the track. If we go that way and back down, the cave picks up again through a crack in the mineshaft wall. It's not far from there." Ashe opened her eyes with excitement.

Jake looked around at the others. He lifted his shotgun and racked a shell ready. "Okay," he said, raising the barrel ahead of him. "Follow behind me, same order as before."

They began to move further down the mine shaft. They were on a downward slope, finding a great deal of debris in the mineshaft. Mostly rock that had let loose and fallen from the blasts that closed up the mine at the entrances. Sometimes an old mine helmet was found, an occasional lantern, a pair of gloves, and then, oddly enough…

"Oh my god oh my god oh my god!" Ashe backed up swiftly from the right wall when her flashlight revealed something wedged behind a large stone on the floor of the mine. The partially smashed top half of a human skull was pushed behind the rock into a small crevice at the base of the wall.

Lydia let out a gasp when she first caught sight of the skull, while Jake and Gabriel looked at it but kept a solid coolness about themselves to try not to frighten the others. Gabriel crouched down to more closely inspect the skull fragment.

"Looks like it's very old and has been here for quite some time. I don't think it's anything to be concerned about," he assured them.

"How did it get in here…and where is the rest of the skeleton?" Ashe asked, looking back and forth between Gabriel and Jake.

There was a faint chattering sound coming from somewhere in the cave. Jake was the first to notice it, and soon the others all took notice of the sound as well. It was getting louder. Something was getting closer, although none of them could tell which direction the sound was coming from.

"Come on!" Jake directed the group, and they started moving further down the shaft at a much quicker pace than they had been before. Gabriel chambered the rifle and kept his eyes behind him as often as he could while continuing to move in the direction of the rest of the group. As he turned his head the light from the headlamp moved around the cave and he wasn't sure if it was a trick of the light, or if he was seeing an array of shadows moving independently along the walls of the mine.

Lydia looked back for only a moment, losing sight of the floor around her. Her foot snagged a mine helmet and she tripped, almost catching her head on the mine wall, at the last instant breaking her fall with her outstretched hands.

Jake stopped when he heard her sudden scream as she began to fall. "Lydia!" He rushed over to her and knelt in front of her. "Are you alright? Are you hurt?"

"I'm okay. I just scraped up my hand a little," she told him.

There was a deep crack in the wall just above where Lydia had fallen. It was only about twelve inches from Jake's face. Jake heard a scratching noise from the crevice and quickly took Lydia by the hand and pulled her up and away from the hole. The rest of the group, along with Jake, stared at the spot in the wall with their light sources fixed on it.

At first, it was only two long, black, crab-like appendages, around 24 inches at least, pushing their way slowly out of the crack. Following the first two cam another eight similar appendages that were slightly shorter than the first two. Once all ten appendages reached out of the crack and firmly placed themselves all around the outside of the crevice, they pushed slowly against the wall. A bulbous black, rounded body covered in short, prickly hair emerged from the crack at the center of the ten appendages. The center of the domed body split open from a slit through the middle of it, revealing a mouth full of jagged teeth. The round body stretched forward as if hidden jaws deformed its spherical shape, appearing as an almost snout-like protrusion between the long appendages.

The group all jump backwards as the thing let out a horrible hissing sound, followed by the flicking of a long, forked tongue. The legs thrust the creature out of the wall and it landed on the ground between them. Behind the head and the legs was a long, snake-like body, about three feet in length, and down the entire length of the remainder of the body were another two-dozen mini appendages that acted as tiny, three-inch legs all the way to the tail end of the thing.

Everyone stood frozen, staring at the thing as it hissed and looked up around at all of them. It was to everyone's shock that Lydia was the first to respond to the thing on the mine floor in front of them. She pulled out the .38 and aimed it directly at the face of the thing, firing three slugs into it and splattering the floor with a dark red spray of blood and whatever else the thing had been made of.

The gun echoed loud in the mine, and everyone stood stunned by what had just happened. Lydia had an unreadable expression on her face as she stood still with the gun still fixed on the carcass of the thing on the floor. Jake reached out and placed his hand on her hand that held the gun, and slowly lowered her hand away from the strange creature.

"What…what was it?" she asked, looking to Gabriel.

"My…brothers and sisters. The ones that fell…some of them had some twisted ideas that they couldn't help but to bring to fruition. For the most part, these twisted abominations stay away from mankind. But they are drawn to things of angelic power." He looked to Miranda. "And that includes you, Miranda."

The sound of the chattering had stopped for the moment after the shot from Lydia's gun was fired, but only for the moment. The sound started again, and Jake directed a high powered flashlight beam down in the direction of the mine from which they had already come.

"Run," he said almost inaudibly at first. Then he yelled, "Run – NOW!"

The walls were lined with more of the same creatures, and they were crawling quickly along every surface of the mine – the floor, the walls and the ceiling, and they were gaining fast.

Jake stopped. He looked to the Miranda, Lydia and Ashe. "You three go on ahead. Gabriel and I will deal with these things. We know they can die. You guys move on ahead and make it to the other mineshaft. We will catch up with you as soon as we can."

Lydia nodded and took Ashe by the hand and led her on to the path between the shafts. Miranda started behind them and Jake stopped her for a moment, telling her, "I know you can keep them safe, Miranda. I have faith in you."

She looked at him for a brief moment, feeling a surge of strange conflict in her heart. She didn't know what faith was, and she certainly didn't know what it meant anymore for anyone to have it in her.

"I will," she told him, feeling cold and detached slightly from herself. She followed quickly behind Lydia and Ashe. Jake watched her disappear into the darkness before turning back to the things coming up fast upon him and Gabriel.

"You have a plan?" asked Gabriel, looking to his side at

Jake.

"Nope," he replied flatly. "Just keep shooting."

Gabriel smiled and nodded, and raised the rifle up. He had readied the extra rounds in his pockets and aimed at the first of the creatures. They both started firing, and the things started going down while other ones made it past the bullets whizzing by and kept coming closer. Each time they were hit they exploded in more of the dark red goo that Lydia had reduced the first one to.

The first one to reach Jake's feet tried to grab at him with its longest two appendages and lunge at his ankles with its snout-like mouth. Jake kicked at it and it flew against the wall, but it quickly regained its composure and launched itself at him once again.

He was angry, and when it scurried up for the second time he lifted his boot and brought his foot down hard on its head, smashing it to the floor. His boot was covered in the thick red goo, but the thing was down, dead.

"Not much to these cavecrabs, are there?" he said to Gabriel as Gabriel kept firing and reloading.

Gabriel ran empty on rounds as one made it up to his feet. He turned the gun around and thrust the butt of the stock straight into the head of the thing, smashing it flat.

"Cavecrabs. Not the catchiest name, but it will do," Gabriel said to Jake as he reloaded once again.

"Go easy on that gun if you can," Jake said. "It's older than I am."

"Not our biggest priority right now I think, Jake!"

Lydia and Ashe made it up to the passage that went across to the other mineshaft, followed close behind by Miranda. They moved through the passage as the loud gunshots from the rifle and the shotgun echoed down the mine chambers. Lydia turned back to Miranda.

"Is there something else we should do?" she asked her.

"No," Miranda said with an unexpected iciness in her voice.

"No?" Lydia replied, taken aback by the way Miranda had responded to her. "Miranda, that is Jake back there! Forget your absentee angel of a father if you want, but Jake? Miri, what the *fuck* is going on with you?"

Lydia had on only the rarest of occasions use the word *fuck*. It was only when she was extremely angry, and usually it was regarding issues within her own family.

"This isn't you, Miranda," Lydia said to her.

"Isn't me?" Miranda responded. "You know me, Lyd? I don't even fucking know me! I can do all of these…these things, but I have no idea what any of it means. The only thing that makes sense to me right now is stopping Lucifer by any means necessary!"

"*By any means necessary?* That's what this is all about for you, isn't it? You don't just want to stop Lucifer from destroying mankind's faith with everything that comes with it. This is about revenge. Isn't it, Miri?"

"It's not that simple. Yes, I want to see him suffer for what he's done to me. To my family. You wouldn't understand. You haven't lost what I've lost, Lyd," Miranda told her.

"I haven't lost? I've lost plenty, Miranda. I thought I lost you. And now we could lose Jake? Gabriel? Maybe our own lives? There is still a lot to lose, and I for one am willing to fight to make sure we don't lose anything else - including our goddamn souls!"

"Maybe you already have lost me, Lyd. I don't even know if I have a soul. I have no idea what I am. All I know is what I need to do."

"Are you going to tell me what that is?" Lydia asked pointedly.

Ashe was feeling the tension in the air between the two friends and slowly crept away from Lydia and Miranda as they had their…discussion. She moved to the corner of the second mineshaft and slipped around it to wait for the two girls to get through whatever it was that they needed to work out. She had been in similar positions before, but they had never (at least as far as she knows) dealt with angels and devils and monsters dwelling in caves.

She felt something hot, accompanied by a strange odor in the air. She turned the flashlight in the direction up the mineshaft and saw, less than six feet from her a large, hairy, apelike creature standing almost seven feet tall. It had to crouch some because the ceiling was not seven feet high at that point. The body was definitely very similar to a large gorilla, but the head had the curled horns of a ram and a snout that looked like a large, angry dog.

The thing looked agitated and began to breathe heavier and faster when Ashe turned the light onto it. Ashe felt such a rush of fear overtake her that she couldn't make a sound. Her entire body was shaking. The hotness she had felt before, along with the odor, was the thing's foul breath.

Ashe unsteadily reached into the little holster that held the pepper spray and unsnapped the canister, and she raised it up to the level of the things face. Before she could squeeze the trigger, the thing let out a deafening roar as it leaned forward toward Ashe. The roar shook Ashe even more and she dropped the can of pepper spray on the mine floor.

Miranda and Lydia heard the roar and rushed to the mineshaft where Ashe was, but not before the thing lunged forward and grabbed hold of Ashe.

The thing was on top of Ashe when they got to her, but something strange was happening. As soon as it put its hands on Ashe, the thing was struggling to get away from her. The sounds it was making sounded more like whimpers and sounds of desperate fear than the sound of an attacking ferocious beast. And by no means was this beast meek or mild. It was a strong, powerful animal (if animal was a correct defining term).

The thing scrambled to its feet and ran in leaps and bounds away from Ashe. Ashe, Lydia and Miranda watched in stunned disbelief as the thing faded from their sight into the darkness.

"What just happened?" Lydia asked, helping Ashe up from the mine floor.

"I'm…not exactly sure," Ashe responded. "I was so afraid…I was literally frozen with fear. When it came onto me, I could feel its rage. Its hunger. But then…it panicked. It was like I was feeling what it had felt, and it felt was I was feeling. I think…I think it felt all of my fear."

"That's incredible," Lydia told her.

Miranda picked up the can of pepper spray and held it out to Lydia to hand to Ashe.

"More potent than a can of pepper spray," Miranda said. Lydia didn't notice that Miranda was holding out the pepper spray to her, so Ashe instead reached out to grab the can. Miranda noticed at the last moment that Ashe was reaching for the can and suddenly pulled her hand away from Ashe as she reached out. Ashe instinctively jerked her hand back away from Miranda with startled confusion.

"Sorry," Miranda told her. "Still skittish about what happened at your grandma's place." She carefully extended her hand and Ashe took the can and put it back into its holster.

"Thank you," Ashe said to her.

Miranda walked on past Ashe and Lydia. "We need to get moving. We're running out of time."

Lydia started to walk on behind Miranda, but Ashe held out her hand and stopped Lydia by the arm as she watched Miranda walk on up the mineshaft. Lydia looked at Ashe.

"I know she is your friend," Ashe whispered to Lydia. "But she's hiding something. I don't know what it is, but it's the real reason she didn't want me to touch her. She was afraid somehow that I'd know."

Lydia looked at Ashe, and then looked back at Miranda. She turned back to Ashe once again.

"I know she is," Lydia told her.

They followed on behind Miranda and caught up to her quickly. There were sounds coming from the mineshaft behind them, and they all stopped and listened. Miranda raised her hand as Lydia raised the .38 and the flashlight and Ashe leveled the can of pepper spray in the direction behind them.

Jake and Gabriel came into view and froze when they saw the three women more than ready to take on whatever might have been coming at them. Lydia sighed in relief as she looked at the two men spattered head to toe in the red goo from the 'cavecrabs'.

Jake smiled widely at the sight of Lydia. Gabriel was happy to see the girls were alright. The guys caught back up with the girls and they all walked on side by side to the space where the original cave that they had come in from continued.

"Run into any problems?" Jake asked.

Lydia smirked. "Nothing that Ashe couldn't handle."

"Huh," Jake said. "I guess that pepper spray came in handy after all."

"Yeah," Ashe chuckled. "It sure did."

They came up to the place where the cave continued into the rocky hill, but now it had narrowed to not more than an eight inch crack that continued deep into the darkness.

"It's there," Ashe told them. "It's only thirty feet away. It's lodged into the rock. About a foot in past where the crack stops."

"How in the hell are we supposed to get to it?" Jake look frustrated. He turned to Gabriel. "What now?"

There was no way that any of them, not even Ashe, could slide themselves into the crack.

"I'll get it out," Miranda said them, raising her hand in the direction of the shard. Her irises changed to their solid black and there was a low rumbling in the walls of the mine. Her impatience was showing. She wanted what she needed to beat Lucifer.

"Miranda, wait," Gabriel pleaded, coming toward her. Her other hand came up and he was pushed back by the invisible force of her will.

"Miranda, it's too dangerous!" Jake said in a raised voice. She twisted the same hand that she raised when Gabriel approached and the other three people in the mine were frozen in place as the walls around the mine began to tremble.

The crack in front of her began to widen. It was twelve inches, then sixteen. Dust and rocks began to fall from the ceiling and walls. Ashe's eyes began to fill up with tears. She was terrified that they would all be buried alive down there. Lydia held her arm around Ashe as they watched Miranda push the crack apart even farther.

Miranda twisted the hand that reached toward the shard and then drew her hand in closer to her chest.

"I can feel it…it's so close," she told them.

The shard broke free from where it had rested for more

than 2000 years, and it flew into her hand. She held it and stopped the force on the walls, but the entire mine structure was still shaking in a chain reaction earthquake caused by the force Miranda had used to pry the cave apart to free the shard. Miranda realized what she had done, but there was no way for them to run out of the mine the same way they had come in and make it out.

She looked to her friends, the girls trembling and in tears and the men standing with horrified looks on their faces.

"I'm sorry…I'm so sorry," she looked at them all. She handed the shard to Gabriel. "Go, take it! Get out of here!"

"Miranda, there's no time," Gabriel told her. "The whole place is going to collapse!"

Miranda looked at her father, and her eyes turned to black once more.

"I can hold it," she said, reaching one hand up toward the roof of the mine and another toward the opposite wall. With powerful force she blew out the wall and opened a clear pathway through the mineshaft wall into the adjacent mineshaft, revealing a clear path to the cave from which they had entered into the mines to begin with.

"Go! Take it and get out of here! I will hold the tunnels together as long as I can!" she told them.

Lydia's face was full of despair. "We can't leave you here, Miri!"

Miranda looked at Jake. "Jake. Take her out of here. Carry her if you have to…I don't know how much longer I can hold this together…"

Jake grabbed Lydia by the arm and led her through to the cave. Jake glanced back at Miranda one last time before passing out of her line of sight. Gabriel led Ashe out behind them, looking back at his daughter with awe for her strength.

In that moment, something had occurred to him about the depth of Miranda's strength and power that he hadn't considered before now - but there was no time to think about it right then. The walls were literally coming down around them.

Jake and Lydia made it out of the cave, and Jake led her far out of the way of the hillside, not knowing what was going to happen when the mines came down completely. Gabriel and Ashe followed close behind - and just in the nick of time - as the giant hill gave out a final groan that shook the surface of the earth for more than a hundred yards around the entire base of the hill. Dust and rock came shooting out of the cave mouth as it completely came down upon itself. Dust bellowed up over the trees and settled all around them.

Jake stared at the shuttered cave in silent disbelief. Lydia was sobbing as she sat on the ground beside him. Ashe held her arm around Lydia, trying to comfort her. Gabriel dropped down to his knees and stared at the hillside. He held the shard in his right hand, but he did not look at it. Instead, he looked upon the hill – the tiny mountain – that stood as a monument to everything that had ever meant anything to him in his life as a man, and everything that he had lost even more.

Ashe felt a strange sensation and looked over her shoulder. As she did, she and the others heard coughing. Ashe stood up as Jake and Gabriel turned to see where the sound was coming from.

Miranda stood a few yards away covered in dust and debris. Her hair was full of rocks and dust, but otherwise she was unscathed. Lydia jumped up and ran to her and hugged her, and so did Jake. Miranda hugged them both back tightly. She meant it, she felt it, and she wanted it.

When they finally let her go, Ashe looked at Miranda

from where she stood. She walked up to Miranda…and punched her with a right hook square in the jar. Miranda went down, to everyone's shock – including Ashe's.

"Ashe!" Jake reached out and held onto her. "She just saved our asses!"

"She almost got us all killed! Isn't anyone aware of that fact?" She was seething with anger.

Miranda sat up on her backside and was touching her chin. She didn't feel Ashe's strike in a physical sense, but she felt the impact on a psychic and spiritual level. Her first instinct was seething rage, but she calmed herself and looked at Ashe and the others.

"She's right. I deserved that. I'm sorry…for everything."

Everyone stood silent. It was true. They were all filled with an uneasy sense about what had just happened.

"I'm sorry. I lost my temper too," Ashe told her.

"It's alright," Miranda said, pulling herself up from the ground. "Nice right hook."

"Grandma made me take self-defense classes when I was a kid," Ashe told her.

A strange shadow passed overhead, followed by another. And then, several more. They all looked up and saw dozens of the same creatures that had recently made a meal of Dean Humphrey, circling and swooping at them from above.

"What fresh hell is this now?" Jake asked as he raised the shotgun to the air, followed by Gabriel with the rifle. Gabriel fired his last rounds at the creatures above.

"I'm out!" he yelled to Jake, followed by Jake's last blasts into the sky.

"Me too," he said. "Get to the SUV! Run for cover!"

Jake, Lydia, Ashe and Gabriel headed for the SUV. Jake

looked back at Miranda, who was standing still watching the things above.

"Miranda! Come on!" Jake yelled to her.

Miranda raised both of her hands to the air, palms stretched up and opened wide. She closed both of her hands into fists and pulled her hands down to the ground. Every single one of the creatures slammed down hard into the ground, straight down from where they had been in the air at that moment.

They were all broken and writhing on the ground. She moved her hands in a series of motions like she was gathering the battered creatures, moving them all with her angelic power to what was once the entrance of the cave. They formed a pile of nearly 30 bodies, some still shuddering in pain. Miranda lowered her hands to her sides. The entire pile of creatures suddenly burst into flames, burning their remains to little more than ash.

Gabriel walked up to his daughter.

"Your power is unlike anything I have ever seen in another angel, save for Lucifer himself. I didn't understand it at first, being that you are only half angel. But you are human as well, Miranda. You have a soul, and a soul, believe it or not, is a very powerful thing in itself. The part of you that makes you human, along with the part that is angel, gives you a strength unlike anything else I have ever encountered. That is how you will be strong enough to overcome Lucifer."

Gabriel reached out and handed Miranda the shard. "Be careful with that. The slightest scratch and you will lose the angelic edge forever. I know firsthand. But I want you to know something. I wouldn't want to go back, Miranda. I loved your mother. It was the most real thing I've every felt. You have her strength in you, along with her beauty."

Miranda took the shard.

"Are you ready for this?" Jake asked her. "Maybe one of us should go with you?"

"No...I need to do this." Miranda took a few steps away from the others and looked back at her friends. They all looked at her in different ways. There was a sadness in her eyes, uncharacteristic of her recent behavior. Lydia was about to say something to her, but before the words could get out, Miranda had vanished.

Ashe pulled out her phone and found to her surprise that she had a good LTE signal. She connected to the internet and tried to find the live stream of the conference.

An emergency alert came across her phone when she first connected to LTE. The tell-tale emergency alert sound came from the speaker, followed by an all points bulletin alert:

"Police in the Upper Peninsula are searching the area in the eastern region surrounding the Eastern Upper Peninsula Correctional Facility for a suspect wanted for questioning in the death of an inmate at the prison. Longtime inmate Daryl Grimes was found dead in the prison visitor center..."

Gabriel's head turned toward Ashe. He rushed over to her and took the phone from her hands.

"Hey!" she snapped at him. He looked to her briefly with an extremely shaken look on his face.

"I'm sorry," he told her. He looked truly worried about something.

"It's...it's okay," she told him, her expression revealed her confusion.

Jake and Lydia walked up on either side of Gabriel and looked at the phone screen.

"What's wrong?" Jake asked him.

The alert continued. "Prison officials are currently

investigating a massive security breach at the prison that coincided with a security systems failure that evidently affected the entire prison."

Gabriel typed in a link to a local television news affiliate and clicked on the link to coverage of the story.

"A major systems failure, a catastrophic security breach, a murder and a manhunt – have you seen this woman?" A drawing of a young woman with the caption 'Artists rendition of prison murder suspect from witness guard' flashed up onto the screen.

Jake and Lydia's jaws dropped. It was an almost perfect rendering of Miranda.

"That's not possible," Jake muttered as he turned away from the phone. "This doesn't make any sense. Who is this guy that was killed?"

"Daryl Grimes," said Gabriel as he handed the phone back to Ashe. He leaned against the SUV, feeling the weakness in his knees.

"Who is Daryl Grimes?" Lydia asked. "Why would she…I mean, this can't be right. Can it?" She started to breathe harder thinking about the frightening possibility that it could be.

"Daryl Grimes is the man who killed the Gales in the fire two decades ago. He is the man who tried to kill Miranda when she was only a child. He is the man…who killed Suzanne, Miranda's mother," Gabriel told them.

Lydia brought her hands up and covered her face. "Oh God…Miri."

Jake stumbled over to the trees and leaned with his outstretched hand on a small oak tree. He picked up a small branch and started beating it furiously against a larger tree, screaming angrily at the treetops above him. He turned to the pile of smoldering corpses across the way in front of the fallen cave.

Ashe sat on the ground with glassy eyes watching the despair of the others. There was nothing she could do to ease their pain.

Gabriel's eyes went glassy as well. He rubbed them and looked at Lydia, and then to Ashe and finally Jake, who was still transfixed on the smoking carcasses by the hillside.

Gabriel raised his eyes toward the sky.

"I'm so sorry, Suzanne. I'm sorry I let things with our little girl get so out of control." He lowered his eyes to the ground.

"Miranda…what have we done?"

CHAPTER TWENTY-TWO

An extended black Lincoln Navigator pulled up in front of the Marshall-Benton Suites Hotel and Conference Center outside of Atlanta, Georgia, just before 1 p.m.

The Archbishop Martin Marseille was escorted to the vehicle by Father Richard Ridley, his most trusted advisor that had worked beside him tirelessly in the months leading up to the Conference.

Father Ridley had been concerned about the Archbishop for the past few days. In his many meetings with Marseille, the normally cool and focused Archbishop had been somewhat agitated. Of course, Ridley believed that it being so close to the main event now, Marseille had reached a new level of anxiety over the final preparations for the Conference. But Marseille was a man who was coolest under pressure, and this was…something else. Ridley had seen on more than one occasion a strange man in conference with Marseille in his office. He had asked Marseille about the man, but Marseille brushed off his questioning, redirecting his attention to the finer preparation details and security issues surrounding the Conference.

Despite Marseille's attempts to distract Ridley from the matter of the man, Ridley held on to his concern. Even now, minutes away from arriving at the Marshalldome Center, there was a shadow hanging over Martin Marseille.

"Your Excellency," Ridley began. "What troubles you?"

Marseille held his gaze out the driver's side rear window of the Navigator, transfixed on the crowds lined up and down the streets and roads leading the entire distance from town to the Marshalldome. If he had heard his longtime friend speaking to him in that moment, he didn't show any sign that he had.

"Martin," Ridley began again, suddenly drawing the attention of the Archbishop.

Marseille suddenly turned to Ridley, as if he had just been startled awake. "What…oh, I'm sorry my old friend. Just lost in my thoughts."

"You have been for the past few days. I had assumed you may be feeling some anxiousness about the Conference, but I fear it may be something more. The man…"

"Oh, Richard! Do not be so concerned. It is God that guides us now. There is nothing we need to fear, for he is on our side. He is…" Marseille seemed to trail off once again before finishing his sentence. "He is…our guiding light."

"Yes, your Excellency," replied Ridley, but he was still not convinced by the Archbishop's reassurances.

The Navigator was escorted by two marked and two unmarked police and federal security vehicles. It was heading to the underground parking structure where all of the special guests and their entourages were led to. The Marshalldome Center had special lodging facilities beneath the conference center for special secured guests, and many of the visiting leaders from the various faiths chose for security and convenience to stay in the plush accommodations that the Marshalldome was providing. Marseille had opted to allow more space for the guests by staying in the nearby Marshall-Benton Suites, which was also owned originally by Peter Marshall – and now by the committee that oversaw the continued operations of the Marshalldome.

Marseille and Ridley were escorted to the rooms outside of the presentation box on the upper levels of the north end of the Marshalldome. The entire building was constructed like most sports arenas and stadiums in the shape of a large oval. It was a very versatile structure that could be used for many different functions, including musical concerts, sporting events and general conferences. One unique feature was the 'Box' - nicknamed with sharp simplicity by Peter Marshall himself.

The Box was a mechanical hydraulic stage that was surrounded on all sides by bulletproof glass. When not in use, the Box was retracted into the stadium walls and the area from which the Box retracted was replaced by additional stadium seating for other events. When the Box was in use, it extended nearly 30 feet out over the lower stadium seating areas (which were commonly not in use during the times when the Box was extended). Today, every seat available was filled, and large monitor screens could be seen from every position in the entirety of the Marshalldome, as well as an abundance of screens and speakers for all of the onlookers in the parking lots and other areas surrounding the Marshalldome properties.

The rooms behind the stadium seating on either side of the Box were the gathering areas for the many special guests in attendance, all of which were gathered in the Blue Room as it was called, comfortably waiting with their personnel and security escorts to be introduced and seated. The Red Room, which was on the opposite side of the Box, was a press designated area. It looked like a high tech military command center, filled with computers and monitor screens and cameras. Reporters from every major news affiliate in the nation, as well as many others from around the world, were all set up in this large communications center. Interviews had been scheduled and conducted throughout the morning with many of the different holy men – and women – who had traveled from around the globe to be in this place.

Marseille went into the Blue Room and greeted personally every single religious leader that was not currently engaged in an interview in the Red Room. He then busily moved on to the Red Room where several of the reporters tried to stop him for a final word before the event began, but he kindly smiled to them and told them there was far too much to do and that he would be available for interviews at a later time. He blessed them and went on his way.

Marseille paused for a moment and scanned the many video monitors along the walls of the Red Room. The Marshalldome was filled to capacity, and the monitors also captured the crowds surrounding the building. Other monitors were showing live news feeds from the crowds gathered around the city, while others showed crowds gathered at churches, temples and gathering places around the world. All eyes were on the Conference of United Faith, and this filled Marseille with an enormous feeling of hope – coupled with a nagging fear he was holding deep inside of his soul.

What he would not share with his longtime friend Richard Ridley was indeed the apprehension he felt about the man who came to him in his office only a couple of nights before, presenting himself as an angel of the Lord. Marseille was a deeply faithful man, and in his many years had seen, experienced and felt many strange things. But never had he seen anything like the display that he saw in his office that afternoon. He did admit to himself that he felt a touch of the divine. But along with that feeling was a sense of fear – fear for what exactly, he did not now. If he were to act on instinct alone, he would have turned the other cheek, despite the powerful presence that this stranger presented to him.

Was this a test of faith? he wondered. If it was, what was he to do? Could he refuse this man? Or was trusting this stranger the leap of faith he must make? Marseille feared he would not know the answer until the final moment the decision had to be made. And the clock was running out fast.

"Your Excellency, it is time," Ridley told his old friend.

Marseille nodded and looked around him. He moved into his position while Ridley prepared the interpreters, gathered in the area to the rear of the Box. The area beneath the Box on that day was sectioned off for a small orchestra, and with a signal from the control room, the music began to play.

Ridley was the first to approach the podium where Marseille's prepared speech along with Ridley's personal notes were waiting for both of them. Ridley was accompanied by two language interpreters who would assist him in the individual welcomes of each of the visiting leaders.

"Welcome, one and all, to the first ever Conference of United Faith!" Ridley announced to the cheering crowd. He raised his hands to calm the masses, and eventually they settled their wild enthusiasm enough to allow him to continue speaking.

"It is my great honor to welcome our guests here on this glorious day." After he spoke, the interpreter to his left spoke in the Hebrew language, while the one on his right repeated the same message in Arabic. These two languages were agreed upon prior to the Conference to accompany English as the primary language, mostly due to the long history and conflict between the Jewish and Muslim world. Today, they would be united as equals under God. On an inset sub-picture on all of the screens was a person communicating using sign language as Ridley spoke.

One by one, each visiting leader representing a religion from around the globe was introduced by Ridley. Each presented them self to the crowd, and each one was met with cheers from everyone in all of the various gatherings in and around the Marshalldome, as well as around the rest of the watching world. After the introductions, they were escorted to their seats assigned around the Box stage. Each was to have their turn to address the crowd, and while each may have their own message to share, the core of each presentation was a show of unity and solidarity like had never been seen before. This was to be a turning point for mankind and mankind's faith in a greater being, bound together in harmony unseen before in human history.

After the final leader was introduced, Ridley turned to look back at Marseille. Marseille gave him the ready nod. Ridley nodded back. As he turned back toward the crowd, he saw the man from Marseille's office standing in the far corner of the Box. He paused, perplexed by the man's presence, but tried not to reveal his concern to the crowds or the peering lenses of the cameras that were fixed upon him. But his subtle sidelining didn't escape the sharp eye of Marseille, who turned as well to see Lucifer standing in the corner.

Lucifer was wearing a long, ivory colored coat over dark clothing. He smiled and nodded as well to Marseille, a sign Marseille took as an acknowledgment of the importance of the moment at hand.

Ridley turned back to the crowds and could almost physically feel the overwhelming anticipation and sense of joy emanating from the masses below and surrounding him. He took a deep breath, and he continued.

"Friends. Brothers and sisters under our great Lord. It is my honor and my privilege to present to you on this gloriously bright and sunny day, the man whose dream it was to make this day what it has truly come to be – with the Lord's guiding hand, of course! Please welcome to the podium His Most Revered Excellency, Archbishop Martin Marseille!"

The crowd erupted in tumultuous cheering. Everyone was on their feet waving and crying and praising God for this day. Marseille moved to the podium and looked out over the crowd. The moment filled him with a joy like he had never felt before. He raised both of his hands to try and calm the crowd, but they were unrelenting. He turned to look over his shoulder and saw all of the men and women who had just been introduced by Ridley on their feet as well in full applause. Tears ran down the faces of many of the leaders looking on at him. As he turned back to the crowd he glanced the way of Lucifer, who was applauding Marseille as well.

He moved his eyes back to the crowd, once again raising his hands until the crowd finally calmed to little more than a murmur.

"Let us pray. Lord, may you bring your blessing upon all of your honored guests gathered here in this place, in this historic time, and to those all around the world who are united as one with us but who could not be here today. Lord, bless my partner who is in your presence, Peter Marshall, who shared in the dream of bringing together, amid our differences, souls with a common bond. In your Holy Name, let your peace and love guide us and help us to continue to move forward as one.

Bless us, oh gracious Lord. Amen."

An *amen* whispered throughout the crowd below and from some of the voices standing near Marseille. Others said their own words of praise and acceptance of Marseille's words.

Marseille looked back out over the crowd, taking in the ocean of faces below.

"We are all here, in this place today, because we all believe…in *something*. Something greater than ourselves, something unseen but felt deep within each and every one if us." He had not looked down once at his written speech, because the words written on those pages were not the ones that he was speaking to the crowd. He was speaking from the heart.

"We believe in a greater being. It doesn't matter whether we call this being God or Allah, Jehovah, or Jesus. It does not matter whether we all believe in a Holy Trinity. What matters most is, as we look into our hearts, what we see and what we feel is what has drawn us to this place in our lives. We feel hope. We are reaching into the unknown for someone or something to reach back out to us. In times of despair. In times of joy. In our every day, all of the little things that we are grateful for and all of the little things that we find ourselves fearful of, we seek hope. And we all do it together in *faith*.

"Faith is our binding principle. We seek guidance in our holy books, and we seek it in our leaders. But ultimately, it is faith that leads us through the darkest parts of our journey through this life. After all is said and done, we are all human beings together in this struggle. We may not always understand why we are faced with the choices that we sometimes must make or the things we must endure. But as long as we have our faith, we can move on, living our best lives, together as one."

Marseille took a moment for himself to look up toward

the glass ceiling of the Marshalldome. The sky was crystal clear blue and the sun shone blazingly bright on the glass. The air conditioning system was working on full power but the building was very warm when filled to capacity on such a hot summer day. The crowd all began to applaud Marseille's words during his moment of pause. He lowered his chin and looked at the roaring crowd, and then looked back to Lucifer.

There was a strange sense of absence in Lucifer's gaze. Marseille was taken aback as he noticed the odd expression. This glorious creature had presented himself with such confidence and certainty just a few days before, and now Marseille could almost see the very same apprehension that he was now feeling himself in the face of the mighty angel.

A shadow passed across the podium, and Marseille turned his head to the glass ceiling overhead. The blue sky was rapidly overtaken by suddenly darkening skies, thick with dark grey, almost blackening clouds overhead. There was a low rumble echoing from outside that turned into a sudden burst of thunderclaps, accompanied by lightning flashes streaking through the overhead clouds.

The chatter in the crowd indicated the beginning of a quiet panic that was rapidly spreading. Lucifer approached the podium where Marseille stood. Marseille turned to him.

"Is this…is this your doing? Am I being judged?" Marseille asked him, his voice trembling.

"No, my friend," Lucifer answered, looking to the skies overhead through the ceiling. "No. If anything, I owe you my thanks. But now, you need to get these people behind us to safety. Go…now!"

Marseille turned and signaled Ridley to come to him. They turned to the many guests and their escorts and ushered them away, out of the box and down the emergency corridors.

None of them knew what was happening. Not even Marseille. The only one that had a clue was standing at the podium overlooking the crowds as a fevered panic was slowly setting in.

Lucifer stood before them all, with the cameras of the world focused on him. This is the moment that he had wanted and craved. This was the moment that he had dreamed of since his grand plan for absolution in the eyes of Amanthus had first come to him. And he knew, as he stood there before all of the eyes of the world a simple truth that had been tearing at him from the inside as he listened to Marseille's words about the power and importance of faith…

This is not the way.

"Ladies and gentlemen," he spoke through the massive P.A. system, "we would like to ask at this time that you exit the building in a calm and orderly manner. There is a minor emergency that is being addressed at this…"

The signal to the speakers began to crackle and pop, and one by one sparks flew from the individual loudspeakers, some of them bursting into flames. A few in the crowd saw and pointed to the flaming speakers, starting a chain reaction that turned into a full uproar of chaos throughout the entire building. People began running for the doors that were in all of the sections surrounding the main room.

What started as a rush to the doors became a riot when the metal framework that held up the glass ceiling began arcing with electricity all across the entire building. People were screaming and running in every direction. Those who fell beneath the crowd were being crushed by those above who were desperately trying to get out, fearful that the whole ceiling above would collapse and kill everyone still inside of the building.

Lucifer watched the scene below in quiet and helpless

desperation. It was a display of pure chaos. The fear within him for the people below was slowly being replaced by a growing rage. He stepped back away from the podium and looked around the Box. Everyone was cleared away from the area. He turned to the cameras and with little more than a thought shut them all down. The images instantly went black around the world.

"Miranda," he said with his fists clenched as his eyes turned to their natural angelic black. "Stop this game. I'm the one you want. Stop frightening these people!"

The collective arcs of energy coursing around the ceiling united as one solid, powerful bolt and directed itself at Lucifer with all of its force, striking the archangel and blasting him through the back of the Box and on through the north end of the building, showering the parking lot and many of the people rushing outside with debris from the building wall. Lucifer was propelled across the crowds, still being pushed by the bolt of energy, almost a half mile into the forest area north of the Marshalldome. He struck several trees as he came in hard across the landscape, knocking them to the forest floor and leaving a trail like that of a downed airliner.

He lay on the ground for a long moment, stunned by the power of the force that propelled him in this spot. He was on his back, staring up at the sky. It was blue once again. The dark clouds had only been concentrated around the Marshalldome. He saw smoke and smelled something burning, finally realizing it was his coat, tattered and torn and still with some flames flickering from the burned edges caused by the force of the artificial blast of lightning.

Lucifer pushed himself up onto his elbows and knocked the flames out from his coat. He looked down the path that had been a lush forest seconds before and saw her standing no more than 75 feet away from where he was laying on the ground. He brought himself to his feet and stood where he had landed, facing her.

"You don't need to do this, Miranda. I'm not going to reveal myself. It was...an error on my part. I know that I cannot do this to these people."

The look on her face was colder than ice. Her blue eyes were full black. She started to walk toward him and raised her arms to her sides as she walked. Broken full-sized trees that had just come down from Lucifer's crash started to fly at Lucifer with incredible force from his right and left sides. Lucifer raised his hands in response and easily knocked the first trees to the side with simple but focused gestures. When a third large tree came at him, he'd had enough of the tree game and redirected it back at Miranda, striking her with incredible force. She flew back into another cluster of trees, knocking them flat to the ground as Lucifer had when he was thrown into the forest with Miranda's initial blast from the Marshalldome.

Lucifer came upon her with almost lightning speed and stood above her. He reached down and grabbed the lapels of her leather motorcycle jacket and pulled her up from the ground with a look of rage on his face. The look on her face held only contempt for his anger and his actions.

"STOP acting like a child having a temper tantrum. Enough of this!" he told her.

She bared her teeth, almost like a rabid animal, and released a powerful force of energy from her hands, striking Lucifer's midsection. The force of her attack sent him flying hundreds of feet into the air. She leapt up at him and caught him by the lapel of his ivory coat when he reached his apex in the air. She pulled back her fist, which was still glowing in the strange black energy that she had struck him with moments before, and punched him hard in the face, sending him flying back to the ground like a missile, making a small crater with the impact that shook the earth for miles around.

Lucifer felt pain, very real and very deep. He let out a cough, which he found odd being that he didn't even have to breathe air. Miranda was back on the ground in front of him. He summoned from deep within the strength to bring himself to the ready, back on his feet.

"Miranda...please. I helped to forge this world. This universe. I made many of the stars that I know you've stared upon on so many lonely nights. *I don't want to hurt you.* We don't need to fight," he pleaded with her.

"Hurt me?" she scowled at him. "*Hurt me!* You have taken EVERYTHING from me! Because of you my parents are dead. My brother is dead. My birth family are all dead - because of *you!*"

"I am not responsible for any of that. I couldn't have been," he told her. "I have to obey the rules Amanthus set forth as well. I may have been able to bend a few, but never break them. And I would not have allowed any of that to happen had I been able to."

"Liar!" she fired back at him, unleashing another blast of the dark energy. But this time, he was prepared for the attack. A split second was all he had to unleash a bright white blinding blast of pure force directed entirely at Miranda, knocking her back about 50 feet and landing her on her backside. Her leather jacket was engulfed in flames.

Lucifer stood stunned by what he was seeing. He knew full well the power of that blast should have thrown her more than a mile. He wasn't even certain if it could or could not have even possibly killed her. He did not want to kill her, just to stop her and make her listen to him. He wanted to reason with her, before something terrible happened to either one of them. But his hopes for that were slipping away with every second.

She was up on her feet once more, throwing the flaming jacket to the side and standing before him in her white v-neck t-shirt and denim jeans that were now tattered with burn holes and tears throughout them.

"There is darkness in you Miranda. A deep rage. I can feel it- even when you are not slamming me into the earth. I know what you did to Daryl Grimes," he told her.

Miranda was caught off guard by this. She had no idea that he could have known what happened to Grimes.

"He was a killer. Like you. He killed my mother. My grandfather. He destroyed my life," she told him.

"Did he? I thought that was me. If you believe that I am responsible for everything terrible that has happened to you in your life, then what of Grimes? No, Miranda. His blood is on your hands, and yours alone. I'm not the monster under the bed. I didn't make Grimes or anyone else do anything. You are responsible for your own actions. You went seeking the truth about where you came from. You went to Aimsley Carter and led David Gale to her and your adoptive family. Yes, Miranda, I know what happened. If you want to find someone to punish, maybe start by looking in the mirror."

His words were harsh, but he knew them to be true. Miranda suddenly looked fragile and weak. Her shoulders slumped to her sides and her eyes returned to their natural blue. Then, they filled with tears that were streaming down her face.

Miranda dropped to her knees and covered her face with her hands as she sobbed into them. Lucifer let out a quiet sigh of relief. He felt for the girl deeply. She had lost so much, and while he knew that he had done none of it by his own hand or by his own will, there was a debt of responsibility that he felt for the pain that she had suffered. She was, after all, his kin as well. He would try to do what was right by her in any way that he could.

Lucifer walked over to Miranda as she was slumped on her knees.

"Miranda," he held a hand outstretched to her. "Let me help you."

Miranda looked up at him. Her face was streaked with dirt and tears and she slowly reached up to take his hand. He pulled her hand gently to help her up from the ground. What came next happened so fast that Lucifer was left reeling in stunned disbelief.

Her hand moved like lightning. There was a strange sensation that Lucifer was feeling. It was a stinging feeling, and then the wet trickling down his face. He reached to touch his face and felt the warm wetness. He pulled his hand away from the left side of his chin and saw the red of blood on his fingertips. No...*impossible*, he thought.

He looked at Miranda. The tears were all but gone. The raging storm was at ease for the moment, but the cold determination was still very present in her eyes. Her ruse was successful. She was indeed touched with darkness, but how much was what Lucifer was left to fear more than anything else.

"What have you done, Miranda?" he asked her. He tried to summon the power from within him, but there was nothing. That was when he felt the essential beating of his heart and the need to draw breath.

Miranda held the tiny sliver from Lucifer's sword still pinched between the index and middle fingers of her right hand. There was an almost imperceptible droplet of his blood still on the shard. As she held it up, the shard collapsed into an ashen dust and disappeared with the passing breeze.

Miranda rose from the ground as a raging wind came out of nowhere. Lucifer was suddenly stricken with pain. He was thrown back against a large oak tree, the force of the impact cracking more than one of his ribs. The pain was excruciating. And his fear was very real.

Miranda floated just above the ground in the air toward him and touched her feet down inches away from him.

"I just don't have the best of luck with uncles, I guess," she said to him. "One tried to use me to get to you, and you…well, you're the devil."

"Miranda," Lucifer struggled to speak with a tightening pain he felt with every breath, "you are more of a devil than I ever was. Please…let me help you…"

"You are going to help me. And don't worry. You are going to survive to watch me punish the one who is truly responsible for all of this. And you are going to suffer for all of it," she said with grim obscurity.

"Who…?" Lucifer started, but before he could say more she laid her hands upon his head and his vision went dark in a rush of pain and emotional overload. He passed out, and when he awoke, Miranda was gone. He was slumped up alongside of a tree. His ribs were healed, as was the small bleeding gash on his face, although there was a dark scar in its place, to remind him it was there - by her hand with his own sword - that she had taken from him his angelic power.

He stood up and concentrated, searching his thoughts. *What was she after? What was she looking for?* He knew she had taken something from his mind and memory, but he didn't know what it was. And then it hit him. He knew what she was looking for, and she had found it.

And for the first time ever, Lucifer had realized what it

felt like to experience the sense of pure, unadulterated dread.

Rick Jurewicz

CHAPTER TWENTY-THREE

The Mojave Desert, California. There were no towns or
roads within several miles of the spot where Miranda now
stood atop a mesa as the sun slowly lowered toward the
western horizon.

No cities. No people. She tried to take in the calm
peacefulness of the beautiful view that was before her. She
turned toward the east with the sun behind her, and she
allowed herself a moment to absorb the radiant glory of the
orange light upon the rocky desert formations that spread
across the landscape. In the distance, beyond what the human
eye could see (but not beyond hers), lights flickered from the
north. It was the distant view of Las Vegas.

She had just turned 14 when the Stratton's had gone on
a family trip to California to visit her father's cousin in
Anaheim. Anaheim was a beautiful place, and for the first time
Miranda had thought that maybe she was a city girl at heart
living a country girl's life. The fast pace and the bright lights did
hold some appeal for her, but it was the collage of culture and

innovation that she embraced the most. It was a two week stay, and for three of those days they took a road trip, renting a car in Anaheim and driving on I-15 across southern California into Nevada to Las Vegas. The interstate ran along the northern edge of the Mojave National preserve, which her father explained was miles and miles of protected desert land.

The days in Las Vegas were spent mostly at a fancy hotel by the pool. It was a nice couple of days away for just the family to unwind and enjoy some quality time together. The highlight of the Las Vegas getaway was a day spent doing a helicopter tour from outside of the city down into the Grand Canyon. Miranda found it both beautiful and overwhelming all at once. The canyon was enormous and she had trouble putting into words how she would describe it, which was one of the things that piqued her interest in journalism. She found that finding creative ways to use only words to convey experiences to others a fascinating challenge.

But that was then, and this is now. And that world…that world was gone now. In only a few short years, it seemed like a lifetime ago. But then again, what is a lifetime? The definitions that bound her reality together before David Gale entered into her once peaceful existence no longer applied to Miranda. She had a new purpose now, and that was the drive that pulled her to this place.

She turned back toward the horizon as the red sun began to kiss the distant edge of the Earth. And while she had seen behind her only moments before the beauty of the light, now that she turned her gaze toward the source of the light, she faced a cold truth; where there is light, there are always shadows.

The shadows of fear.

The shadows that fall in the face of love and of loss.

The shadows that are cast by the things that you trust and hold dear.

And always, looming deep within the furthest reaches of the soul –

The shadows of fate.

The storm inside of Miranda was churning, and the time had finally come to let it out. She raised up her arms and she concentrated, with more focus and determination than the last time she had done this very same act. The sky began to crack and the clouds appeared out of nowhere as if they were called from a faraway place to rush suddenly to this spot, and with them came the winds with hurricane force.

The fire-like lightning raged across the sky, tearing across the horizon in every direction. Stray streaks of lightning struck the ground around the mesa on which Miranda stood, throwing up flames that rose almost as high from the ground as the mesa itself stood from the desert floor.

And then, the first of the mightiest bolts came crashing down less than a quarter mile from Miranda, impacting the Earth with such a powerful force it pushed the desert floor up hundreds of feet around. The first was followed by a second one, slightly closer but to the north of Miranda, toward the lights of Las Vegas.

Lastly, the third and final fire-bolt blast came down to the south of Miranda, only a few hundred feet away. The clouds quickly gave way to a crystal clear, starry night, and Miranda stood atop the mesa, waiting.

The three arrived, gently rising up from the floor of the desert and coming to rest before Miranda, side-by-side atop the mesa. Miranda looked at each one with fascination. Much like Lucifer did, and her father, Gabriel, the three angels that stood before her looked entirely human, like anyone else she had ever known.

"Who are you?" said the female angel that stood between the two men. She had long wavy curls through her thick red hair. She was a tad taller than Miranda, wearing long leather boots and a dark shirt and a vest that, in Miranda's eyes, made her almost look like a pirate. She wore tight bands around her wrists, and even in the darkness of the fallen sun, Miranda could see the maroon hue in her eyes.

"My name is Miranda Gale," she told them. "I am the one who freed you from Hell."

"How is that possible?" asked the angel to her right. "Only an angel or Amanthus itself can open the gates to Hell. It is forbidden for any angel to do this without Amanthus' consent." He was much taller than the rest, with dark skin and short, black hair. There was little extraordinary about the way he was dressed. A plain white, tight long-sleeved shirt that showed off a very muscular physique beneath. He wore black trousers and combat style boots. He had a short trimmed mustache and goatee on his face. On the right side of his face beneath his right ear was a three-inch tattoo-like image of a reapers scythe.

"I can. And I did," she told them.

The third one looked keenly at Miranda. "You're not an angel though, are you? You are…both angel and human? The offspring of a union between our kind and man. Endowed with great power, but bound by no one." This one looked like a man of forty years, with flecks of silver in his hair that was pulled back into a pony tail, leaving a small clump of strands hanging down along the right side of his face. He was dressed in a long dark-brown robe over a beige shirt, with small ties down the middle of the shirt. He wore plain, dark brown trousers and brown boots. His physique was slender but muscular, and he had a peaceful look about him and a generosity in his gaze. Miranda had learned though, all too well, to be distrustful of the apparent generosity in others.

"I am the daughter of the archangel Gabriel. My mother was human. Her name was Suzanne Gale."

"I am Veramlus," said the angel with the long silvery hair. He held his hand toward the other male angel with the dark skin. "This is my brother, Kaborus. And this is…"

"Oh, hush Veramlus. She knows exactly who we are. Don't you, sweetie?" interjected the female angel with the long red hair.

Miranda looked at the red-haired angel keenly. "You are Ember, I take it?"

"Indeed. So, the question isn't who we are at all. The question is *why* we are here," Ember said, first fixed on Miranda, then looking back upon her two angelic brothers.

"I want to offer you something that we all want, and I believe we can achieve it by all working together. You are the three other archangels that fell with Lucifer. The other angels will not interfere with anything that happens in this world. They are forbidden to. This I have learned."

"And what of Lucifer? He fell as well. Have you released him, too? He is far more powerful than all of us, and he did not have the…same ideals that others of us had," said Kaborus in his deeply resonate voice.

"Lucifer has been stripped of his power," Miranda told them. "He is no longer a threat."

"And your father?" asked Ember. "Is he not a threat?"

"No. He has suffered the same fate as Lucifer. It is only the four of us now."

"And what is it you want to do?" asked Veramlus.

"I want us to take vengeance upon Amanthus." The

three stared in apparent disbelief as Miranda spoke the words.

"That's…that's not possible, is it?" asked Veramlus. "We cannot beat Amanthus."

"No…we can't," Ember replied.

"Amanthus…God, whatever you call him. He is all about his structure and rules. He created man and he loved man. But for Amanthus, it's all about the rules. Maybe he cannot be destroyed, but the idea of God can be torn down and destroyed. He wants their worship in return…their love. I want to show the world that he truly has abandoned them…that he isn't worthy of their love. I want him to feel the pain of loss that he has made me feel by turning his back on…*all of us*."

"So…we get vengeance for two millennia in a cold and unfeeling netherworld. And you get to feel better by breaking his toys? Is that it?" asked Ember in a snide tone.

Miranda turned to Ember with a sharp glare. Her eyes began to turn to black.

"Hold up, girl," said Ember, raising her palms up toward Miranda. "I'm in. All the way. But you – you're half human. Are you willing to turn against your own kind if need be?"

"The part of me that was human…it died not long after I lost my loved ones," Miranda said with her eyes lowered to the ground. "Now, I'm just a monster. Like *you*."

"A little harsh, but I'll go with it," Ember replied. "Kaborus…up for some payback on dear-old Dad?"

The dark angel grinned from ear to ear, nodding reassuringly at his fiery sister.

"Veramlus?" she asked him.

He looked unsteady and unsure, but even still, he was hurt by being sent to Hell. He nodded as well.

"Yes."

"There you have it, sweetie. Looks like your four horsemen are ready to ride."

Ember's smile widened from ear to ear, and Miranda returned the smile.

But behind Miranda's smile was her pain, and it had built to a desperate pressure point that fueled the dark rage that had been building inside of her since the moment she watched a helpless Aimsley so senselessly cut down by a bullet from a man under the orders of her own flesh and blood. It didn't matter whether she saw the monster within her coming more from the angel part of her being or the human part. There was enough monster to go around, human and angel alike.

She believed all that remained in place of what had once been her soul was that burning rage that fueled her desire for vengeance…and that rage was what she wanted to return to Amanthus with furious force.

This was a declaration of war.

This was Miranda's war…and Hell followed with her…

EPILOGUE

Just to the west of Denver, Colorado, you will find a section of the world famous Rocky Mountains. This collection of ranges, known by its popular nickname *the Rockies*, stretches across the North American continent some 3000 miles, from northern Alberta, Canada as far south as New Mexico. To the east lies the Great Plains and to the west, beyond the mountains is the region called the Basin and Range Province, spanning several of the western continental states of the U.S.

There are some sections of the Rockies that span more than 300 miles wide. The southern Rockies, in the areas just west of Colorado, have some of the highest peaks with elevations exceeding 14,000 feet. Many of these mountains have roads that trail up these peaks that have become popular tourist attractions for hikers, adventurers and sightseers.

Across the mountain range, those who traverse it will find areas of truly harsh and challenging terrain. And once you go off the beaten path, it is not only the terrain itself that makes the journey a dangerous trek. The wild country of the Rockies is rich with wildlife. It is the natural home to black bears, mountain lions and coyotes, as well as so many more creatures native to the lands along the mountains. It is in the nature of all creatures that, if a threat is perceived, they will defend themselves and their offspring at all costs.

Exploring the range is not for the faint of heart. The early settlers of these parts found this out even before these lands had become part of the fledgling nation called the United States of America.

But then, and still today, there was one section of the southern Rockies where no one– not mankind or angel kind – ever set foot upon. It was a remote 25 square mile area on a mountain that had no name and was not marked on any map. There was a single road that wound its way up a part of the mountain to a very remote rustic cabin, but no one ever gave the road consideration to drive up it. It would be passed as a side road off of a major highway, but in the instance that it was given any thought, it was disregarded just as quickly as if those who gave it notice experienced some trickery to the eye or perhaps a sense of déjà vu. But if a person ever were to venture down this road, they would find it impassible and turn around, going back in the direction from which they came. This was what was prescribed for this place long before anything else had happened in this world. It was as it was at the instant of creation, and no one knew precisely why. No one but God himself.

The resident of the cabin on the unnamed mountain made his trek out on the trail that he had cut through the thick brush a great many years before. He was dressed how he often was – a heavy red and black flannel shirt with a khaki canvas hunting vest over the shirt. Rugged and worn blue jeans covered his legs, held in place by a thick leather belt with an oversized buckle that had an embossed Texas steer across the entire buckle.

The man had made trips to town now and again, purchasing clothing and sometimes ammunition and a few odds and ends, along with a plentitude of books, usually 50 to 100 per trip. The last trip he made into the nearest town where he could buy books was about five years ago. The time before that was around the year 1954 or '55. He wasn't quite sure because he never really paid much attention to time. It was fair, because time never paid that much attention to him either. While he looked as if he were a man in his late forties to early fifties, his exact age was unknown, even to him.

On the trip in '54, he remembered picking up a fairly new novel called *The Old Man and the Sea* by a gent named Ernest Hemmingway. It was a short novel, but one that he found himself reading over and over again. Maybe it was the struggle of man against nature that appealed to him, or perhaps it was the familiarity with the sense of solitude that the main protagonist, an old Cuban fisherman named Santiago, felt alone on the vast sea in his battle with a mighty marlin. Whatever it was, he seemed to have a fondness for the classics.

On the more recent trip, he picked up the hat he was now wearing, a tan Austrailian bush hat with the left side of the brim snapped up on the side. He had almost round, Lennon-like glasses, with flip-shades down as he walked toward the sun up the mountain trail.

He stopped suddenly and brought his right hand down to his side with the palm out facing to the back in a gesture that indicated 'hold on." Close behind him, a German Shepherd that the man called *Marlin* – named after the great fish in the Hemmingway book – stopped dead in his tracks at his master's gesture. The dog did not whimper a whisper, keenly sniffing the air for whatever it was the man might have seen. It didn't take long to snatch the scent from the air.

The man slowly pulled the large scoped rifle from over his left shoulder and brought it around to his front, lifting the stock to his right shoulder. He peered through the scope in the direction of a large bull elk in the distance following the path. He set the crosshairs on the elk and watched it for a minute before finally chambering the bullet.

Three birds flew up near where the elk was standing, and the elk suddenly turned its head, startled by the birds, but it did not move any further. The man was about to pull the trigger when suddenly he seemed distracted by something else. He lowered the barrel of the gun and the elk lumbered peacefully away down the trail.

He looked down to his right at the dog. The dog faithfully looked up at his master and sat on the ground, on the spot, and was wagging his tail.

"You smell that?" the man asked the dog, who only responded with a brief yet excited whining sound.

The man looked off toward the east and lifted the flip-shades from the glasses. His hazel eyes peered into the hazy distance from the side of the mountain. To anyone else, there may have been nothing to see but the distant horizon. But this was not anyone else. And he saw something that he had never anticipated ever seeing before, not until this moment. He saw trouble coming his way.

"Best be getting back, Marlin. We're going to be having some company."

The Red Road Tavern just outside of Franklin, Georgia was a tiny yet typical roadhouse bar.

At just after 2 p.m. on a Wednesday afternoon, you will find just what you might expect to find patronizing the establishment at that time of day. You have your run of the mill regulars that have recently lost or cannot find either their latest job or the love of their life. But on exceedingly unusual occasions, you may find something far rarer indeed.

"I'll have another…one of these…whachu call it?" the highly intoxicated blond man slurred out as best as he could in his current state. He was missing a shoe, which he could not explain, although he was quick to point out to the barkeep after the first few drinks that the sign on the door said "No Shoes, No Shirt, No Service", and that he indeed did have a shirt (a little torn and slightly bloodied), and he had one shoe, so the plurality of the "no shoes" on the sign had been covered by his remaining shoe. The barkeep was in no mood to argue as long as the guy had the cash to pay and he didn't stir up any additional trouble.

"It's called Jack Daniel's on the rocks," the barkeep told him as he poured him his third drink. "You don't look much like you know your way around whiskey. Restroom's that way if you start feeling sick."

"I'm…just fine," said the man as his head sank slowly closer to the bar top. The glass of Jack was shifted slightly to the right and his nose sank to within inches of the surface of the bar. His eyes were open and he took notice of his reflection in the smooth polished bar top.

"It's…so…shiny," he murmured to himself.

The front door of the bar opened and the barkeep looked up to see the visitors stepping in through the main door.

"Good afternoon, folks. What can I help you with?" he said to the four people entering the tavern. There were two men with brown hair, one older and one younger, accompanied by a young blonde woman and a girl with black hair with blood-red streaks.

"Just looking for a…friend," the younger of the two men said to the bartender.

"Well, let me know if there's something else you need then. Not much here but these ol' dregs," the barkeep told them, motioning to the three drunks sitting at different places at the bar.

The older of the two men, alongside the younger girl with the jet-black hair with red streaks, walked up behind the man whose nose was almost touching the bar top now.

"Lucifer," the older man said aloud, perking the blonde man's head up from the bar surface. His vision was slightly distorted as he tried to make out in the mirrored glass across the bar the details of the man's face who stood behind him.

"No wonder why the past few hours I've been tracking him I've felt dizzy and goofy," said the girl with the black and red haired.

"Lucifer. Brother. It's me. It's Gabriel," he told him, placing his hand upon Lucifer's shoulder.

Lucifer slowly turned around and squinted in Gabriel's direction. Then he looked at Ashe, who stood puzzled in astonishment at the man who was at one time thought to be the 'Devil'. She wasn't overly impressed.

Lucifer then turned his head toward the two others standing behind Gabriel, almost as if he'd looked through his brother. Jake stood a ways away, glaring at Lucifer. The former archangel and once right hand of Amanthus could see in Jake's face a man who looked like he wanted to march over to him and tear his head from his shoulders. This prompted Lucifer to look to the girl beside Jake, who had a similar look on her face as well. He then finally turned his attention to Gabriel.

"Gabriel? Brother?" he whispered, almost confused.

Gabriel looked to Ashe. "Ashe…would you give me a hand?"

Ashe took her hand and touched Lucifer's. It was like a supercharged hangover cure, rushing through his mind and body, bringing to light in vivid waves the memories of the last few days of both Lucifer and of Ashe and the others. When she pulled her hand away from his, she was deeply shaken by what she had seen. She almost had tears in her eyes.

"What…what did you see?" Jake asked. "What happened to Miranda, you bastard?!" yelling at Lucifer, who was now suddenly stone sober, yet visibly shaken.

"I…" he started, looking at Jake, and then turning again to his brother Gabriel. "She…"

The being that helped shape the worlds and form the stars was at a loss for words as the four of them looked down upon him. Gabriel placed his hands on Lucifer's torn shirt and pulled him up from the barstool, bringing Lucifer's face within inches of his own. Lucifer could see both the fear and the fury in his brother's eyes.

"WHAT HAPPENED TO MY DAUGHTER?"

To be concluded…

The Lightbringer

ACKNOWLEDGEMENTS

Words cannot express the gratitude I have for everyone who has shown me their support and enthusiasm for the work I have done so far, first with the novel that precedes this one, *In the Shadows of Fate*, and also for the kind words and praise I have received from so many people for my first collection of short stories and poems, *Once Upon a Wicked Eve*. One always appreciates hearing the kind words of friends and family who have read my work, but when I started to have complete strangers approach me to tell me how much they love my writing and how eager they were to read more, it has been quite overwhelming. I thank you from the bottom of my heart.

It is truly a labor of love, weaving these tales and creating these characters, and an honor to share their stories with all of you.

To my wife, Nikki, one of the most avid readers I have ever known, I thank you for your keen eye and invaluable proofreading skills. But most importantly, I thank you for your endless love and support of all that I do.

I thank my wonderful son Dylan for being there with me at the very beginning of this story, allowing me to bounce ideas and thoughts off of him well before I could ever imagine what this would become. To Kaitlyn, the newest member of the family, thank you for being another ear to listen to my craziness and another smile to brighten our world.

And finally, a few special notes of thanks. To my Dad, thank you for always being encouraging and for always being there for our family, and for just being the father that you are.

Uncle Tom and Krys, thank you for the special place you hold in our lives. And to our great friends from Petoskey, Michigan - Alex N., Devin Y., Alex B., and so many more friends and family that are too numerous to mention here - each and every one of you, in your own special way, help greatly to make this magic possible!

Rick Jurewicz

The Lightbringer

Also from Rick Jurewicz

In the Shadows of Fate

Once Upon a Wicked Eve:
Dark Tales and Dreadful Wonders

About the Author

RICK JUREWICZ is an avid lover of fantasy, sci-fi, horror and dark drama, and has been writing short stories and poetry most of his adult life, some of which has been featured in print publications and online. *The Lightbringer* is Rick's second novel in the *In the Shadows of Fate* series.

Rick and his family are lifelong residents of Northern Michigan.

Find out more and follow Rick

Facebook.com/RickJurewiczWriter
Instagram/RickJurewicz

www.ingramcontent.com/pod-product-compliance
Lightning Source LLC
Chambersburg PA
CBHW072127250626
47159CB00007B/2591